One of Us

Also by Scott Nadelson

Fiction

Aftermath

Between You and Me

The Cantor's Daughter

The Fourth Corner of the World

Saving Stanley: The Brickman Stories

Nonfiction

The Next Scott Nadelson: A Life in Progress

One of Us

stories

Scott Nadelson

Winner of the G. S. Sharat Chandra Prize for Short Fiction
Selected by Amina Gautier

BkMk Press
University of Missouri-Kansas City
www.bkmkpress.org

BkMk Press
University of Missouri-Kansas City
5101 Rockhill Road
Kansas City, MO 64110
www.bkmkpress.org

Executive Editor: Christie Hodgen
Managing Editor: Ben Furnish
Assistant Managing Editor: Cynthia Beard

Cover photo by Alexandra Opie

Financial assistance for this project has been provided by the Missouri Arts Council, a state agency.

See page 299 for a complete list of donors.

Library of Congress Cataloging-in-Publication Data

Names: Nadelson, Scott, author.
Title: One of us : stories / Scott Nadelson.
Description: Kansas City, MO : BkMk Press, University of Missouri-Kansas
    City, [2020] | Summary: "These eighteen stories feature Jewish
    characters across the twentieth and twenty-first centuries and dealing
    with the tensions between individual and group identity. Several are set
    in New Jersey, Oregon, and North Carolina in the 1980s and 1990s, as
    well as 1930s New York or Soviet Union. Some are set in Europe, shortly
    before, during, or after the Holocaust. Historical characters include
    artist Louise Nevelson and actor Zero Mostel"-- Provided by publisher.
Identifiers: LCCN 2020038839 | ISBN 9781943491254 (trade paperback)
Subjects: LCSH: Jews--Fiction. | LCGFT: Short stories.
Classification: LCC PS3614.A34 O54 2020 | DDC 813/.6--dc23
LC record available at https://lccn.loc.gov/2020038839

ISBN: 978-1-943491-25-4

This book is set in Adso and Iowan

Contents

7   *Foreword by Amina Gautier*

9   Squatter

13   *Liberté*

27   One of Us

43   Sweet Ride

67   Caught

77   Safe and Sorry

95   Perfect Together

115   Trust Me

133   Butterfly at Rest

147   The Depths

161   Parental Pride

167   Enzo's Last Stand

183   The Payout

203   In Black and White

219   Last Bus Home

241   The Cake

255   Cut Loose

269   Going to Ground

296   *Acknowledgments*

For Alexandra and Iona, the three of us.

FOREWORD

With stories largely set on the northeast corridor at the end of the twentieth century, or in Europe during World War II, the past bleeds over into the present in *One of Us*, blurring the historical and the contemporary. Identities and the boundaries within which they exist are defined and then redefined once more when characters board ships and take sail, visit correctional facilities, attend synagogue, or hide in plain sight. In "Liberté," a woman leaves her marriage and sails to Europe in order to pursue a career as a painter. On board, she meets a Parisian novelist who pursues her despite his anti-Semitic leanings. In "Trust Me," a man overwhelmed with love for his daughter can't seem to stop disappointing her. He continually mucks up his visitations with her—picking her up late for his weekends with her, forgetting her birthday and so on. It's complicated, to put it mildly. In *One of Us*, characters can't help but to come up short as they try to bridge the gaps between who they are and who they wish to be. From the silent scornful bullying of congregants who shun a disgraced family, to a young man whose Aryan features allow him to move through Berlin unmolested while he watches other Jewish countrymen rounded up for the camps, to the emergence of a liberal community's latent racism rearing its ugly head when zoning laws permit the inclusion of affordable housing units and, by implication, an influx of black and brown residents, these stories challenge the ways we identify in terms of nation, race, class and religion and ask readers to consider who really belongs.

—Amina Gautier

Squatter

He broke in the day after we'd moved out, so he'd likely been watching the place for some time—maybe since the realtor first put a sign in the yard. That was three months earlier, but we'd yet to get an offer on the house. It was mid-2011, the market still sinking to undetermined depths, and even at thirty thousand less than what we'd paid for it, few people were interested in walking through. But *this* guy wanted to live here. He clearly appreciated the work we'd put into the old bungalow, remodeling kitchen and bathrooms, refinishing floors, replacing rotten boards on the back deck. Afterward, from scattered evidence, we pieced together his visit. On the sliding glass door, two greasy smudges, the imprint of forehead and nose as he peered in to make sure no one had stayed behind. Then, around the side, footprints in the oxalis, where he tested each window until discovering the one with a broken lock. What a thrill to feel the sash budge and then, crouching in the camellia, listen for the alarm that didn't sound. And how carefully he climbed in to avoid knocking over the lamp, to keep from soiling the armchair we'd left to stage the place for potential buyers. There were other things we'd left, too: half a dozen dishes on the kitchen's open shelves, a few cast-iron pans, air mattresses on cardboard boxes made up to look like beds. And in the garage a case of Riesling my father-in-law had given us when he thinned out his wine cellar, cast-offs we'd been storing for a year and never intended to drink. The stuff was sweet and warm, but our guy couldn't believe his luck when he found it, dragging the box inside, setting it in a place of prominence on the old farm table we used as a butcher-block island in the middle of the kitchen floor. We hadn't left him a corkscrew—how thoughtless!—but he was resourceful enough to punch the cork in with a butter-knife chisel and saucepan hammer. I don't know if it was before or after opening the first bottle that he decided to get some food. But eventually he let himself out the back door—which he left open a crack, maybe forgetfully, maybe for fresh air—and returned with a bag from Safeway. And what did he pick out? A tub of salad greens, bottles of oil and vinegar, scallions he sautéed in one of the cast-iron pans on the vintage Chambers stove we'd found on Craigslist. Salad! Sautéed scallions! Did he always eat this way? I want to believe it was a special night for him; that the house, though small and old and surrounded by decaying apartment buildings and group homes for the mentally ill, was the most elegant he'd occupied for years; that he admired the people who lived here and had restored it so affectionately; that imagining them made him want to live as they did, cooking healthy food, drinking hand-me-down wine they couldn't afford to buy themselves. And what a night it was! The first bottle he finished while cooking, leaving it empty in the kitchen sink. The second he drank while eating his salad and a bag of tortilla chips on the air mattress in what had been our bedroom. Only he didn't realize it was an air mattress at first, because he sat on it hard, collapsing the cardboard boxes underneath. Salad dressing and wine spilled on the sheets, but he enjoyed his meal anyway, left the plates on the mattress, and fetched a third bottle of Riesling. That one he drank in the front bedroom, which had been my office, this time taking the boxes away first and laying the air mattress on the floor. Did he browse the dozen or so books I'd left on the shelf and appreciate my taste in literature? Did he pass the time with a Chekhov story—"The Kiss," maybe, or "The Darling"—or peruse recipes in my vegetarian cookbook? All I know for sure is that here he spent the night, getting up only once, as far as I could tell, to relieve himself on the baseboard in the corner of the room. And why not? For tonight, this was his house, and he could do with it what he pleased. If that meant splattering urine on the wall and floor after downing three bottles of warm white wine, so be it. Why begrudge him that, when I'd enjoyed so many nights here, strolling in the garden, cooking dinner on the Chambers stove, making love under the cracked plaster ceilings, conceiving my daughter. How could I walk away from the place just because it felt too small now that I had a child, the neighborhood too dodgy, the school district's rating too low? Shouldn't I have done more to honor all I'd put into it, all it had given me in return? I want to believe my guy took in the perfect tight grain of the old floorboards before lying down and shutting his eyes. I want to believe he caught a glimpse of the moon made wavy by the leaded window, that the surprise of it tickled out a little hiccup of laughter. I want to believe he slept a heavy sleep in my old office, that he dreamt rapturous dreams. Because I know it must have been a rough awakening when the realtor opened the lockbox and jingled the key early the next morning, leading in a young couple who wanted just this kind of old place with a big yard, so long as it was free of rot, and its roof didn't need replacing, and its sellers could come down another twenty thousand off the asking price. How cruel to face the daylight slicing through the tall windows; to scramble up from the floor and crouch in the closet, waiting to run out the front door; to hear the couple exclaiming over high ceilings and laminate countertops they'd mistaken for real marble; to hear the realtor shouting after him and telling the couple to call the police; to feel the pavement rattling from shins to throbbing head; to pass *For Sale* signs in the yards of sagging bungalows with patchwork siding and crumbling chimneys and weedy lawns; and to know, once more, that nothing as ecstatic as love's first flare ever lasts.

Liberté

◄○►

In order to devote herself wholly to art, Louise Nevelson—born Leah Berliawsky—has left her marriage of thirteen years. She's been drawing and painting since childhood, but at thirty-three she's hardly more than a novice. She has never had a show of her work, has not yet discovered her medium. It will be many years before she's famous for her massive monochromatic assemblages, considered a queen of modern sculpture. Famous, too, for her bold style—colorful headscarves and enormous fake eyelashes—and brash, uninhibited speech. When asked, in her late sixties, how she's maintained such vitality for so long, she'll reply, Why, lots of fucking, of course.

In the early summer of 1933, however, she's both unknown and relatively inexperienced with men. Since separating from her husband, Charles, a shipping executive whose family—wealthy and cultured Jews who cherish art and music but laugh at those who dream of making it— has oppressed her since their wedding, she's had only one affair. Her lover was another American businessman, whom she met on her first crossing to Europe a year ago, her first, that is, since emigrating from Russia at six years old. And though the newness of the affair excited her, as well as its illicit charge—the businessman was married, his wife joining him in several weeks—she found sleeping with him largely dispiriting. Like Charles, he was overly solicitous, asking constantly after her comfort. With both she has just barely glimpsed what she guesses to be the dark and thrilling possibilities of sex, the struggle and near-violence of it, terror and triumph outweighing simple pleasure.

She found her three months in Berlin, chaste while studying with Hans Hofmann, far more rewarding than those hours naked in a stranger's cabin. And so now she decides to make another trip, this time planning to spend several months in Paris to learn contemporary technique. So at least she has told herself, though a part of her knows she may never return. She will do whatever she must to become the artist she has long believed herself capable of becoming, no matter the sacrifices.

―◦―

About leaving Charles, she feels little remorse. She was always honest with him, and he knew what she wanted when they married. If he didn't believe her when she confessed her ambition, that is his fault, not hers. He acquiesced to the separation with little argument, though she knows he is hoping she will soon come to her senses and return to him. Or more likely, that she will find it too difficult to survive on her own, that his money, if not his love and loyalty, will draw her back. But unlike her shipboard lover, whose manufacturing interests were only mildly affected by the crash, Charles may not have money for long. His family's business has suffered enormous losses over the past four years and is now on the verge of collapse. More than her own survival, she fears for his. What will Charles do with himself if he can no longer spend his time tracking shipments and accounts? What purpose will guide his days?

Any discomfort caused by deserting her husband, however, is minor compared to the guilt she carries over abandoning her son. Myron—who prefers to be called Mike—is eleven years old and bewildered by the changes thrust upon him. Last summer she sent him to stay with her parents in Maine, and though she tried to tell herself he'd be perfectly happy there, her mother spoiling him with her baking, her father, a builder, teaching him to how to frame a house, she nevertheless imagined him smothered by the same boredom that had driven her to marry the first wealthy man she met, when she wasn't yet twenty-one. At the time Charles lived on the twelfth floor of a building on Riverside Drive, and she believed it was the city she was marrying as much as the man, the opportunities such a move would afford her. If she'd known he would soon pack her off to the suburbs to be surrounded by his brothers and sisters-in-law and cousins who would judge every word she spoke, she would have refused his offer instantly, or so at least she tells herself now.

She agonizes over Mike, and yet the thought of her own suffocation were she to stay overwhelms all others. She books her passage and sends her son back to Maine.

◄○►

The ship, a single-class steamer bound for Le Havre, is called *Liberté*. A fitting name, she thinks, though worries about Mike's unhappiness keep her from feeling terribly free until the second evening out from New York, when she meets a handsome Frenchman, a doctor named Destouches. Louis-Ferdinand Destouches. He says the name as if she might recognize it, and when she doesn't, shrugs to confirm she couldn't possibly.

This takes place in the ship's narrow dining room. When she enters, most tables are already occupied by families and large parties of young people traveling together. Those few passengers on their own wander the edges, looking for friendly faces. She finds herself seated with five strangers, all men. More Americans on business, two disembarking in Portsmouth, another traveling on to Frankfurt. The remaining two are heading to Paris, and before the entrée is served, both have offered to take her to dinner there, or to a show. All five laugh at her jokes, and the two closest to her pour wine into her glass as soon as she empties it. They smile feral smiles as she unwraps her stole to reveal athletic shoulders—she was captain of her high school basketball team, as well as its sole Jew—and a long neck. The most attractive of them has bits of bread stuck between his teeth, the tallest unappealingly bushy eyebrows. One of the others—she can't tell which—smells ripely of sweat.

The Frenchman approaches just as the meal ends. When she stands, he takes her hand lightly and releases it before introducing himself. His accent is so thick she has a hard time understanding what he says. But she thinks he tells her she has the appearance of an artist, the only one on the entire ship. He is sloppily dressed but fierce looking, with a large head, dark hair combed back from a widow's peak, prominent cheekbones, dazzling blue eyes. He's an inch or two shorter than all the other men, but the low tones of his voice and his way of leaning forward as he speaks diminishes them. He is bold yet nervous, fidgeting with his tie as if it chokes him, and after saying a few more words she can't make out, gives a nod, shuffles backward, and disappears into the crowd exiting the room.

One of her dinner companions suggests stepping outside to look at stars, but she excuses herself, says the wine has made her dizzy. In her cabin she studies a picture of Mike, dapper in a tuxedo, though dour, taken just before attending a concert with Charles's insufferable relatives. Later, when most people are asleep and the passageways are quiet, she does go out on deck. The stars are hidden behind clouds she can't see. Beyond the ship's lights, everything is black. She can't distinguish ocean from sky.

—◦—

She spots the Frenchman again the next day, soon after lunch. He is seated in a card room in which the tables have all been moved to one side. A thin stooped man stands next to him, handing out books to people waiting in line. The Frenchman, Destouches, signs them, hands them back with a little dip of his head, unsmiling. She learns from another passenger—a sharp-faced Parisian who looks at her with disdain, as if in not knowing already she is either ignorant or mad—that in addition to being a doctor, he is also a novelist whose first book was published to great acclaim some months earlier, called a masterpiece by many critics, herald of a new French literature, one more raw and honest and free than any previous. He writes under a pen name, Céline, in tribute to his grandmother. He is returning home after traveling to California in hopes of having the book made into a film. Will it be? Louise asks, but the woman shakes her head. Cowards, she says. Communists. The producers were warned before he arrived, alerted to his political leanings, and as a result they all declined. What those political leanings are, the woman doesn't say.

Céline. Once Louise hears the name she can't connect him with any other. She doesn't stand in line for a book and doesn't think he has seen her before she walks away. But when she arrives for dinner, he is waiting for her. His slender companion hands her two copies of the novel. In one is just his signature, he says, the other a special inscription. The book is thick, at least five hundred pages, and heavy, and to hold two she must use both hands. The simplicity of its cover appeals to her. White, with red and black type, no image. She likes the sound of the

17

title, too, but knows enough French only to decipher *voyage* and *de la nuit*. A voyage of the night strikes her as both mysterious and enticing. The meaning of *au bout* she will have to do without.

The slender companion vanishes, and Louise joins Céline at his table. He speaks quickly, with vehement gestures, and again she misses many of his words. He jumps from topic to topic, but always follows a central thread: the essential corruption of humanity, the yearning for filth even among the most so-called refined of society—he mutters this while jutting his chin at a well-dressed couple across the table—which itself is a cesspool, needing to be emptied and scoured. Everything he says is bitter and morose, and yet there's a charm in his passionate insistence, a relief after so many years of listening to Charles and his relatives speak with mild disinterest about even those things they claim to value most. He stares at her as if he will soon pounce and clamp his jaws around her neck. She wants to hear him say more about how he recognized her as an artist just by looking at her, but for now he talks only about himself, about his family, his mother who traveled house to house selling liniments and herbal remedies so he could study legitimate medicine.

I'm peasant stock, he tells her. Last of a line. When you have a head like mine, you know you've reached the end.

After the meal, she expects him to invite her for a drink, maybe at one of the ship's several bars or maybe in his cabin. And she is prepared to accompany him to either. Instead he delivers his nervous bow, tells her how much he has enjoyed their conversation, asks if they might continue to talk tomorrow. His companion has reappeared, bony and silent, and the two of them hasten below deck. In her cabin, she flips through his novel, unable to read any of it. Like the text, the inscription is in French, the handwriting loose and rumpled like his suit, and she can make out only a handful of simple words: *bien* and *au* and *courage*. Another looks like *ravissant*, but she can't be sure. The image of Charles comes to her for no reason she can imagine, taking off his trousers and carefully folding them before joining her in bed. She has a headache but cannot sleep. She goes upstairs, finds a bar, orders a whiskey on ice, and interrogates the bartender about which cocktails he enjoys mixing most and why.

‑‹◦›‑

The crossing takes seven days, and a part of four she spends with Céline. At times they sit on deck, enjoying sun and a light breeze. On a stormy day both are mildly seasick and huddle on velvet sofas in a deserted lounge, where Céline smokes to calm his stomach and Louise drinks to settle hers. He still asks nothing about her life, why she's traveling to Paris, what sort of art she hopes to produce, but she takes his silences as opportunities to tell him about her failed marriage, her previous work with Hofmann, her plans for the summer. If I like it, perhaps I'll stay, she says. She does not mention Mike, though almost immediately a vision of him springs to mind, standing on the shore of Rockland, staring out over the ocean into which his mother has disappeared. Céline, brooding or nauseated, says nothing.

Later, when the sea has calmed and they have returned to the deck, he tells her that Paris is a toilet, full of nothing but thieves and con artists, and yet compared to America it's an oasis, a place where you can speak your opinions freely and not fear reprisal. She recalls what the woman said about Hollywood producers and wonders what opinions scared them off. It's the only place to live, he goes on, a disgusting city but an honest one, where all depravity is on display. He has seen it first-hand, patients coming to him with wounds from scuffles, with horrifying sexual diseases, everything left to fester because all have been contaminated by the pestilence of contemporary life.

Every time he mentions his work as a doctor, she is surprised anew. Afterward she quickly forgets how he makes his living. It's as if the information won't stick in her mind, crowded out by the heft of his novel. Or maybe it's because she can't imagine going to him for medical attention. With those harsh, inward-focused eyes and large hands with blunt fingers, how could he possibly ease someone's suffering?

As if she has spoken the question aloud, he says, waving a hand, It's mostly pointless, this whole, how you say, enterprise. He heals those he can, but soon enough they are ground up again by the machinery of decadence, of the world going to rot. In times like these, he goes on, who should rise to the surface, like shit floating on a flooded river? Yes, the Jew, the bottom-feeder, thriving on the foulness and decay of a poisoned culture, poisoning it further, until those few left with dignity must burn everything down and plant new seeds in the ashes.

His face is flushed as he speaks, flecks of spittle at the edges of his lips, and yet his voice remains calm, with the lilt of amusement. When he finishes, he smiles and apologizes, not for his sentiments, but for his mixed metaphors. Louise tries not to reveal anything by her expression, though she can't help leaning away. Surely he knows what she is, if not from her features, then from her name. And yet he keeps staring at her with the same hunger, the same ferocious need. Only now he is finally ready to act on it. He moves toward her, sweeps an arm across her shoulders, bends to kiss her. She turns away, swivels out of his grasp, hurries inside without looking back.

But for the rest of the day she is less horrified than fascinated. It's an important discovery, she thinks, a profound one:

that someone can detest what he desires or desire what he detests. Which comes first, the wanting or the loathing, she doesn't know.

-◄o►-

On the last day of the voyage, she takes her meals in her cabin and does not encounter Céline again before the ship docks for the last time. She doesn't see him on the train from Le Havre and learns from the sharp-faced woman that he disembarked at Cherbourg. She assumes that will be the end, she won't hear from him again. But he soon contacts her in Paris, sends a note to her hotel, invites her to lunch. He does not apologize for what he has said nor for trying to kiss her afterward, does not acknowledge their last meeting in any way. His note is brief and self-deprecating. *Dear Miss Nevelson,* he writes in English. *By now you must have been married over and over again. What passion will be left for me?* During the summer she sees him once, and though he flatters her with compliments, he is otherwise distracted and distant, avoiding all serious topics. She finds herself both relieved and dejected when they part. He kisses her cheeks lightly, the smell of tobacco lingering until she is well down the street.

Later, she learns from an acquaintance that she is not Céline's first American infatuation. He once lived with a girl from California, with similarly strong shoulders and elegant neck. Not long ago, this girl returned to the States and married, leaving Céline heartbroken. To find that she served as someone's replacement is less insulting to Louise than sad. She pictures Céline entering the ship's dining room, scanning the tables for a passable likeness. She imagines Charles similarly scouting for someone new in the lobby of a theater or the reception hall of his synagogue, someone who will both remind him of what he has lost and help him forget.

Her time in Paris is, on the whole, disappointing. She sees much artwork that moves her, attends parties, has many flirtations. But the mood is generally bleak. Too many people are out of work. There are fears of more anti-parliamentarist demonstrations like the one in February that left fifteen dead. She considers returning to Berlin, where she was so much happier last summer, but she meets a number of German artists and musicians and writers who have fled since Hitler became chancellor, all of whom warn her to stay away. Hofmann, she learns, has left, too, emigrated to New York. So why has she come at all?

Mostly, though, her disappointment is personal rather than political. Her friendships feel shallow. The prospect of establishing a career in Europe seems more daunting the longer she stays and the more she sees. Here the tree of modern art is massive, with many limbs, thick and healthy and intimidating. She could be no more than a small leaf, clinging desperately to a twig. But at home, in the country Céline described as a swamp of naïveté and repression, she might grow to be a branch, or perhaps, with enough effort, a part of the trunk.

She visits Chartres, Versailles. Depressed, she travels to the Riviera, sleeps with a sailor in Nice, and boards a ship home from Genoa. She arrives just as summer ends, when Mike is due back in school, and pretends this has been her plan all along.

‑◦‑

To her surprise, Céline writes to her in New York. They begin an extended correspondence, the strangest of her life, part seduction, part debasement. He invites her to come live with him in Italy, or perhaps he will move to America, even if it is a reeking bog filled with the dregs of the earth—though now that Germany is being purged, he writes, France, too, is overrun with slime. Why she puts up with these letters she doesn't know, except that they captivate her, so many contradictions on display. Or perhaps she is simply lonely, longing for any interest to distract her from the sight of her empty bed.

By then she has settled into an apartment on Fifteenth Street and Third Avenue. It's a large space though sparsely furnished, with a bedroom for Mike and a studio for herself. While Mike is in school, she spends her mornings painting. She takes classes at the Art Students League, with Hofmann again, and George Grosz, both of whom are shaken by their flight from the darkness that has so quickly consumed their home country. She wishes she could offer them some comfort, but their distress puts her off, makes her keep her distance. She wants only to admire them, see them as great men, full of wisdom and fortitude they can pass on to her. She tells neither about her exchanges with Céline.

When Diego Rivera comes to New York to work on several commissions, she is enlisted to help paint one of his murals, not the monumental *Man at the Crossroads* at Rockefeller Center, but a smaller one called *The Workers*, close to her apartment. She is in awe of Diego, approves of his appetites. His second wife, Lupe, shows up at one of the many parties he throws, kisses everyone, dances with her eyes closed. She is beautiful, though less mesmerizing than his current wife, Frida, still in her twenties and shy, though with a calm poise that makes Louise forget she's almost a decade older. Both women smell faintly of semen when they hug her goodbye. She doesn't think Diego loves them so much as he feeds on them. They set flame to his passions, stoke his work. If she weren't afraid of draining what little fuel she has for her own work, she might offer up her heat to him as well.

Instead she begins to experiment with sculpture, plaster figures painted in primary colors. They don't satisfy her, except that she can feel herself searching for form, knows for the first time that she will eventually find it. She shows pieces in group exhibitions, but galleries turn her away. She occasionally considers throwing herself out a window, but her studio is on the first floor, the sidewalk only ten feet below the sill.

—◦—

Céline's letters increasingly confuse her. After Hindenburg's death and Hitler's ultimate ascent to power, he writes sincere condolences, saying he hopes any friends or relatives she has in Germany have managed to escape—and if not, that he may be able to help with arrangements. But then he castigates the French government for accepting refugees, whose stink pervades the air whenever he walks through the streets. Sometimes she doesn't respond for months, and then he pleads with her not to abandon their friendship: it is too important to him, he writes, she is the only woman in his life who is both beautiful and intelligent, and knowing such a possibility exists has been crucial to maintaining any hope for a world so deeply mired in excrement.

And then he visits her in New York. When he calls, Mike is in school, and she doesn't hesitate to invite him to her apartment. She gives him coffee, and he sits across from her, smoking, smiling a pained smile. She wears a loose dress with a low neckline and no sleeves. She has downed a tumbler of whiskey and left the door to her bedroom open. She thinks, I am free to do whatever I please. She can gratify herself or harm herself as she chooses. There is no one to stop her, no one to judge. Céline leans forward, elbows on knees. His voice is low, desperate. How would you like to marry me? he asks.

She thinks she ought to laugh but doesn't. She knows he is serious. She pictures Charles again, when he proposed at her parents' house in Rockland, when she was just a girl yearning for the promise of city life. She thinks of the brutality of that sailor in Nice, the hammering of his huge body that both unnerved and enthralled her. She sees shit floating in a swollen river. Which is worse, she wonders, the fanatic who wants what he hates or the one who wants what hates her?

After the war she will read about him in *Life* magazine. Collaborator. Nazi spy, propagandist. She will learn about the vile pamphlets he has authored, calling for the extermination of all Jews in France. She will tell those friends who knew of their correspondence that she is appalled, disgusted. She will give away the books he inscribed for her, toss his letters into the fireplace. She will regret doing so, not right away, but later, after Mike has grown up and moved out, while working on the first of the many walls of black boxes for which she will become known around the world, filled with arrangements of found wooden blocks and cylinders that suggest the messy intricacies of mind and heart. She will think he was one of the few who understood her, because, like her, nothing could ever appease him. And she'll think, I wasn't ready then.

You know, dear, she says now. You would be worth more dead than alive to me.

She isn't quite sure what she means by it. But he doesn't object, just nods, shows his woeful smile, finishes his coffee and cigarette. At the door, he tells her not to worry, she has all the strength she needs to thrive, he glimpsed it in their very first encounter. But then he asks, as he steps into the hall, Is this a world worth thriving in?

Before she can answer, he's gone.

ONE OF US

—◄○►—

We all expected Arlene Besunder to disappear for a while. She'd stop coming to Sisterhood meetings, drop off the Purim carnival committee, skip the annual gala. She'd retreat, as any of us would have, until the noise died down. And if it didn't die down, if the issues couldn't be resolved? Then she'd pack up the six-bedroom colonial in Union Knoll, move to a town some miles away, join a new synagogue, a new Sisterhood, a new Purim carnival committee.

What else could she do? Her husband, Glen, had been indicted for defrauding the state of New Jersey. The story broke on the front page of the local paper. TV vans parked outside her house for three days. Faced with such exposure, how could she not want to hide herself away?

Yet there she was at services at the end of the very same week, one of the first people in the sanctuary, flanked by her two teenage children, Todd and Naomi. It wasn't unusual to see just the three of them there on a Friday evening, as Besunder often traveled for work. They took their usual spot, four rows from the front, just to the left of the center aisle, where the rabbi couldn't fail to see them over the top of the bimah.

Did she have no shame, no self-respect? Wasn't she embarrassed in the least?

Of course, Besunder's arrest was embarrassing for everyone. After the news broke, none of us could say our pride in Temple Emek Shalom hadn't been shaken. He was on the board of directors, after all, one of the leaders of the congregation. Just inside the lobby doors, his name topped a list of major donors on a bronze plaque molded in the shape of stone tablets. He'd twice served as president of the Men's Club, and when he was in town for Shabbat, he was often called on to lift the Torah and carry it through the sanctuary so we could kiss it with our tzitzit or the edges of our siddurs. During the kiddush afterward we'd usually see him chatting with old Rabbi Aronson, who gazed on Besunder with a beneficent expression suggesting gratitude and admiration.

But then, Rabbi Aronson offered most people that look: grieving widows, boys whose voices cracked during haftorah practice, parents who sought his counsel about a daughter's drug addiction. He was past seventy, white-haired and beginning to stoop, and perhaps he was growing deaf. He'd also come of age during a more innocent time. Maybe he couldn't distinguish between a man of character and a charlatan.

Could we? Why hadn't we suspected Besunder all along?

True, we'd always recognized he was different from most of us. He wore his expensive suits as if they were overalls, yanking at the sleeves and then rolling his shoulders to set them straight, stripping off the jacket in the middle of meetings. He hadn't gone to Brandeis or Yale or RPI—not even to Montclair State—hadn't earned a degree in finance or medicine or engineering. Had he even graduated from high school? We weren't sure. But he talked enough about his origins for us to know he'd grown up a virtual orphan in Elizabeth, his parents abandoning him and his sisters into the care of neglectful grandparents when he was a toddler. Not yet fifteen, he swept floors in a foundry specializing in manhole covers. "I'm still just a lowly janitor," he'd say to Rabbi Aronson, loosening his silk tie, flashing a platinum Bvlgari on his hairy wrist.

Of course he was no longer just a janitor. He'd built the biggest cleaning and maintenance company in the region, servicing office complexes and industrial parks all over Morris County and beyond. He had seventy people on his payroll, plus dozens of temps, and worked with all the major firms in the area, including those that employed many of us: Prudential, AT&T, Warner-Lambert. Who didn't admire a self-made man? He was like our immigrant grandparents, scrappy and ingenious, lifting himself from bleak poverty to a level of wealth most of us—even some of the lawyers and doctors and investment bankers among us—could only imagine.

So we'd accepted him into our ranks, voted him onto the board, shook the etrog and lulav in the enormous sukkah he built in his backyard. He played up his rough edges, talking brusquely, apologizing when profanity slipped into his speech. He alluded to unsavory characters in his past, to youthful brushes with the law. And we enjoyed his stories, pretended to cringe at the profanity, laughed when he gestured at the new stained-glass window he'd paid for in the sanctuary, winked, and said, "Good thing I settled all my debts, or someone might come collect."

We remained aware of our differences but decided they mattered less than all we shared. And we waited eagerly every year for the end of the gala, when we'd tear open his donation envelope and glimpse the figure on the check he'd slipped inside.

◄○►

What we might not have realized, or perhaps we didn't care, was that his biggest contract was with the state. His crews took care of government facilities from Trenton to Newark, repainting stairwells, repairing roofs, replacing ancient furnaces. Certainly, we knew he had close relationships with county freeholders, with state assemblymen, with the lieutenant governor, who once accompanied him to our Passover potluck. But why should that have given us pause? Why would we think to question his motives, we who never bent the law beyond writing off a few charitable donations we hadn't made?

One of those relationships must have gone sour, or else someone lost an election, because on a Tuesday morning in late fall of 1989, police cars greeted Besunder when he arrived at his office. According to the indictment, summarized in both the *Star Ledger* and the *Daily Record*—the latter of which included a mug shot, spread across two columns—he'd been overbilling the state for years. He'd charged for servicing buildings that had been abandoned for decades, others that had been demolished. "A simple accounting error," his lawyer told the reporters. "Not a criminal conspiracy." In both articles, the lawyer hinted that the blame lay with a civil servant who oversaw the contracts.

At first we believed this story, or tried to, and hoped that the civil servant would step forward and accept responsibility. But when subsequent articles laid out the evidence against Besunder, our outrage quickly flared. He'd swindled us the same as he'd swindled everyone else. Hadn't the state taxes withheld from our paychecks helped finance his house and landscaping and that enormous sukkah in which we'd eaten Arlene's mediocre kreplach? We debated whether to print a statement in the monthly newsletter, condemning Besunder's behavior. We considered taking down the plaque in the lobby. We suggested that Rabbi Aronson deliver a sermon on the dangers of avarice.

But how could he, when Besunder's wife and children were right in front of him week after week, offering up their praise to HaShem like the rest of us? They, too, had been betrayed, or at least the children had been, though we couldn't help believing Arlene must have known what her husband was doing, must have given at least her silent consent.

But if she felt betrayed, as we said we did, or experienced the guilt of complicity, as many of us admitted experiencing only to our spouses in the privacy of our bedrooms, she didn't show it. During the silent Amidah, she stood longer than anyone else, swaying and mumbling, eyes closed, as the rest of us shifted uneasily in our seats. It was as if she were daring us to sully her husband's name in her presence, keeping us in check with her vigilance. She was an imposing woman, straight-backed and bosomy, with hair in a ballerina's bun that stretched the skin on her temples and showed off flashy earrings, big gold discs with gems dangling from their rims. She kept her gaze fixed on the rabbi through the service, never glancing around or behind, but still she somehow projected the appearance of keeping an eye out, cataloguing our looks of disapproval. She knew exactly who was judging her, who was talking behind her back. And when all this blew over and we came to her for help with the carnival or the trunk sale? Then we'd see what our judgments had earned us.

—◦—

The truth is, as much as we'd enjoyed Besunder's company, envied his success, and benefited from his generosity, we'd never been able to stand Arlene. She was dour and assertive, quieter than most of us but powerful in her silence. At Sisterhood meetings she'd sit stonily as we discussed possible speakers for a lecture series, uninterested, it seemed, or more likely, out of her depth. But when we'd finally settled on a slate of scholars and writers—experts on Jewish women's history, on the design of Holocaust memorials, on the legacy of Emma Goldman—she'd heave a sigh, shake her head, and ask in a hushed voice that made us lean forward to hear, "Can't we bring someone who won't put us all to sleep?" Then she'd suggest a popular children's book author, who also happened to be her cousin's friend. He'd already agreed to come, she informed us, and for half his ordinary fee.

Every year, after we'd spent months planning, she'd take over the Purim carnival the day we began setting up, arriving with bags of decorations and masks that terrified the little kids and balloons that filled the gym. She didn't listen to any suggestions, and when we challenged her, she'd remind us, without a hint of self-consciousness, how much money her family had contributed to the shul in the past year.

We didn't know the history of the Besunders' marriage, or, frankly, what Besunder had ever seen in Arlene. She wasn't attractive or charming, though she did have a pleasant singing voice. Had they met after he'd already started his business, or did their connection date from his time as a janitor? We wanted to believe the latter. Not only that she, too, had come from humble roots, but that she was an imposter in her role as benefactress and wealthy matron. We imagined her in the slums of Elizabeth—an aspiring showgirl, maybe, or better yet a streetwalker—before Besunder swept her away and set her in their ill-begotten castle atop Union Knoll. This was the way we made sense of her loyalty, even after he'd disgraced her and her family—and all of us—with his shady dealings, about which, after a few months, his lawyer refused to comment in public.

We knew this silence could mean only one thing: a plea bargain was in the works. Thank goodness, we thought. We'd soon be able to put all this behind us. Arlene could no longer deny, in her mute, stoic way, who her husband was—who she was—and where her money had come from. Yes, we'd lose their sizable donation, but we'd make up for it with our combined efforts. We could all give a little more, we told each other, we could stretch and sacrifice for the sake of the community. After all, hadn't most of us held back a bit, knowing Besunder would make up for our shortcomings?

Most important, Arlene would finally stop coming to services, would finally stop making us pretend that nothing had happened. Surely she wouldn't show herself when her husband was a convicted felon, when he'd admitted his wrongdoing and accepted his fate. Surely she had too much dignity for that.

◄o►

Once again the editors of the *Daily Record* printed the story on its front page. Besunder agreed to plead guilty to a single charge of conspiring to commit fraud in exchange for his testimony against the civil servant who'd taken a cut of profits from the servicing of buildings no longer in use. The evidence against him must have been damning, because even with the deal, the conviction carried a thirteen-month sentence at the minimum-security camp at Fort Dix. The civil servant, on the other hand, went away for seven years.

The news generated a fresh bloom of embarrassment, as the article mentioned Besunder's involvement at Emek Shalom, even quoting our board president, who, when asked whether the synagogue would return any donation found to be tainted, said, noncommittally, "Mr. Besunder has been a very generous member of our community, but we do not condone any criminal activity and will cooperate with law enforcement."

Even worse, the story began to spread among our children. During dinner they'd pass on what they'd heard from other kids at Hebrew school—that Besunder had buried two mil in his backyard, bundles of crisp twenties, and that the spineless prosecutor was letting him keep it all—and we'd answer sharply, "What business is it of yours?" Then, softening slightly, we'd recite the old proverb about gossip: "If you didn't see it with your eyes, don't witness with your mouth." The kids would try to argue on a technicality—they'd seen the newspaper, hadn't they? didn't that count for anything?—but we'd just raise a hand and stare sternly at our plates, signaling that they'd better not push their luck.

Once more we exchanged concerned phone calls and spoke privately to Rabbi Aronson. Should we release a statement? Should he deliver a sermon? For the sake of the children? Yes, yes, we all agreed. As soon as we knew for sure that Arlene and her kids wouldn't be back.

We waited for Friday with a sense of giddy anticipation, ready, finally, to move on, to see ourselves once more as a community full of integrity and goodwill. We were so excited, in fact, that we finished our dinners quickly and arrived twenty minutes early. The sanctuary buzzed with our murmurs and lighthearted laughter, as we took in the empty space in the fourth row. Rabbi Aronson stepped up to the bimah, the cantor cleared his throat, and still we whispered and tittered.

Then the doors flew open, and in walked those three Besunders, Arlene marching straight down the center aisle, shoulders back, head held high, a wisp of lace pinned to the top of her tight bun, the two kids trailing behind. We were aghast, shocked mute, many of us forgetting to stand when the service started. Once again Arlene stayed up longest during the silent prayers, sang the Adon Olam in her soft, tuneful, almost sultry voice, and afterward perused the snack tables in the ballroom, sidling up to the rabbi with a cup of punch in one hand and a pistachio pastry in the other, remarking on some detail from the week's Torah portion and complaining that there'd been a few wilted petals in the flower arrangement on the dais. "The florist should hear about it," she said. "We shouldn't have to pay for next week's delivery."

She accosted others, too: the board president, members of Hadassah and the gala steering committee, any of us who hesitated for a moment to look her in the eye. She spoke to us haughtily, with contempt, defying us to send her away. And what could we do but smile and compliment her dress or her earrings and say that we looked forward to seeing what decorations she'd come up with for this year's carnival?

—◦—

Only then did we really turn our attention to the younger Besunders, whisper among ourselves how heartless it was to make them suffer any further humiliation. During services they were hunched and miserable, Todd ducking down into his tallis, Naomi hiding behind her siddur. During the Amidah, they sat as soon as they could do so without calling attention to themselves, and they kept their heads lowered as their mother dipped and bobbed above them. They vanished as soon as the service let out, waiting in the car, we guessed, while their mother tormented us at the kiddush.

If she didn't go away for our sake, for the sake of the congregation, we muttered later in our bedrooms, changing out of suits and dresses and tucking jewelry and watches into cherrywood boxes and drawers, then at least she should consider the impact on her children. Couldn't someone suggest as much?

We suspected all this was hardest on Todd, a junior at Union Knoll High and a generally well-liked kid, short for his age but athletic, a starting left fielder on his school's baseball team, a wrestler who'd placed two years in a row at the state championships. Our own children—the awkward ones, the ones who, like us, struggled to thrive outside the safe confines of Emek Shalom, in that broader, supposedly secular but seductively Christian world of sports and cars and proms—wanted to be like him, and we were often envious on their behalf. Todd's life, as we saw it, had been a series of easy triumphs, and his father's incarceration was a blow for which he'd been entirely unprepared. His friends didn't know what to say so avoided him altogether. His girlfriend tried to offer comfort, but he pushed her away. His wrestling coach, a stocky and sadistic former state champ who'd lost in the first round of the 1976 Montreal Olympics, rode him for not practicing hard enough: if Todd couldn't hack the pressure, he said, he should stick to pussy sports like baseball.

We heard about these things from our children, who heard about them from other kids at Todd's school, but even without firsthand testimony we could tell he was experiencing the kind of shock and grief that comes only from believing you're going to have a comfortable life and then discovering the world and everything in it is a reeking pile of shit. That's not to say all of us felt sorry for him. Not, for instance, those of us whose sons were considered odd-looking by the square-jawed standards of the time—narrow chests, bushy eyebrows, teeth crooked even after braces came off—or who were crippled with shyness. Sons who, because they didn't play sports or take apart car engines, were pegged as gay by their classmates, the more enlightened of whom—round-faced girls with plucked eyebrows and powder covering blemished noses—would offer to set them up with a boy in their drama club, the rest settling on the expected taunts of *faggot* and *butt-plugger* and spreading rumors that they had AIDS.

These boys had few friends in school, even fewer in the youth group whose meetings and events they kept attending mostly to have an extracurricular activity to list on college applications but also as a screw-you to the other kids who wished they'd disappear. They joined us, their parents, at services for similar reasons. They'd stopped believing in God years earlier, and we'd told them, tearfully, that their spiritual life was their own, and if they wanted to skip Kol Nidre to go to the movies with Catholic friends, as their sisters—pretty and promiscuous—had done a year earlier, that was their choice. But they didn't have anyone to go to the movies with, so they stuck around Emek Shalom, their motivations, now that we thought about it, so like Arlene Besunder's that, despite ourselves, we couldn't help but admire her for the way she made us squirm, her stiff posture and fixed gaze speaking louder than her voice ever had: *Here I am. Deal with it.*

◄◦►

All this is to say, many of us hated kids like Todd Besunder and were happy to see him laid low by tragedy. A wrestler especially, who could get away with calling our sons *faggot* while he wore leotards and rolled around on mats covered with another boy's sweat. Of course we wouldn't have objected if our sons were gay, though it would have meant uncomfortable conversations with their grandmothers. But the fact was, despite their disinterest in sports and cars—and pretty much everything else—most of them were straight. It wouldn't have taken a gifted therapist to diagnose them with depression, though they wouldn't visit one until well into their twenties.

We'd find nudie magazines in their closets and under their beds, along with stains on their sheets or pillowcases or at the ends of their socks. They spent their nights fantasy-fucking those round-faced drama girls with plucked eyebrows, or the wrestlers' cheering girlfriends, or the stuck-up youth-group girls with their nose jobs and designer purses and practiced ways of pretending our boys weren't in the room.

◦

Maybe they even fantasized about Naomi Besunder, a striking, though glum, girl of fourteen given to wearing baggy, unflattering clothes. If we didn't know better, we might have assumed she simply took after her mother, with her sour expressions, her bluntness—"you're wasting your time," she told Rabbi Aronson when, after her bat mitzvah, he tried to convince her to enroll in high-school Talmud study—her sullen silences. We might have imagined her one day taking over Sisterhood meetings and Purim carnival setups, undermining our daughters just as Arlene had undermined us.

But we understood that nothing could be further from Naomi's thoughts. She wouldn't take part in anything that made her the center of attention. Long before her father's arrest, she'd wanted only to be invisible. What most of us knew—or maybe all of us—was that an early bout of severe colitis had left her with a permanent shunt and colostomy bag, and she lived in a state of permanent apprehension lest her peers find out. As a result she had as few friends as our awkward boys and kept mostly to herself. We'd always been careful never to tell our children what we knew, understanding how brutal and intolerant kids could be, and now, watching her sitting in the fourth row of the sanctuary, while her mother davened in defiance—or was it some attempt at penance? was Arlene actually trying to atone?—and Naomi hid her face in her prayer book, we agonized on her behalf. She was the only one we truly pitied, the one who deserved better after all she'd already suffered. For Naomi's sake, we said to each other on the phone, one of us should tell Arlene to stay at home.

And yet, in Naomi we also glimpsed Arlene's only weakness, and recognizing it, we couldn't help wondering what might happen if we were to exploit it. We'd protected Arlene all this time, one of us said as our indignation thickened, and this is how she shows her gratitude. And then—accidentally, or perhaps unconsciously—we let slip at dinner the source of Naomi's dreariness, and seeing the horror and delight on the faces of our children, made them promise to keep the secret. And because they were children, they did so for half a day at most, and then all the kids in the Hebrew school, all the kids in the high-school Talmud study, and all those in Naomi's youth group knew. At services they now pointed and giggled and whispered, and every so often we'd hear one of the younger ones, who didn't know any better, blurt out the phrase they'd all been passing around like pieces of discovered afikomen, plucked from its hiding spot and broken into equal portions: "Shit sack."

Or maybe it was one of the awkward boys who first said it out loud, one of those tired of being called *butt-plugger* by Todd Besunder and his wrestler friends. And who could blame him? "I can smell that shit sack from here," he'd say, ten rows back, his voice raised just enough to make Arlene Besunder stiffen even more than usual, her chin rising an extra degree, as old oblivious Aronson asked us to stand for the Shema. Poor Naomi, we thought, with her pretty face hiding behind her dark hair, her damaged body pumping feces beneath the waistband of her baggy dress. Callous, selfish Arlene, we thought, keeping the

kid on display, week after week, daughter of a criminal, pariah
through no fault of her own. Wouldn't she spare her now?

And out of concern, one of us told our kids to be kind to
Naomi, maybe even to seek her out after services one Friday
evening. "Show her some sympathy," we said, and perhaps
suggested they wait for her at the synagogue's back door so
they could catch her before she slipped out to the parking lot.
Is it our fault that so few kids are capable of sympathy, especially
when, like dogs, they smell fear and gather in packs? They did
as we asked, a group of ten or twelve crowding the door to the
parking lot just as Naomi and Todd came down the back stairs.

We don't know for sure what happened then. We were all
up in the ballroom, sipping punch, snacking on fruit—we avoided
the sweets as best we could—smiling our pained smiles at
Arlene. We can guess, of course: one of our kids asked Todd
about the money buried in the backyard, and another said, no,
they probably hide it in their underwear, they've got it on them
now. And then a third pointed to Naomi's pelvis and said, "The
shit sack. I saw it move!" And when Todd wrestled him to the
ground, the rest of the kids kicked and shouted, "Your mother's
a whore! Your father's a lying thief! You'll go to prison one day
just like him!"

It was as if all the words we'd thought but hadn't said for
the past eight months—imagine, eight months of holding our
tongues!—came exploding out of our children's mouths, an
eruption of anger and cruelty and truth-telling. It's a wonder
the doors didn't blow off their hinges, that the dome of the
sanctuary didn't topple down.

By the time we reached them, it was all over. Todd and
Naomi had escaped into the parking lot, had locked themselves
away in the Besunders' BMW. Arlene was the first down the
stairs, and she cried out in a voice that even then was quieter

than ours, that strained to make itself heard above our murmuring behind her. "What did you do to them? What did you say?"

Our kids only shrugged. Several snickered. One boy wiped blood from his lip.

Then, her face pale, veins showing on her taut temples, she turned to us.

What did she expect? Our support? Solidarity? Compassion?

Once more we smiled at her. Only now with wide joyous grins. We couldn't help it. It was impossible to hide our pleasure.

Her eyes went big with astonishment, it seemed, though afterward we assured each other that none of this could have possibly surprised her. "This is how you treat one of your own," she said. "You're no better than—"

No better than whom? We wouldn't ever find out. Before finishing, she threw open the door and strode into the orange glow of the parking lot's overhead lamps. For a moment we thought sparks were flying from her heels before realizing it was just light reflecting from bits of mica in the blacktop.

–◦–

And that was it. We showed up for services the following Friday remorseful, our kids reprimanded and ready to apologize. We knew it would be good for them to express their regrets, to learn to put on a sorrowful face. But the seats in the fourth row on the left side of the center aisle were empty. They stayed that way as Rabbi Aronson welcomed us. We were still braced when he reached the Kaddish, but by the time the Amidah began, we breathed easier. Such relief we'd never experienced before—not in a rush as we might have expected but a slow seeping that spread outward from chest to limbs to digits. Later some of us tried to describe the feeling: the unraveling of hundreds of tiny knots, steam rising from a field on the first sunny morning of spring.

Our kids felt it, too. We saw it in their flushed faces, their glances up at the dome overhead. There was plenty of time for them to learn to humble themselves, we thought, and if our lives were any prediction, they'd have no shortage of opportunity. So instead of giving them any more chiding looks, instead we squeezed their shoulders and offered up vigorous praise to HaShem, many of us standing and swaying for a good fifteen minutes, losing ourselves in the ancient words, the sounds of them rich and glorious in our heads, while the room itself remained silent. And afterward we all enjoyed brownies at the kiddush, free of guilt and worry.

We didn't see Arlene again. Or any of them. They sold the house and moved ten miles west. Besunder served five of his thirteen months and came back to open a successful real-estate agency in Sussex County. The children transferred to Roxbury High, where Todd wrestled his way to the state championship for a third time. How Naomi made out there we didn't know, though one of our kids spotted her a year later at the Rockaway Mall, wearing dark eye makeup, torn tights, and combat boots.

They joined Temple Beth El in Budd Lake, which soon had a refurbished Ark and a Torah rescued from a Tehran shul ransacked during the revolution. We tried not to envy the exuberant Purim carnival there, to which, after it was written up in the *New Jersey Jewish Herald*, people flocked from all over the state. We resisted the impulse to contact their Sisterhood president to find out whether Arlene was driving them all crazy. We told each other to enjoy thinking of her belonging somewhere else.

SWEET RIDE

◄○►

The van shows up while Noah's in school. He spots it when the bus drops him off one afternoon in early fall, a rusty hump in the strip of woods separating his family's driveway from the Weiners'. Whether someone has driven it there or had it towed, he can only guess. It's at least a decade old, dirty beige with a flaking red stripe around its center, porthole windows on its sides. Its back fender is missing, a corroded tailpipe exposed. Birch leaves soon cover its roof and hood. Snow follows. In spring its tires sink in mud, which the sun then bakes into hard clay. Weeds grow thigh-high in front of its doors. Noah never sees it move.

But he knows its engine turns over, and that Carl Weiner keeps enough gas in its tank to let it idle for an hour at a time. Every evening Carl sits in there with the doors closed, stereo cranked loud enough for Noah to hear drumbeats all the way in his bedroom on the opposite side of the house. From the kitchen he watches smoke seep from the driver's-side window, exhales coming ten or twelve seconds apart. His mother catches him staring, and her face settles into a look of pinched consternation, the same one she turns on him when he comes downstairs for a glass of water late at night to find her and his father snuggled together on the couch, flushed and whispering.

"Give him some privacy," she says. "If you were out there, would you want someone gawking?"

Not long after, he hears her on the phone, and from a few of her muffled phrases—*temporary, I'm sure* and *just needs time to get back on his feet*—he knows she's talking to Carl's mother, Jackie Weiner. They play bridge once a week and work together on a shared garden that straddles their backyards, but they aren't really friends. Jackie's a loudmouth, according to his mother, her husband Bruce a shlub. To Jackie, he's sure, his mother's a snob. She probably thinks better of his father, who's breezily sociable and generally disarming, though that's never kept her from gloating whenever Bruce, a sales executive at a pharmaceutical firm, gets a bigger bonus or a raise.

"Have you thought about finding him a counselor?" Noah's mother asks, and then winces while listening to the response. "I'm not suggesting anything, Jackie. I'm just trying to help."

When she finally puts the phone down, his father makes a dismissive gesture, flicking invisible lint from the front of his shirt. "Not everyone needs a shrink," he says. "Kid's just down in the dumps. Who wouldn't be after getting kicked out of two schools in two years?"

"When people ask me what I think, I tell them," his mother says. "If she didn't want my opinion, she should have called someone else."

Noah's older sister, Judith, rummaging in the refrigerator, rattles jars and clears her throat. "He didn't get kicked out," she says. "He dropped out."

"What's the difference?" her father asks.

"Free will," Jude says.

"As opposed to what, divine intervention?"

"He chose his own destiny."

"Sure," their father says. "He chose to fail all his classes, throw away his parents' money, and come crawling home."

—◦—

Whether Carl has dropped out or been kicked, Noah doesn't know. Only this is certain: After graduating from Union Knoll High School with high honors, class of 1987, he left for college at Vanderbilt. But as a sophomore he transferred across the North Carolina border to Appalachian State. He lasted nine months there before coming home to New Jersey. Now twenty, he rides his bike to a job as checkout clerk at ShopRite and sits in a disintegrating Chevy G20 in the evenings, smoking and listening to music turned up loud.

Noah has just turned fourteen. He's a quiet kid who does well enough in school not to get questioned by his parents, though not well enough to get singled out by teachers or by those kids who'd delight in torturing the smarts out of him. He plays passable shortstop on the junior-high baseball team. He cleans his room without being asked and calls his grandparents every week. But this version of him has recently come to seem like an easy default, not necessarily the person he has to be. Over the past year he's discovered that he no longer cares very much about things that have long interested him: baseball, fishing, exploring the woods behind his house. Nothing has yet replaced these interests, except for girls, who remain a mystery far out of reach. He now has the feeling he's been waiting for the right time to become something else, or something more. He has several close friends but has begun looking around to see if others might prove more exciting. It's strange to realize he doesn't know where to direct his attention, what to hope for, and for months a vague, uncertain expectation has been building in him, a sense that he'll soon be swept up by new and, so far, undetected desires. The appearance of the van speaks to this feeling, though how he's not yet sure.

He's known Carl most of his life. Despite their age difference, he can tell that something has happened to Carl while he was away, that he's been altered in that time. It isn't just the hair he's grown out, or the fringed leather jacket he wears over ragged T-shirts instead of the polos he favored in high school. There's something uneasy in his smile the few times he's greeted Noah.

On a sunny afternoon in late spring, after the bus drops him off, Noah comes upon Carl flat on his back beside the van. By then Carl has been home seven or eight months, but the van looks no different than when Noah first saw it. Carl pulls his head from the chassis, says, "Noah Gottlieb. The little prophet. Ready to help me build my ark?" and then touches his hand to his cheek as if to make sure his mouth is behaving as he expects. He pretends to work for a few minutes and then pushes himself off the ground with a grunt, flexing his arms. There's a smudge of grease on his chin, so precise Noah can't help thinking Carl has wiped it there for his benefit. "How long will it take?" he asks, meaning to fix the van, but Carl only glances at him oddly, and answers in the voice that has gone raspy in the two years he's been away, making Noah lean forward to hear him. "If I knew that, man, I'd have the key to the kingdom."

As far as Noah can tell, he's made only one improvement. The new stereo fits its compartment awkwardly, the deck poking out an extra inch past the dashboard, wires dangling below. Carl fishes a key from a hiding place under the front fender, revs the engine a few times, and pulls a box of tapes from beneath the passenger's seat. The only music worth listening to, he says, was played by bands you would have seen in Golden Gate Park in 1967: Jefferson Airplane, Big Brother and the Holding Company, Country Joe and the Fish, the Grateful Dead. "But only the early stuff," he adds. "When they didn't waste everyone's time with twenty-minute drum solos."

His favorite, though, is Moby Grape. Hands down. Ever heard of them? Noah gives a half-shrug, half-nod to signal that of course he's heard of them, who hasn't? But Carl doesn't acknowledge the gesture. Best band in the world, he says, but hardly anyone even knows the name. In his voice is a mixture of indignation and pride, suggesting, Noah knows, that only a select few, the rare and worthy, can appreciate true genius. He pops in a tape, lights a cigarette, and closes his eyes. Noah doesn't mind the music, which is bluesy and raw, with jangling harmonies, but it doesn't make him bob his head in the dreamy way Carl does, shaggy hair fanning his eyes and swirling clouds of smoke blowing out of his nose. Instead Noah drums one hand against the van and keeps the other in his pocket. It's the first time he's heard a bootleg, and there's something unhinged about the live recording, sudden changes of volume or bursts of static, people shouting in the background even during the ballads. At any moment he expects to hear one of the amplifiers blow or the musicians throw down their instruments and run into the crowd.

"If I could go back in time and see them at the Fillmore," Carl says between songs. "I'd quit this place in a second. Never give it another thought."

But the Haight isn't the Haight anymore, he adds. The closest thing is what he's found in North Carolina, up in the mountains. He's going back as soon as he's saved some cash, fixed up the van, dealt with some lingering hang-ups. Then he'll stay down there for good. It's a chance for him to become part of a family, a real one, not like these people who believe they can control his thoughts just because they fed and clothed him for eighteen years. He flicks a hand in the direction of his house, and Noah considers relating his mother's assessment of Carl's parents: *loudmouth, shlub.* But by then another song has started, and Carl disappears behind his mask of hair and smoke.

Noah doesn't know what the Haight is and hears it instead as "the Hate." Why anyone would want to go there he has no idea. And when Carl mentions hang-ups, Noah thinks he's talking about the telephone. In general he doesn't understand what Carl's looking for, what sort of family he wants. But he recognizes the longing in Carl's voice, one he's experienced often enough, staring out his bedroom window at the bland curve of Crescent Ridge Road, the silent house across the street occupied by a couple whose kids have grown up and moved away, an old basketball hoop on the garage missing its net, the door of their mailbox always left open like a slack tongue. He doesn't know what to dream about, but dreaming for its own sake makes all the sense he needs.

When Carl flips the tape over, Noah asks him to turn up the volume.

"Hell yes," Carl says and twists the knob.

—◦—

The days Jude doesn't have tennis practice, the high-school bus drops her off twenty minutes before Noah's. He shouldn't be surprised to find her sitting on the hood of the van one afternoon, but the sight of her leaning back on her elbows, heels on the fender, knees sticking through ripped denim, makes him hesitate on the sidewalk. Carl hunches on a rock nearby, smoking and bobbing, face hidden in waves of dark hair. It's a warm day, and he has his shirt off, the top button of his jeans undone, and this time a grease smudge mars his chest, just as carefully placed, Noah thinks, as the previous one on his chin.

But this isn't what bothers him. It's that the driver's-side door is open, and out of it churns the same bluesy riffs, the same loose beats and rough harmonies. Isn't he the one who agreed the Grape is the best band in the world, though he first heard of them only a week ago? Hasn't he proven himself worthy? He hates the idea that anyone else in the neighborhood, much less his own sister, might be among the chosen.

Only then does he really take Carl in—this new permutation, so unlike the one he knew he can't quite believe they're the same person. The former Carl had fluffy hair, combed straight back from his forehead, a Star of David on a silver chain around his neck, a narrow chest that seemed to swim in oversized shirts, a studious squint that made his features look too big for his face. Now he's straightened his posture, and his shoulders turn out to be broader than Noah realized. Framed by long hair, the sizeable nose and ears are imposing rather than ungainly. More hair grows in a triangle on his chest and circles each nipple, and on his right shoulder is a black tattoo of what appears to be a figure-eight toppled onto its side.

He knows Jude is also studying Carl, sneaking glances as he sucks long drags from his cigarette. She doesn't move to the beat, just chews the fingernails of her left hand and spits whatever she's loosened into the weeds. Do the tapes make her nervous, too? She doesn't wave to him when he approaches or even look up as he sits in the grass a few yards away, trying to bob his head in rhythm with Carl's. Carl doesn't greet him, either, not even when the song ends and he surfaces from what seems less trance than a state of forced bliss, painful because it's so fleeting. He raises his head slowly and forms that odd, closed-lip smile that doesn't quite settle into a comfortable shape, instead rising and slipping and rising again into something closer to a grimace. "So?" he asks. "What do you think?"

Noah wants to be the one to answer. It's his chance to show Carl he's chosen wisely in playing the music for him first. But he struggles to find any words. The right words, the ones Carl wants to hear. How are you supposed to talk about a song? He can imagine describing the way it makes him want to jump up and kick at the weeds or at the van's tires, the bouncy frenetic energy that seems to have nothing to do with Carl's languid head-bobbing. Is it possible they're hearing two different songs? Or that Carl is hearing it wrong?

"Subliminal," Jude says before Noah can come up with anything. She, too, has her eyes closed now, and instead of chewing her nails she presses a finger to the bridge of her nose. The word doesn't sound appropriate, no closer to the music than Carl's movement. In fact, it sounds like gibberish, and though he knows he's heard it plenty of times before, now he can't call up its meaning. He makes a noise of disapproval, halfway between a cough and a chuckle, to let her know she's full of shit.

But it doesn't matter what he thinks. She has Carl's full attention now. The labored smile fades, and he peers at her with surprise as if he's only just noticed her sitting on the hood of a beat-up van no one ever drives. And seeing him scrutinize her that way releases Noah from his jealousy. He wants her to open her eyes and realize she's being assessed, maybe admired. She doesn't get a lot of glances from boys, and though she never confides in him, Noah always knows by her extended silences, her sudden irritability, when she's suffering from an unrequited crush. It's been a regular feature of his childhood to wish Jude happier than she is.

Few people would call her attractive, and certainly no one would use the word *pretty* to describe her. She has unruly black hair, more bushy than curly, made stiff by too much hairspray and cut with bangs that tumble in a tight wave over dense eyebrows. Her nose is long, her mouth set in a downward curve that makes her seem more stern than she really is. Altogether her look is severe, unapproachable. He tries to guess at its appeal, especially when she plays it up as she does sitting on Carl's van, wearing dark eyeliner to match her hair, tight jeans with strings hanging from holes in the knees, chunky silver rings on slender fingers with unpolished nails. Carl might notice the long legs muscled from tennis, the prominent collarbones, the lips waxy with Chapstick. Whatever he sees, Noah wants Jude to know about it, and he clears his throat to say something about the music and make her look up. He still has nothing in mind and has no idea what will come out if he gets the chance. But he's hesitated too long.

"You got a good ear," Carl says and looks away.

Jude keeps her eyes closed and waits for the next song.

◄◦►

Noah doesn't find it strange for a twenty-year-old college dropout to take an interest in his sixteen-year-old sister. It doesn't occur to him to think of it as inappropriate or creepy or illegal. If anything, the prospect of a romance excites him. He wants kids to see him around with Carl, to wonder and envy. He imagines the three of them riding to Lenape Lake once summer starts, pulling up to the little beach in the freshly painted G20, catching looks from the jocky delinquent types who always claim the sunbathing dock floating thirty yards out in the brown water shimmering with oil slicks. He wonders if Jude has a similar vision in mind, but when they leave Carl's yard, she doesn't mention him, not even tangentially, except to say, "Don't tell Mom we've been hanging out over there."

"I'm not an idiot," he answers.

"Fooled me."

"I'll tell Dad instead."

"He never pays attention to what we do."

"He would if he saw Carl checking you out."

"No one checked me out."

"He must need glasses."

"You don't know what you're talking about."

"You had your eyes closed. Too busy dreaming about his chest hair." He runs a hand down his own chest, hairless beneath his shirt, and lets his voice go high, though Jude's is deep, close to husky. "So soft, but manly."

"Idiot," she says.

After that, nothing. She doesn't deny the attraction any more than she admits it. But her silence undermines Noah's attempts to needle her, and after trying a couple more times, he quits. Instead he watches the way she runs the ends of her hair through her fingers whenever she speaks to Carl, eyes flitting up as soon as he turns his back. When they aren't listening to music, Carl rants about how much he hates it here, how terrible it is for the soul, how they should get out the first chance they have. "This place, man," he says. "It chews you up and spits you out, and you just go along with it because you don't know any better. And if you stick around until you're an adult, then you're just this walking gob of chewed up . . . I mean, you're a fucking spitball."

Noah doesn't know what he objects to, exactly, what he wants to warn them away from. Is it their neighborhood, their town, New Jersey? Or being twenty and stuck living with your parents after an aborted attempt to escape? He's heard his mother use the word *depressed* when talking about Carl, but the term doesn't mean much to him. Whatever failures or disappointments have sent him home after a year and a half of college seem part of an important reckoning. If he sounds a little lost or lonely or desperate, isn't that only because he's trapped in a house with people who have no vision for their lives beyond going to work and playing golf and saving up for a vacation to Bermuda?

"My folks are pissed off all the time for no reason," he says. "Yours, too, I bet. Because they're bored out of their minds. But they go around pretending this is exactly what they want. It's a simmering pot of repression. One day the lid's gonna blow right the fuck off."

If Jude sees him any differently, she keeps it to herself. Maybe she's too flattered by his attention to question what prompts it, or maybe she thinks she can help him, ease the loneliness and lend new purpose to his days. In either case, she doesn't shy away. When her tennis season ends, every day Noah comes home to find her sitting on the hood of the van, listening to music while Carl works—or pretends to work—underneath. The days grow hotter, and she exchanges jeans for shorts, T-shirts for tank tops. She paints her fingernails and works hard to keep from chewing them. Instead of ChapStick, she wears dark red lipstick. She smiles dreamy smiles. In the evening, she snaps at her parents when they ask innocuous questions about her day. In turn, their parents speak to each other tersely. Noah senses something momentous coming. Even trouble he'll welcome as a balm to the tense anticipation that now makes nights in the stagnant house unbearable.

Enough, he thinks. Just get it over with.

-◄○►-

One afternoon, Carl says, "I'm riding into Chatwin. There's a place there . . . Better see it for yourselves. Wanna come?"

He doesn't look at either of them as he speaks, and his voice is even more hushed than usual, caught, it seems, halfway up his chest. Jude hops off the van without a word and heads toward their garage to get her bike. Noah expects her to give some sign that she doesn't want him to tag along. But when he doesn't follow, she calls over her shoulder, "We're on our own tonight," which means their parents will be out to dinner and not home before eight. Then he expects Carl to object or at least make a show of disappointment. Doesn't he want to be alone with her? But instead his voice returns to ordinary: relaxed and raspy, confident and secretive. "You got to be cool about this. Can't tell anyone."

Downtown Chatwin is only a four-mile ride from their quiet street in Union Knoll, with its brick-fronted colonials and sloping lawns, but the world changes along the route. Past Lenape Lake, sprawling waterfront homes give way to turn-of-the-century bungalows with sagging front porches and flaking paint. Then, where Lakeview Road widens and turns into Russell Avenue, come tilting row houses followed by sooty apartment buildings with rusted fire escapes. At its end is Victory Park, the old town square. The neighborhood around it was once a shopping district, but most foot traffic has been siphoned away by the Heritage Mall, built a few miles farther south. The square still vibrates with the aftershocks of recent collapse. Sheets of plywood cover the plate glass of the appliance store and the Woolworth's. The old brick library has been abandoned for a new building beside the mall, and the marquee of the once-grand movie theater advertises only second-run horror flicks like *Puppet Master* and *Psycho Cop* and *Halloween 5*. The pedestrians who used to stroll through the park have since left it to groups of men who share wine bottles and sleep on benches when the weather turns warm.

Noah has passed through this part of town before, plenty of times, on the way to Temple Emek Shalom, where he had his bar mitzvah just over a year earlier. But rolling through on a bike is nothing like being in a car with glass separating him from those crumbling buildings and boarded-up stores. There's nothing between him and the ancient trees of the park, which cast deep shadows across the paths, a rotting picnic table visible beside a statue covered in pigeons. The men drinking on the lawn watch them as they ride past, and he pedals hard to keep up with Carl, who stops at the southeast corner of the square. Jude pulls up a few seconds later. Noah hops off his bike and starts to chain it to a lamppost, but Carl says, "Leave it there, and you'll have a long walk home."

He leads them to a squat brick building, old but intact, and then to a blank steel door between a shuttered storefront and a still-operating pawn shop, with stacks of stereos behind barred windows. The door is painted black, no sign to mark it, not even a street number, only a button that makes no sound when Carl presses it. Then he gives Noah a wink, an awkward one because it isn't accompanied by a smile. Is it supposed to be reassuring? Carl's dismounted from his bike, but Jude stays on hers, one foot still on a pedal, both hands on the handlebars. They wait thirty seconds, maybe longer, but nothing happens. Carl cups his hands around Jude's ear and whispers something that makes her squint and pick at her lower lip. Then one of his hands slips around to her back, fingers spread between her shoulder blades.

The park's trees have just finished leafing out, their green impossibly bright against the backdrop of filthy brick and stone.

One of the men has broken away from the group and started toward them, cutting straight across the overgrown lawn, skirting another statue, this one of a Revolutionary War hero in a tricorn hat. He wears a knit cap and a heavy camouflage jacket, though it's hot enough for Noah to sweat in short sleeves, and he has a mustache that cuts all the way across his face to connect with bushy sideburns. Out of a nearby storm drain comes a funky smell, rotting leaves, maybe, or the last whiff of an animal that died a week earlier.

From across the street the guy calls, "It's your lucky day."

"Don't answer," Carl says and presses the button again.

"I said it's your lucky day. Don't you want to know why?"

When he's halfway across the street, he pushes up the cap and locks eyes with Noah. And then Noah can't help himself. He wants to know what the guy considers lucky. He calls back, "Why?"

Then something buzzes and clicks. Carl yanks the door open, and they roll their bikes inside. The guy's face appears in the gap, closing in on them, but the door swings shut before he reaches it. In front of them a narrow set of stairs leads to a hallway lit by a single tube in a fixture with no cover. Noah's shirt is smudged with chain grease by the time they make it up and lean their bikes against the wall. At the end of the hall a dark curtain fills a doorway with no door, bluish light seeping around its edges, along with a kind of music he doesn't recognize, a jumble of reverberating hums. Carl's hand is on Jude's back again. Noah has the feeling that he's pushing her forward, though maybe she passes through the curtain on her own. Carl goes in after her. Noah hesitates a moment, standing alone in the empty hallway, listening to the strange music, and then follows.

The feeling that accompanies him through the doorway is a strange mixture of elation and letdown. He's never seen anything like it, and yet it's exactly as he's expected, exotic but

ordinary. Tie-dyed tapestries with vaguely Indian patterns—
elephants parading in a circle around a feminine figure with
too many arms—cover the walls and windows, and drifts of
pungent smoke graze the low ceiling. Elsewhere, skulls and
roses and dancing bears. Shelves display hand-blown glass
pipes, and knitted ponchos hang from clothes racks.

The only astonishing thing is that a place like this has been
here all along, just a few miles from Union Knoll. For some
reason he thinks of his father taking the train into Manhattan
every day for work, the disappointment he must feel every
evening when he returns. Noah wanders through the warren
of narrow rooms expecting to hear someone tell him he isn't
allowed to be here, breathing in the incense and ogling the
pipes, browsing racks crammed with import records and bootleg
tapes. The latter are arranged not by band name, it seems, but
by quality: those with typed or photocopied covers at the top,
those handwritten in the middle, those without covers at the
bottom. Some of the tapes have no writing on them at all,
nothing to identify their contents, and they sell for a dollar
each. "Mystery selections," Carl says when Noah crouches down
to examine them. "Most of it's crap, but you'll occasionally pull
out a diamond." Carl scans the cassettes quickly, slipping a few
out to read song titles, giving a whistle when he comes across
something that entices him.

The only names Noah recognizes are Led Zeppelin and the
Who. He guesses Carl won't approve of either. Since he doesn't
know what else to look for, he grabs a couple of mystery tapes,
along with one from the typed bunch whose name appeals to
him. On the spine it reads, QUICKSILVER WINTERLAND 1968,
and on the cover is a blurry photocopy of four skinny, long-
haired boys leaning against a brick wall, one with a big belt
buckle and a top hat too small for him squeezed down onto his

forehead. "You got a good eye," Carl says. It sounds too rehearsed, too much like what he's said to Jude, for Noah to take it as genuine praise. He has twelve bucks in his pocket, most of three weeks' allowance, and the tape costs eight. He puts the mystery selections away. Jude, who has a weekend job at a bakery in Lenape, spends three times as much on an ankle-length skirt made out of the same material as one of the tapestries. She holds it to her waist, twirls, and lets out an uncharacteristic giggle too girlish for her and altogether phony.

"Made for you," Carl says.

Back on the street, Noah expects to find the guy in the knit cap waiting to confront them or to hit them up for money. But he's nowhere in sight. The sidewalk outside the pawn shop is empty, though the square itself, with a convergence of one-way streets and stoplights on every corner, is choked with traffic and honking horns. Their bikes beat it out of there much faster than the cars. When they make it back to Carl's yard, Jude unfolds the skirt and reveals what's hidden inside: a glass pipe, purple and blue like the fabric, blown in the shape of a butterfly.

"You bought that?" Noah asks, though he already knows the answer.

"Who'd pay twenty-five bucks for a hunk of glass?" Jude says.

Carl gives her that naked stare again, no smile, no softness around the eyes. For a moment he says nothing. Then: "Goddamn." Jude shrugs and chews her nails. To Noah, he says, "Did you know you had an outlaw in the family?"

"Too bad we don't have anything to put in here," Jude says. She holds the pipe up to the sun, still high above the horizon, and a blue shadow falls across her cheek and jaw.

"I might have a little something," Carl says.

Then they both look to Noah, as if he's the one who should decide what will happen next. He can't tell if they want him to stick around, to stand in the way of what's coming, or if they're waiting for his blessing. He studies the tape he's bought, the unfamiliar song titles. Then he mutters something about heading home to listen to it while doing algebra homework. They seem more nervous than relieved when he stands up, Jude playing with her hair, Carl brushing leaves from the van's roof.

"There's lasagna in the fridge," Jude says. "Stick it in the oven for forty-five minutes. Three-fifty. Or eat it cold. It's not bad that way."

"After you listen to that," Carl says, "algebra'll never be the same."

Noah wheels his bike across the wooded strip to his driveway, stows it in the garage, and looks out the kitchen window. The back door of the van hangs open, and Jude crawls in. He cuts a piece of cold lasagna and brings it to his room, where he won't be able to see what's happening. He puts his headphones on, too, so he won't hear anything but the Quicksilver cassette, which is badly recorded, guitar fuzz hardly distinguishable from tape noise and applause. Without Carl listening along with him, the music sounds muddy and amateurish, and it distracts him too much to do any homework. So he just lies on his bed, picturing the elephant tapestries and the butterfly pipe, the guy in the knit cap and army jacket who told him it's his lucky day. Is it?

Jude comes home a few minutes before their parents pull into the driveway. Her face is pale, her lips swollen. She isn't carrying the patterned skirt. Though the tape has come to an end, Noah keeps his headphones on as she passes his bedroom and pretends not to notice the red mark on her neck.

"Who left the lasagna sitting out?" their mother calls up the stairs.

"Who knows where the time goes?" their father sings in response.

A couple of hours later, when he takes off the headphones and gets into bed, drumbeats pulse through the screens of his open windows.

—◦—

The next morning he wakes to find Jude sitting on the end of his bed. The red mark on her neck has purpled into a bruise, and her face is drawn and dark but calm. "I don't want him to leave," she says.

He pushes himself up and blinks away a dream he can't remember. The back of his throat immediately begins to burn. "Is he going to? Now?"

"He didn't say when. Soon, I guess."

"Are you going with him?" he asks and feels ridiculous for the next question, which he can't stop himself from asking. "Can I come, too?"

"He has a girlfriend down there."

He knows he should feel anger on her behalf, betrayal, but it stirs only distantly, something he might reach for if he can get rid of the burning that has now crept into his nose. He wipes a hand across his eyes in case they've started to leak.

"He shouldn't have messed with me," Jude says.

"Is the van ready? He said he won't leave until he can drive it."

"We'll find out," Jude says. "Get dressed."

Their parents have already left for work. Clouds have formed overnight, and by the time they make it outside, backpacks on as if they're going to the bus stop, it's begun to drizzle. All the shades at the Weiners' are lowered, and they creep beneath the birches, crunching leaves as quietly as they can. Jude finds the key under the van's front fender. Without turning the ignition, she eases off the emergency brake and rolls it backward out of the yard. To keep from making extra noise, they leave the doors open until they reach the street. Then Jude turns the key. The engine sputters and rumbles. They slam the doors hard, Jude presses the gas, and the van jerks forward.

Raindrops patter the scummy windshield, but the cracked wipers only mix water with dirt and decomposing leaves to make a brown film on the glass. Where the window cranks should be, rusty bolts poke out of ragged holes. The driver's window is stuck open less than an inch, the passenger's not at all. Jude's hair, still damp from the shower, clings to her neck, and Noah's back has begun to sweat. The inside of the car steams. Before they make it to the end of the street, he leans forward to clear away condensation with a forearm.

Because Jude doesn't yet have her driver's license—she's had her learner's permit for all of a month—they stay off busy Lakeview Drive, which often has speed traps at the top of Crescent Ridge. Instead they snake a circuitous route of back streets and then down the long stretch of Lenape Road, which skirts the far edge of the lake, a steep bank to the water on one side, a rock wall on the other. The road is narrow, and the van keeps pulling to the left. Whenever a car approaches from the opposite direction, Jude jerks the wheel, and they swerve toward the guard rail and the brown water, pocked by raindrops, lapping at the rocky shore below. Before they're halfway along the bank, a big black pickup catches up to them and rides their tail. Their back window is too dirty to see the driver's face clearly, but Noah thinks he can make out a baseball cap and sunglasses, though the clouds have darkened further, and a row of lights blare on top of the truck's cab.

The speed limit is twenty miles an hour, and Jude holds steady between twenty-five and thirty. But when the truck won't back off, she taps the brake once, twice, and then speeds up. It does back off then, but only for a moment. When it charges, it comes with horn sounding, silver grille suddenly filling the side mirror. Noah thinks for sure it will hit them, and not just a nudge, either. If they're lucky, they'll skid into the guard rail and slide to stop, but he pictures instead the van plunging nose-first into the lake, water seeping through the stuck window, the dim light growing dimmer as they sink. And all he can think is that in either case, this will be over before it has gone very far. He doesn't know how to feel about that. A part of him is disappointed. He still wants something big and new and transformative, something to carry him forward into the rest of his life. But another part has been trying to get up the never to tell Jude they should turn around and go back, return the van, and pretend they've never touched it. He closes his eyes and waits.

But there's no impact. When he opens his eyes, Jude still has control of the van, that sharp face of hers—beaky nose, chapped lips, wild hair—set perfectly still above the steering wheel, frozen not with fear but furious concentration. The pickup has jumped into the eastbound lane, horn louder as it comes even with them. Hit us, asshole, he thinks, and reaches over Jude's arm to punch their own horn, which only squawks a little, hardly audible over the grind of the engine. Jude bats his hand away. When the truck makes a move to pass, she jams her foot on the accelerator. She holds it there even when she sees another car coming toward them, a little red compact, small as a rodent. Noah thinks, road kill. The truck edges forward, and through the window slit he can see the passenger, also in a baseball cap but backwards, fat red cheeks, mouth opening and closing, fingers jabbing. Jude half-stands to keep the gas pedal down. "Hell are you doing?" he asks, but he already knows. Too many people have been fucking with her. The whole world fucking with her. She's had enough.

The truck slows and shimmies back into place. The red compact ticks by, too fast for Noah to see the driver's face, distorted, he imagines, by the flash of mortality. Eyes wide or squeezed shut? Mouth open in a scream or pulled back in a cringe? Why does he care? He's sweating harder now, soaked under the armpits and thighs, droplets rolling from his lower back into his underwear. Jude eases her foot off the gas, leans forward to clear the windshield. Her arm comes away wet, the dark hair slicked down over pale skin. The bruise on her neck bends around taut muscle.

"It stinks in here," she says. "Is that you?"

His smell isn't worse than any others in the van: mildewed fabric, spilled beer, stale cigarettes. But because he doesn't want to check to see if the truck is charging again, he pretends to fart and fan it toward her.

"I'm gonna puke," she says.

"Better breathe through your mouth."

Here, finally, is the end of the bank, old stone gateposts on either side, the road widening as it curves into a tunnel of trees. Before reaching it, Jude glances in the rearview mirror and slows to twenty miles an hour. "Oh dear," she says in a lousy British accent. "I believe I may have been driving too fast."

Noah doesn't want to laugh but can't help it. "We shouldn't like to get a ticket," he says, his accent even worse.

Jude snorts. "Heavens, no. That would be terribly inconvenient."

Once they start, they can't stop. "One should always obey the posted signs," Noah says, busting up before he's gotten the last word out. They're laughing hard when the pickup wheels around again into the other lane, clear now for at least half a mile, and comes even with them. In the gap above the window, there are the fat cheeks again, even more flushed, the backwards baseball cap, the enraged mouth shaping words they can't hear. Jude touches two fingers to her lips and blows a kiss. The pickup roars in front of them, around the curve and out of view.

As soon as it's gone, their giddiness fades. Jude's face settles back into a hard scowl. The rain picks up when they come around the ridge and drop toward Chatwin, washing the windshield nearly clear. Noah fishes a tape from the box beneath his seat. Its cover sleeve is creased and dirt-stained, unmarked except for a handwritten note: *Decent Sweet Ride. Best Omaha ever!* He slides it into the deck, but after only half a song Jude pops it out. For a second her eyes leave the road to study the label, nose wrinkling as if this is the source of the nasty smell. "I meant *sublime*, not *subliminal*," she says, though this new word means no more to Noah than the original. She reaches across her body and shoves the tape out the barely opened window. Noah turns to see where it lands but can't follow it. "He's going anyway," Jude says.

"He should have left you alone."

"Everything he said was straight out of some bad movie from the sixties."

"Who gets a tattoo of a figure-eight, anyway?"

"It's an infinity sign."

"It's infinitely stupid," he says and feels the burning in his throat again. This time he can't stop himself from crying. He doesn't know why. The grind of the engine gives him cover as a sob, one he can feel more than hear, escapes his mouth. He pulls another tape from the box. Without glancing at its cover, he leans across Jude and tries to toss it out of the van, but it bounces against the glass and lands in her lap. She retrieves it, and this time with her eyes set on the road, slips it out the window. After that, Noah keeps handing her tapes, and she sends them flying, one after another. A few of them he glimpses as they hit the pavement, one plastic casing shattering to let magnetic tape flutter in the middle of Russell Avenue.

By the time they make it to Victory Park, the box is empty. Traffic is light around the square, the drenched lawn beneath the trees deserted. Shallow puddles cover picnic tables and benches, and when they get out of the van the smell of damp moss masks any coming from the sewer drain. Noah hopes to see the guy with the knit cap and mustache, this time tell him it's his lucky day, but there's no one in sight. Jude pulls the key out of the ignition and leaves it on the driver's seat. Noah lets the passenger door hang wide open.

"How do we get to school?" he says, grabbing his backpack. He doesn't quite mean the question, just has a sense that he's supposed to test out his voice to see how far they've come, to decide whether he's willing to keep going. "Should have brought our bikes."

"They can do without us for today," Jude says. "We'll hang out in the mall until it stops raining."

But then she hurries across the street to the unmarked door beside the pawn shop, presses the button that makes no sound. He calls to her, "Haven't you stolen enough already?"

"Just a second," she says.

He joins her and waits. When the door clicks, she props it open with a knee and fishes something out of her pocket. The glass butterfly. It smells musky and singed, and a few dark specks stick to the inside of its blue stem. She sets it down on dirty tiles and lets the door close.

"Ready?" she asks.

"Ready," he agrees, though for what he has no idea.

CAUGHT

◄○►

He'd seen her. The one they'd called blonde dynamite. It was early 1944, in a café on Kurfürstendamm. He'd taken a table in back, near the rear exit. Through the closed door came the sound of rain in the alley, the smell of rotting vegetables. He had little appetite for coffee, even less for public spaces, but if he didn't leave his furnished room on Wielandstrasse for at least a few hours a day, his landlady would grow suspicious. He always faced the door to the street and kept his feet flat on the floor, ready to spring and run. Most nights he dreamed of shots fired at his back.

This afternoon he'd hardly touched his coffee when the young woman entered. Tall and shapely, with striking eyes and a dimpled chin, a scarf covering her head. Ella Goldschmidt. He was sure of it. By then she was legendary among the community of so-called U-boats: Jews living illegally around Berlin, most carrying forged papers and blessed with Aryan features. A photograph had circulated, though Bruno hadn't seen it, only heard a description of the blue-eyed beauty who'd once been one of them. Ella, too, had lived underground, using a false name, until a friend betrayed her, turned her over to Dobberke, head of the collection camp on Grosse Hamburger Strasse, who threatened to deport her parents unless she cooperated. Now she'd been working for him almost a year. According to rumors, she'd turned over hundreds, many her former schoolmates, sent them all to the trains heading east. And after Dobberke deported her parents anyway, she kept at it, even more ferociously. Maybe to save herself, maybe for her own enjoyment. She made men go wild for her and in the throes of passion got them to divulge the hiding places of cousins, ex-girlfriends, co-workers. She'd report them all, including the lovers, as if it gave her extra pleasure to wield such power over them.

So at least Bruno imagined. Thus far he had been both careful and fortunate not to cross her path. Fortunate in other ways, too. He'd lost contact with his family three years earlier, but they'd left him enough to live on for the remainder of the war. He was a good-looking boy, as German as any of his peers. His entire childhood, no one in his house had spoken a word of Yiddish. They'd celebrated Passover with four glasses of wine as prelude to an elaborate Easter brunch with neighbors. By nature he was reserved but intrepid, willing to take risks when he recognized the possibility of reward. These past five years he'd frequently depended on women, often homely ones, too surprised and grateful for his affection to question his motives. They'd take him into their beds, they'd feed him, they'd help him find new accommodations. He told them he was hiding to avoid military service, he didn't want to be sent to the front, he was too much of a coward. And they took pity on him, these brave girls with long faces and blemished skin. They forgave his cowardice. They would have taken his place at the front if they could.

He wished one were with him now, to deflect the attention of the woman entering the café, who untied her scarf, shook out thick blonde curls, and scanned the room for a table for too long, with too much deliberation. He lowered his face to his cup, as if to make sure no coffee would spill over the edge when he sipped. He felt her eyes pass over him, or imagined they did, lingering a moment and perhaps taking in the worn collar of his shirt, the unpolished toes of his shoes, any hint that he'd been in hiding and unable to attend to daily upkeep. She would know the signs. She'd once lived them, and since being recruited by Dobberke, had studied and exploited them. Yes, he was sure she could see he hadn't shaved this morning, though he was mostly smooth-cheeked, only a few light hairs sprouting along his jaw and on his chin. He was caught, after all this time. How fitting and absurd that it would end with a beautiful woman, after he'd passed time with those he would not call so, for so long.

His feet already pressed against the floor, backside just lifting from the seat. Before standing, he forced himself to look up. If Ella's gaze had touched him, it had since passed on, now focused on a couple across the room. A girl in a black raincoat, a man still wearing a hat. Too obvious, Bruno thought, too nervous. With such poor skills, how had they stayed free so long? Ella spoke to the waiter, who raised eyebrows in alarm. He deposited his tray on a counter and disappeared into the kitchen. Bruno stood slowly. He knew he had only a few minutes before Dobberke and his men arrived. He wanted to warn the girl in the raincoat—pretty but too thin, big eyes swimming in their sockets—and her companion in the gray tweed hat, but to do so would risk too much. He took his time putting on his coat. The key, he knew, was to show no fear. A man expecting arrest would be arrested. Now Ella did glance at him as he fed buttons through buttonholes. For a moment she held his eye and smiled. A smile, he thought, of recognition. There was no doubt, she saw in him one of her own, one who'd get away with escape today only because she let him, because she had easier prey. Next time, who knew?

He turned to the back door. If he ran, he might trigger her instinct to chase, like a dog's. He forced his feet to move slowly, even when they crossed the threshold into the alley, the cold rain blown by a sharp breeze into his eyes and over his cheeks. He kept a casual pace down Kurfürstendamm until reaching the intersection of Joachimsthaler Strasse, where he slipped into a movie house. A picture was already playing. He watched without seeing, keeping an eye on the entrance. When it ended, he stayed and watched through again. Only when the screen went dark a second time did he leave, heading straight to the apartment of a girl whose face had been scalded in infancy, a red mark, smoother than the dull skin around it, crossing from left temple to lower right jaw. He told her he'd had a run-in with a recruiter for the Wehrmacht, described a close call and his cunning dodge. She held him for a few hours before finding him a new place to live. He switched rooms. He bought new papers. He survived.

◄○►

More than a decade after the war's end, he attended Ella Goldschmidt's trial. It was in the old courthouse on Turmstrasse, built like a medieval fortress with turrets on each corner, high vaulted ceiling in the lobby. But Room 500 was small, drab, devoid of character. He crammed in with three, four dozen others. Families of her victims, survivors of the camps, people who'd read about her in gaudy headlines in *Nacht-Depesche* and other tabloids. The bloodthirsty, the curious, the bored. They jeered and whistled as she entered in a new maroon dress and matching shoes, with ramrod posture, hair recently styled and loose to the shoulders. She looked hardly older than the last time he'd seen her, though thirteen years had passed, ten of which she'd spent in a Soviet labor camp, convicted already by a military tribunal on the other side of now-divided Berlin. That would make her thirty-seven, while Bruno was thirty-five. The number still surprised him, he who'd once believed with certainty that he wouldn't live to see twenty-five. Even if he somehow managed to hide day after day, year after year, he'd thought, surely the world couldn't withstand so much chaos and horror, couldn't possibly continue turning for so long.

And yet here they both were. If not age, then imprisonment should have worn her down, and manual labor, and illness. In the camp, she'd contracted tuberculosis. So he'd read in one of those tabloids he'd tried to resist, finally picking it up from a newsstand despite knowing it made light of her victims' deaths with its pretense of shock and outrage. "Jewess Sent All Her Friends to the Gas Chamber!" read one of the headlines. Perhaps if he stood closer he might have seen how the disease affected her pallor, hollowed her cheeks, but from the back of the gallery he could make out only the color from the blush she'd applied, the dark lipstick that seemed to harden her indifference to the angry glare of the prosecutor, the somber demeanor of the judge. She didn't turn toward those who shouted and whistled at her, didn't face the first witness to take the stand, a former schoolmate whom she'd trapped in early 1943. This was soon after she'd first become a catcher for Dobberke, who'd reported to Höss, who'd reported to Eichmann. She stared straight ahead at the wood-paneled wall between judge and gallery, a pair of white gloves pinched lightly in one hand.

The witness described how she'd come to him asking for help, claiming she needed new papers, that her false identity had been compromised. Moments after he brought her to the forger, soldiers appeared. Even then she feigned innocence, the witness went on, weeping as all three were arrested. But when they arrived at Grosse Hamburger Strasse, she dropped the act, walked free through the prison halls, laughed with Dobberke, taunted those locked in tiny cells, deciding on the spot who would be deported to Theresienstadt, who to Auschwitz. He was sent to the latter, he said, though he escaped by breaking through rotten boards on the transport car and throwing himself from the train. As he spoke, the courtroom quieted, and by the time he ceased, it was silent. Ella's fist crumpled the gloves, but otherwise she showed no hint of emotion.

Bruno remembered this forger, the one who'd provided his first papers, on them a name he could no longer recall since afterward he'd changed it so many times. Now that he'd reclaimed the original—Bruno Gelbert, Bruno Gelbert, he'd recited often in the first years after the war ended, in disbelief, still prepared to give it up at any moment—he felt, with unease, that the young man who'd carried those other names was a different person altogether from the one in the courtroom. This Bruno Gelbert had taken a degree in biology, one of the first to graduate from the Free University, and now worked in a laboratory testing drinking water. He'd married a woman ten years his junior—with clear skin and bright eyes and a coy smile—who'd been a child in Tübingen during the war, daughter of a soldier killed at Stalingrad. Yes, a different person, wilier and less fragile than the one who cried at the birth of his daughter, who flushed with shame when his supervisor suggested ways he might work more efficiently.

That other young man, who'd moved from room to room, who'd gone to bed with girls he cared nothing for in exchange for their protection, who'd snuck out of a café knowing that soldiers would soon swarm an oblivious couple several tables to his left, had thought highly of himself for his daring and evasion, had believed it was his acumen and effort alone that kept him alive, while the Bruno in the courtroom now knew it was simply chance, out of his control. The same fickle, indifferent chance that had sent the forger to his death and allowed the first witness to escape.

When the latter returned to the gallery, Ella spoke only one word: "Lies." She said the same after the next witness described her chasing a man down a crowded street, shouting, "Criminal! Jew! Stop him!" to bystanders who tackled and held him until Gestapo police arrived. She said it without anger, without passion of any kind, the only inflection a glib arrogance not so different from that of the prosecutor who strutted in front of each witness, a dark-haired Bavarian with a drink-reddened face and double chin. How had *he* survived the war? What dubious acts had *he* committed to come through unscathed? Not so different, either, from the derisive laughter of those in the gallery, one of whom quoted another tabloid headline, "The Catcher Caught!" It was an arrogance Bruno knew well, that of people who believed they were responsible for walking free while others were in chains, convinced they'd worked for their good fortune, that their unique qualities had merited it.

His thoughts had been similar as he'd left the café. The couple had been less savvy and therefore deserved their fate, while he'd earned his. Such convictions were necessary then. They helped him get through each day. It was an illusion, of course, to think that all he needed to survive were his natural abilities and enough will. But without it he would have given up the first year.

And he guessed now, watching Ella Goldschmidt sitting stiffly before the stout judge, that she'd nurtured the same illusion, continued to hold onto it still, unaware how desperately she clung. Fear might have driven her to send hundreds to their deaths, fear of her parents' deportation and her own, but fear alone wouldn't allow her to live with what she'd done, to deny it with such half-hearted gestures, as if the accusations were nothing more than mildly insulting. Those people she'd caught were merely weaker than she was, less ingenious, less resourceful. When she'd smiled at him in the café, she was acknowledging the instincts they shared, which set them apart from the girl in the raincoat and the man in the hat.

Bruno had hoped to spot those two in the courtroom, though he realized it only now. Why else would he have come? It was his opportunity to see that they'd survived despite their bad luck in the café, despite his having turned his back on them. He scanned the faces around him, trying in his imagination to scrape away ten years from these pitted cheeks, or those sunken eyes, or that sneering mouth. Who knew if he'd recognize them even if they stood right beside him? Yet this was all he wanted, not revenge or even justice, just a glimpse of good fortune having landed, a nearly weightless bird, on someone else's shoulders with the same caprice or happenstance as it had on his.

"All lies," Ella said after a third witness described the outfit she'd worn while out searching for U-boats, a tailored green suit and matching cap, which she'd boasted was her "hunting outfit." And again after the fourth, a middle-aged man who'd lost his wife and three sons to the ovens, told how she'd spied his family with opera glasses during a children's play and had them arrested as they left the theater. Not smarter, Bruno wanted to tell her, not savvier, just luckier. Luckier to be heartless and cruel and selfish when compassion and dignity would have gotten her killed. And the couple in the café, unlucky and dead, but fortunate never to wonder as Bruno did if they'd been just like Ella Goldschmidt, willing to do anything to survive.

But then he was luckier than Ella, too. He'd never been forced—never been given the chance—to doom others in order to save his parents or himself. If he had, he wanted to believe he would have acted differently. Of course he would have. But because he could never know for sure, he almost pitied her as the first day of her trial ended and she strode out of the courtroom with the same rigid posture, the white gloves now pulled to the elbows. He almost tried to forgive her as someone in the gallery spit in her direction, a bit of white froth landing several inches short of her shoes. He didn't return to Turmstrasse the next day, or any other day. He'd seen enough, more than he needed. But a part of him remained in the courtroom, heard the testimony against her many times on sleepless nights, when his wife and daughter were lost in dreams. He didn't know if he'd ever fully leave it.

The trial, on the other hand, lasted less than two weeks. The tabloids announced Ella's conviction and sentence: ten years imprisonment. Then they forgot about her. Some months later he read in a legitimate newspaper that her lawyers appealed the sentence, which was remitted for the time she'd already served. She was freed to live the rest of her life.

SAFE AND SORRY

◄○►

Rabbi Markoff, the chaplain, kept typing as the officer—the chunky, sour-faced one who'd introduced himself as "Charles, but around here everyone calls me Chuckles"—led Josh Kaplan into the tiny office.

"Getting any sleep yet?" the officer asked, hanging on the doorframe.

"Does it look like it?" Markoff answered.

"Looks like someone's been pummeling you under the eyes."

"I'll sleep when she's in college," Markoff said with impatience, staring hard at his computer screen.

"I never lost a wink when my kids were born," Officer Chuckles said. "Wife did the night feeding. Why should both of us be up all hours?"

"My wife's a radiologist. She needs rest. If we had to survive on my salary, we'd live in a tent." Markoff punched out a few more words on his keyboard until the officer left. "Have a seat," he said and read over what he'd written. Kaplan, the new statistician from the Research and Evaluation Unit of the Office of Policy and Planning, eased himself into the chair beside the desk and glanced at his hand, as if he could find the time there, or the weather, or a message from his girlfriend asking him to pick up sushi for dinner. He didn't know what to do without his cell phone to occupy him, but he'd had to leave it in a locker in the waiting room, along with his wallet and keys—everything but his driver's license, which he'd handed to an officer behind shatterproof glass in exchange for the visitor's badge clipped to his shirt. "They last updated our software in 1998," Markoff said, before clicking his mouse and whisking a box off the screen. "It's a miracle I can send an email."

"I'm glad you could make time for me," Kaplan said.

"When you get back to headquarters, tell them I'm not kidding. If they don't upgrade soon, I'll start communicating by carrier pigeon."

"I'll see what I can do."

"Anyway, welcome to our live-in meditation center. And remind me what it is you need from me."

Kaplan had been working for the New Jersey Department of Corrections for five months now, but this was his first visit to an actual prison. His job was to deal with numbers, not people. When he'd finished his doctorate a year ago, with a dissertation on the effects of commuting on mental health, he'd expected to land a corporate job, or at least an academic one, but that was soon after the economy had tanked. The firms he was interested in downsized, and the colleges he applied to instituted hiring freezes. Only the state was bringing on new people, thanks to federal stimulus funds, and friends told him he was lucky to find any position, given how many of them were moving back in with their parents. He knew nothing about corrections when he started. His only experience with prison was as a boy watching *Scared Straight!*, which had had its intended effect, terrifying him into law-abiding behavior through most of his adolescence, until, for a brief time during college, he decided he was no longer concerned with consequences.

Now he was tasked with assessing the impact of chaplaincy programs on recidivism rates, and over the past few weeks he'd received spreadsheets from ministers, pastors, and priests at facilities around the state—including from East Jersey State Prison, where *Scared Straight!* had been filmed. But when he contacted Meadowbrook State Penitentiary in North Chatwin, just a few miles from where he'd grown up, the reply was curt: when the DOC finally updated their computer system, they might have data in electronic form. In the meantime, he was welcome to come any time to look at their files.

He supposed the ones he needed were those in cardboard boxes crammed into the office, which was hardly more than a closet, with a window looking out on the chapel, a low-ceilinged room with dingy carpet, sparse bookshelves, folding chairs arranged haphazardly. Any hope he'd had that the files might be organized or systematic fled the moment he'd walked in. His report would be spotty and largely useless, though he'd submit it all the same. Better safe than sorry, his father had always said, about everything—and despite never having taken a risk in his life, he'd died of a heart attack at fifty-four. What would he think of his only child walking into a maximum-security prison, hiking up five flights of stairs, and passing convicted drug dealers, carjackers, armed robbers—and sure, even murderers—hurrying from jobs or showers to their cells for count?

Now, to distract from the unease that had been bubbling since his director had told him, a week ago, that he would indeed have to look at the files in person, he asked, "Are there many of us in here?"

"Many of who? Bureaucrats?"

"Jews, I mean."

"A handful," the rabbi said, his look of bored irritation giving way to one of mild interest. "Hard to get a minyan together. Our people," he added, with a wink, "tend to prefer federal accommodations."

"I was surprised to find a rabbi, that's all," Kaplan said. "I wouldn't have thought there was much demand."

"I serve people of all faiths," Markoff snapped. He didn't look much like a rabbi, at least not like the one Kaplan had known as a boy, when he'd squirmed through Saturday morning services and squawked through bar mitzvah lessons: bearded, mostly deaf, fond of quoting the Rambam. Nor like the one who'd directed his Hillel chapter in college, an aging hippie in sandals and tie-dyed tallis. Markoff was clean-shaven, maybe thirty-five, no yarmulke or fringes. His boyish face settled back into sleepy composure. "Ecumenical, we call it."

"Of course. But I imagine a lot of these guys are interested in finding Jesus, right?"

"I'm familiar with the New Testament. The Koran, too. Even the Bhagavad Gita. I point people toward useful passages." He let out an abrupt, wheezy laugh. "Except for the passage that leads out of here. They don't give me the key to that one."

His computer made a bleep, and his gaze drifted back to the screen. Through the window, Kaplan could see a few men wandering into the chapel, wearing blue overalls stenciled with the state seal and the letters DOC, the same as on the letterhead in his office. They pulled chairs into a circle and lowered their heads—waiting, it seemed, for something to fall on them.

"I just figured they'd, I don't know, be more comfortable with a priest. Someone who could take their confession."

Markoff looked at him with renewed attention, one eyebrow lifting. "You think that would help them?"

"They must be carrying around a lot of guilt," Kaplan said. "Just seems like it would be easier if they had someone who could give them, you know . . ."

"Absolution?"

"After a few thousand Hail Marys, or whatever."

Again Kaplan glanced at his hand. He'd known he'd have to give up his phone before passing through the metal detector, but he hadn't realized how vulnerable it would make him feel, stripped of his only connection to the outside world. When he raised his head, Markoff was staring at him with a pleased, smug expression, as if reading his mind and thinking: a little discomfort would do him good.

"It's an interesting topic," Markoff said. "Forgiveness, that is. But I was under the impression you were here for other reasons."

"Yes," Kaplan said. "Your files."

But before he could go on, the rabbi was looking over his head, then rising. "Excuse me a second," he said.

It took Kaplan a moment to realize why. Someone else had come into the office and stood just behind his chair. Officer Chuckles, returned already to hustle him back to his regular life? The relief was surprising only in its swiftness and force. His legs moved into place to get him up and out. What did it matter if he hadn't even looked at the files? What could he possibly find in that mess of boxes, only a few of them labeled, the years handwritten, some in Sharpie, others in pencil?

But it wasn't the officer. When he tilted his head back, he saw a big man, dark skinned, head shaved. Blue overalls. Tattoos on every knuckle. By instinct Kaplan flinched, then tried to hide it by readjusting his visitor's badge. Over him, the inmate and Markoff exchanged an elaborate handshake with at least three separate stages, beginning with fists coming together and ending with fingers snapping apart. Afterward Markoff said, "All hands on deck?"

"Not yet. Soon. Could be within the hour."

"Family's been called?"

"So I hear. We'll see if they show."

"When it's time, come get me," Markoff said. "Doesn't matter what else I'm doing," he added, tipping his head toward Kaplan. "And if you're in count, tell them they better send someone for me."

"On it, G."

—◇—

Then they were alone again. Markoff dropped back into his chair and gave Kaplan a look of confusion, slightly disgruntled, as if he couldn't remember who he was or why he was sitting there. Kaplan kept playing with his badge. "I better get started," he said.

"That's Rashid," Markoff said. "He runs the hospice."

"Someone's dying?"

"All volunteer, of course. The state doesn't give us a dime."

"I thought we had what's-it-called."

"Compassionate release?"

"I saw the report. Haven't had a chance to read it."

"Depends on the sentence. And whether the family's able to take them in. Or willing."

In the chapel, the men had stopped praying. Now one had a book open in his lap, but he didn't look down at it, just made big swooping gestures with his arm and called up to the ceiling. The others were cracking up, two holding their bellies, the third snapping his wrist next to his head. A different officer appeared in the doorway, the one who'd greeted Kaplan in the waiting room and read him a list of rules and disclaimers—"Visiting a correctional institution carries an inherent risk of being assaulted or taken hostage. You okay with that?"—before escorting him through the metal detector and three electronic gates. This one was older and leaner than Chuckles, less boisterous, with a solemn voice that whistled out from behind a thick gray mustache. He took a step into the chapel, and the rabbi leaned over his desk, rapped the window with a knuckle, made a sign with his hands to settle down. The men took big breaths and wiped away tears.

"So you were saying," Markoff said, an eye still on the window. "You're interested in forgiveness."

"I don't know about interested," Kaplan answered. "I just figured that's what these guys . . . the inmates, what they'd need."

"And you don't think Judaism cuts it?"

He guessed Markoff was making another joke and expected him to laugh, but his face stayed serious, even stern.

"Catholics always just seemed to have it easier," Kaplan said. "Say a few words, and all your sins . . . you know."

"I wish you would have told me this sooner. All those years I wasted at Hebrew Union."

Now Markoff did laugh, wheezy shudders that made his face scrunch up as he rocked forward and slapped his knee. When he recovered, he passed a hand over his eyes and nose, stretching out the skin in order to reset them to neutral.

"So pretend I'm a priest," he said. "Tell me what you want forgiveness for, and I'll send you off to say some Our Fathers."

"Me?"

"Of course, if you're more comfortable with secular approaches, you could always try a counselor."

"I wasn't talking about me. The inmates . . . the men in here. I imagine they must have things to get off their chests."

"Our newest counselor is straight out of graduate school. Nice enough kid, but whenever I try to talk to him about someone's baggage, he throws around terms like 'predictor models' and 'pathophysiology.' I prefer 'baggage.' Not scientific, maybe, but you can feel the weight of it, can't you?"

The men in the chapel had quieted, the one with the book scanning a page with his finger, the others leaning toward each other to whisper. The lean officer had backed out of sight, though Kaplan could still make out his shadow falling across the carpet just inside the doorway.

"I don't do shrinks," he said.

"Don't get me wrong. A good one can be helpful."

"Not if your mother's one."

"Fair enough."

"And she tests out behavioral therapies on you when you're five."

"So you can try me instead. Who do you want to forgive you?"

"I wasn't talking about me," Kaplan said. "I'm only here for the files."

"They're not going anywhere," Markoff said and flapped a hand over his shoulder. "And anyway, you'd be better off talking to the guys. Ask them some questions."

"I need hard data. I didn't come to make a confession, if that's what you think."

"I don't think anything," Markoff said. "I'm no good at guessing motivations. Especially not in here. Why people do what they do? Why they want what they want? That's a mystery I leave up to those"—he pointed up, gave his finger a little twirl—"in a higher pay grade."

After this he folded his hands in his lap and waited. Kaplan stared at the file boxes that formed a short wall behind him.

Full of baggage. Impossible to sift through and categorize. "It's just that, if I were in this place for something I did, it might give me a chance . . ." He trailed off, flipping his badge up and back down.

"Is it your parents you want forgiveness from?" Markoff said. "That's the usual story. You mentioned your mother."

"I don't care what she thinks."

"Or a child. Maybe you've got a kid? If so, tell me it eventually gets quieter."

"Do I look that old?"

"You don't have to be. Not if I read the biology books right."

"No kid," Kaplan said. "And not my parents. There's just my mom and stepdad. My dad died when I was eighteen."

"I'm sorry to hear it."

"And I don't need him to forgive me from beyond the grave, if that's what you—"

"Who, then?"

"I don't know. Nobody."

"Tough to get nobody to forgive you. You might as well come up with a name."

"It was just a girl."

"That's not uncommon, either."

"A woman now, I guess."

"So you're no longer in touch."

"I hardly even knew her."

"I see."

"It's not what you think."

"I don't think anything," Markoff said. "I'm just listening."

"I didn't get her pregnant or force her to have an abortion or anything like that."

"I don't make guesses," Markoff said.

"I didn't hurt her, either. Not directly, at least."

"Maybe you should back up. Slow down and tell me from the beginning. How did you know her?"

"In college," Kaplan said. "I was, anyway. My sophomore year. She wasn't a student. I met her through some friends. Acquaintances, really."

"Where did you go?"

"Excuse me?"

"What college?"

"Lehigh."

"Oh yeah?" Markoff tapped his chest. "Bucknell. Go, Bison!"

Kaplan thrust his chin at the file boxes. "Which should I start with?"

"Lehigh has a pretty active Hillel, if I remember right. Were you a member?"

"What does it matter?"

Markoff shrugged. "Sorry. Go on. This girl you met through friends."

"Acquaintances. Local guys. Not the most refined bunch. I'd go over to their house once in a while to . . . purchase certain things."

"I understand."

"Sometimes I'd see her over there. Usually hanging out on a couch, watching TV. Super skinny girl with hair in her eyes. Always looked half asleep. Sweet, though. She'd say *hi* to me and smile. I usually brought a six-pack for the guys who lived there, and I'd hand her a beer before I gave any to them."

"I'm guessing you weren't twenty-one as a sophomore."

"Big crime, I know," he said and waved at the file boxes.

"It's all relative," Markoff said. "I don't judge."

"The guy who oversees the hospice," Kaplan said, hoping to change the subject. "Who was in here before."

"Rashid. Used to be Nation of Islam. Mainstream, now. We've had some pretty interesting conversations about Farrakhan."

"What did you say he's in for?"

"I didn't."

"Is he due to get out soon? I can include him in my report."

"Time's relative, too," Markoff said, the sleepy impatience returning, his eyes going half-lidded. "So you had a fake ID. And?"

"Look, Rabbi—"

"Please, call me Gary."

"You don't need to hear my stupid drama. I don't even know why I thought of it. It happened almost ten years ago."

"Which would have been, what, a year after your father died. Or a little less?"

"Something like that," Kaplan said.

"Well, we're into it now. Might as well finish. Or else you'll leave me hanging."

"I don't remember what I was saying."

"You'd buy some beer and bring it over to this house, where you'd make certain purchases. And you'd see this girl."

"I don't know if she lived in the house or was just visiting. Didn't seem to be anyone's girlfriend. Maybe a sister. But she was nice to me, and the guys always needled her, telling her she was trying to get with a college kid. They told her if she thought she was too good for them, maybe she could whore herself out in my dorm."

"Classy guys."

"One day I showed up with a whole case. My friends and I were throwing a party, and we bought loads of this cheap stuff—"

"Yuengling!" Markoff cried. "I haven't had that swill for fifteen years."

"That's right," Kaplan said. "I forgot the name."

"Eastern PA classic."

"We had more than we needed. And I thought we could use, you know, a little something else. So I went over to the house. It was way out on the edge of town, and none of my friends ever wanted to go with me."

"But you didn't mind?"

"Made me feel dangerous. Like some kind of outlaw. I can't imagine doing something like that now."

"But you'd just lost your father—"

"And I went a little wild, I guess."

"You wouldn't be the first."

"Anyway, this time the girl answered the door. Said none of the guys were home. That I should come back later."

When he hesitated, Markoff asked, "And did you?"

"I asked if I could wait. Held up the case of beer. Might as well have a couple before they came home and polished it off, I said. And she let me in."

"Nice girl, like you said."

"I wish she would've told me to fuck off and go away."

"Please, I prefer without the cursing," Markoff said. "I hear it enough, walking around this place, but in my office—"

"I'm sorry."

"No need to apologize. Go on. Please. She let you in with the case of Yuengling—"

"G. It's time."

The voice made Kaplan start. When he glanced behind, there was Rashid again, tall, broad, dark, and looming. His hand leapt back to his badge, and this time he yanked it hard enough that the clip came loose from his shirt.

"Family?" Markoff asked.

"No word," Rashid said.

"All right. Let's go."

Markoff was up and heading out, leaving Kaplan with the mountain range of boxes, the sight of which suddenly made him so tired he closed his eyes. But then he felt a tug on his shoulder.

"Come on. No time to waste."

"The files," he said weakly.

"They're still not going anywhere. And you need data for your report. The good kind. What's it called. Empirical, right?"

When he stood, the badge slipped from his fingers. It hit the floor, skidded, and slid beneath Markoff's shoe. The rabbi picked it up, waggled it up and down, and handed it back.

"You don't want to lose that," he said. "Unless you're interested in staying the night. This is," he added, with a wink aimed over Kaplan's head, "a bed and breakfast, after all."

—◦—

He'd never told the story to anyone. Not to his mother, who'd sent him her sixteen favorite books on grieving; not to his girlfriend at the time, or his current one; not to the rabbi who'd advised his Hillel chapter, which he'd quit soon after. He remembered certain details of the house as if he'd just stepped out of it. The mildew smell that rose from the couch the moment he settled onto its cushion. The hole punched in the drywall beside the kitchen door. The collection of Pez dispensers—Charlie Brown, Bart Simpson, Boba Fett—carefully arranged on a windowsill. He could see the girl's long bangs, the dark eye makeup, the dimple that formed when she smiled, a missing molar noticeable only when she spoke. He could hear her gulping down beer so fast she reached for a second can before he'd finished half his first.

He didn't remember what was on TV, only her feet tucked onto the couch beside her, not far from him, and a blanket spread over both their laps. That, and the feeling that he could be anywhere, watching anything, so disconnected had he become from the person he'd once believed himself to be. Fuck everything, he'd been telling himself since his father's funeral, volunteering to buy beer for his friends with the fake ID he'd paid for with $300 of his inheritance and offering to buy weed and mushrooms, too, though it meant driving to a sketchy house on the outskirts of town, where four boys in backwards baseball caps and gold chains liked to show off their skills with butterfly knives and bo staffs. Fuck everything, he told himself again now, shifting closer to the girl and imagining the boys coming in to find their arms around each other, mouths pressed together. That was what he wanted, more than the kissing itself—to hear the boys ribbing them in their mean-spirited way, welcoming Kaplan into their world, enticing him to abandon his cozy, sheltered existence for a new, dicey one as their peer. Why not, now that his father was dead, the safe life he'd modeled exposed as a sham, as precarious and fleeting as any other?

But they weren't kissing when the boys came home, or even touching. At least three inches still separated her feet from his leg. He was finishing his first beer, and she was on her third. They'd hardly spoken. The door flung open, and the boys burst in, already shouting. His car was parked on the street in front, so they couldn't have been surprised to find him there. But they didn't taunt him for being alone with the girl. They yelled and cursed. Two pulled Kaplan off the couch and pinned him against the wall. The others stood over the girl, who cowered, hands over her face. It took him a minute to understand what they were saying: that she'd been stealing from their stash, giving it away to every guy she was fucking, and now this rich asshole?

He protested, said she hadn't given him anything, told them to check his pockets, which the two holding him did, coming up with the roll of cash he'd collected from his friends. They took it, gave him nothing in exchange. They told him to get out, to never come back. When he reached the door, he heard the horrifying smack of skin on skin, a sharp cry, and looked back to see the girl with her face buried in the musty couch, her sobs muffled but audible, the two boys leaning over her, one with fist raised. "Out," another said. "Now."

He assured himself they were done hurting her, but he knew better. He knew, too, that they'd hurt him worse if he tried to help her. And yet he was sure he should do something other than walk out of the house and drive away, back to the comfort of classes and parties and a girlfriend who was studying to become an engineer like both her parents. But that was all he did.

What would Markoff have told him if he'd managed to get it all out? Probably what he told many of the men in here, what Kaplan had tried telling himself: that he'd been young, that he'd made mistakes, that he couldn't change the past, that all he could do was try to be a good person from now on, that he shouldn't hold it against himself forever. That maybe going to services would help, or volunteering for a charity. That he really ought to consider regular counseling.

But now Markoff was busy arguing with Officer Chuckles, who blocked their way to the infirmary. The four men who'd been in the chapel were with them now, Markoff a head shorter than all of them, including Kaplan, whose own head topped out at Rashid's ear.

"He's not supposed to leave the chapel," Officer Chuckles said.

"It's a roving chapel," Markoff replied, dancing fingers in the air on both sides of his head. "It goes where I go."

"Sorry, reverend. I'm just trying to follow the rules."

"If that man dies before we get in there—"

"What's the problem here?"

The second officer joined them, the lean one with the dense mustache, and the sight of him made Officer Chuckles straighten his shoulders and take a step closer. "Chaplain's taking this visitor to an unauthorized—"

"How's the bambino?" the second officer asked.

"Bambina," Markoff said. "Let's just say she's got healthy lungs."

"Earplugs," the second officer said. "Best investment you'll ever make."

Officer Chuckles took hold of Kaplan's arm. "He's only supposed to be in the chapel office, looking at, I don't know—"

"Excuse me, gentlemen," Rashid said. "We don't have much time."

"Let them through, Charles," the second officer said, and Markoff, puffing up his chest, pushed past. Officer Chuckles released Kaplan and glared at him as he walked by. Kaplan gave his badge a tug to make sure it was attached securely.

As they made their way down the hall, passing a pair of classrooms where a dozen men typed on computers even older than the one in the rabbi's office, Markoff tried to introduce him to the others, struggling to recall his name before giving up. "He's an ally at DOC headquarters."

"Josh Kaplan. My friends call me *Kap*."

"He's finally going to get them to update our software."

"I'll see what I can do."

Rashid shook his hand, but only in the standard way. "Joshua," one of the men from the chapel said. "Nice to meet you."

The infirmary was smaller than the chapel but brighter, with two rows of beds, twenty total, and a desk behind which an orderly read a magazine. Markoff marched down the aisle, whispering, "It's time," as he passed the beds, half of them occupied by men sleeping or reading, one drawing in a sketch pad. A pair slid out from beneath their blankets and followed. At the back of the room hung a curtain, a handwritten cardboard sign pinned to it. *Meadowbrook Hospice*, it read. Behind the curtain were two more beds, only one taken. A small head visible above the edge of a pilled sheet, a few wisps of hair over a forehead wrinkled and yellow as parchment, white eyebrows above closed lids. Dry lips moved, and Rashid bent close.

"We're here," he said. "With you all the way."

Kaplan squeezed into the tight space with the four men from the chapel, the two from the infirmary, Markoff and Rashid, all of them shoulder to shoulder. Flies landed on the bed and took off before anyone could swat them. Kaplan had no idea what he'd put in his report. "What's he saying?" he asked.

"Nothing but Spanish for the last week," Rashid said. "Only word I understand is *padre*."

"Doubt his dad's still around," Markoff said.

"A priest?" Kaplan asked.

"They're all the rage these days, apparently." Markoff stepped up and waved his hand over the dying man's forehead, vertically then horizontally. "Can't hurt, right?" He shrugged and grinned sheepishly, then said a few words in what sounded like Latin, though Kaplan couldn't be sure—it might just as easily have been pig Latin. The dying man's lips moved again. The blanket rose and slowly descended. No one mentioned what he'd done to spend his last years, months, hours in this place. Had everyone already forgiven him for it? What if he died before they could?

"In my dreams," Kaplan muttered. "I do terrible things."

No one seemed to hear him. Markoff cocked a finger at each of them and counted. "Not bad," he said. "A minyan, for a change. Let's send him off right."

Rashid held the man's hand and recited something in Arabic. In shaky harmony, the four men from the chapel began a hymn Kaplan didn't know. Markoff chanted a prayer Kaplan vaguely remembered from childhood, snippets of Hebrew that had stuck in his mind, though distantly and without any connection to meaning. He mouthed the words he could recall and hoped they'd serve some purpose, even if he didn't understand them.

Perfect Together

◄○►

Today development stretches in a solid block from the heart of Union Knoll over Crescent Ridge. Aside from the massive sports complex on Route 46, the reservoir behind it, and a few small parks to the south, no open spaces show on the map. Just streets branching off of other streets, the shortest ending in cul-de-sacs, in a pattern less like a grid than a network of veins, or maybe nerves, organic if disorderly, and surprisingly attractive when viewed from above.

But when I was growing up, there was still plenty of room to build. Ours was the first house on our street, then one of only two side streets in the neighborhood, both emptying onto Lenape Road, which snaked over the ridge and dropped to the flat plain of Chatwin below. Some of my earliest memories include the sound of bulldozers scraping boulders. Drumming hammers during the day were as common to me as chirping crickets at night. Every week my mother went from sideboard to hutch to end-table, righting knickknacks knocked askew by dynamite blasts that cleared granite for a new street higher up the ridge.

All this prepared me early—or should have—for frequent and constant change. Where one day there was a small patch of woods to play in, the next there would be a mess of tumbled logs. Then a pit, then a frame of two-by-fours, then a sprawling ranch or boxy colonial like my family's. As they crept higher up the ridge, the houses grew bigger and gaudier, the driveways longer and steeper, the cars in them newer and more luxurious. A clever developer renamed the neighborhood Lenape Heights to match its new status, though those of us who'd lived there from the beginning continued to call it simply Crescent Ridge.

By the time I was twelve or thirteen, I'd gotten to know several of the builders, and after school I'd hang around one of the jobsites, watching a frame go up, listening to the men cursing the heat or bragging about their prowess with women or wishing loudly for a cold beer. They'd ask me to pass up a tool or a box of nails, and I'd wander through the half-finished house trying to imagine where the kitchen would be, or the bathrooms, deciding which of the many bedrooms would have been mine if my parents were rich rather than just well-off. Occasionally they'd let me hammer a board in place, and once a younger shirtless guy taught me how to work the controls of a backhoe. I suppose people were less concerned about liability then, because his boss was watching and didn't object. Most days they let me take home an armful of wood scraps for the tree fort I was banging together in my backyard.

One builder especially liked having me around. I didn't know why, but neither did it occur to me to wonder. His name was Mike Piluso, and he ran a small operation out of Union Knoll, a single crew of eight men who'd take most of a month to put up a house. He didn't subcontract out anything but electrical and plumbing, and he was known for doing the best work around. Other contractors took on twenty, twenty-five new houses at a time, but Mike did no more than three or four on any given street. I thought of him as an old guy, though he was probably in his late forties or early fifties, with thinning gray hair and a dense mustache that ran the full length of his upper lip. He was missing part of two fingers on his left hand, the middle and ring ending just above the first knuckle. "Dumbass with a table saw," he said the first time he caught me eyeing them. I'd noticed them before but didn't have the courage to ask what had happened. "Better for me to sit back and watch other people use the tools."

He wore a wedding band on one of the stumps, and sometimes he talked about his children, a boy close to my age and a girl two years older. "They're good kids," he said. "Deep down, anyway. Even if they don't always show it." The girl struggled in school, fought with her mother about curfews, threatened to move in with her boyfriend, an eighteen-year-old living on his own in Boonton, if they didn't occasionally let her stay the night at his apartment. Mike worried he'd find himself a grandfather, he and his wife on the hook to take care of an infant. The son was brighter and a good athlete—starting forward on the Union Knoll High School freshman soccer team—but he, too, caused Mike plenty of grief: taking the car out for a joyride and coming back with a mangled fender, getting arrested for shoplifting at a baseball card show at the Heritage Mall, smoking in the basement and leaving singe marks on the couch. "I should make him come work with me after school," he said and then laughed an empty, dry-throated laugh. "Except he'd probably burn down a jobsite. I'd do better hiring a vagrant off the street."

He'd tell me all this as if he were talking to one of his crew or maybe to another contractor, since his employees tended to steer clear of him unless they had to ask for instructions or clarify a detail of the specs. He kept a close eye on them, occasionally calling out when someone was being lazy or careless. "That wheel's wobblier than a hen in a whorehouse!" he'd yell to one of his guys pushing a barrow full of bricks. "Tighten it the fuck up!" I didn't know what a hen would be doing in a whorehouse or why it would wobble there more than elsewhere, and I didn't ask. But I could tell it was lonely being boss, and I was glad to be able to follow him around as he checked on work in progress. He carried a level wherever he went, pressing it to newly hung drywall and countertops and watching for the air bubble to settle between the two black lines. If it didn't, he'd lean his head back and mutter indecipherably, then take a deep breath and say, as if it were a tragedy, "Everyone's fucking human." More than once I listened to him bawl out one of his guys for being off-square before making him tear out and start again.

Sometimes he'd wave me into the trailer he kept on site, hand me a Coke from a mini-fridge, and spread a blueprint across a folding table. "These people," he'd say, gesturing at the nearest window. I knew he meant "these rich people" and was grateful that he didn't include my family and those who lived in humbler dwellings like ours in his judgment of the neighborhood. "They want everything under the sun. Marble fireplace. Three-car garage. Skylights in every room, including the johns. But they don't really want to pay for it. The shit doesn't pencil out." He'd walk me through the design, pointing out ways he could simplify or cut corners if he could stomach shoddy work. "That's why most of the bids go to the bigger firms," he said. "They'll throw up three dozen units in a month, and in ten years it'll all be falling down. But these people—" Again he waved a hand at the window, at the houses he was building, the families who hadn't yet come to occupy them. "All they care about? Are the countertops granite, are the floors real oak, and can you see the moon when you're taking a dump? Makes a guy want to give up his principles and cash in."

Then he leaned back in his chair and took a long pull from his Coke bottle, the finger stumps weirdly naked against the clear glass. The hammering outside went in and out of rhythm, and I wondered if the framers ever tried to work to a single beat. "I don't know why I'm telling you all this," he said. "Not like you're gonna get into this business. Not if you're smart. What's your dad do again? Was it accountant? Insurance?" I told him, and he winced. "Right. Fucking pharmaceuticals. Even more crooked than real estate. If you're smart, you'll run from all of us."

—◦—

This was in the mid-1980s. Our governor was Thomas Kean, a popular Republican from a long-standing political family whose cultured accent reminded people of the Kennedys, even if his policies didn't. Around this time he appeared in a TV ad from the state tourism board, touting attractions from Atlantic City to the Delaware Water Gap and ending with the catchy slogan, "New Jersey and You: Perfect Together." The ad played on all the local stations, so often I found myself reciting the slogan out loud, trying to mimic Kean's inflections, his dropped Rs. Though I knew my parents had voted against him twice, I liked the governor, and a part of me believed that when he said "You," I was his primary audience.

But even then I had an inkling that not everyone in the state felt the same way. Things were more perfect for some than for others. The New Jersey of that time was a rigidly segregated place. It may still be, though now I live far away, and because my parents have retired to Florida, I no longer have a reason to visit. Back then Union Knoll was mostly Italian and Irish Catholic. Lenape was largely Jewish. Almost all the Puerto Ricans in the county lived across Route 46 in Lakewood. And Chatwin was the only township with a sizeable Black population, the poorer segment of which was relegated to a neighborhood of tightly packed row houses and sooty apartment buildings constructed on dry riverbed and known, unfortunately, as *the Bottoms*. Our synagogue was on its north edge, and every time we came close, my father would nudge his door lock down with an elbow. Crossing boundaries was dangerous, I learned without ever being told, and should never be taken lightly. Safer for everyone to stay where you belonged.

But there were also threats to this order. Around the same time as the big houses were going up on the ridge, people in the neighborhood, including my parents, talked heatedly and often about what was known as *the Mount Laurel decision*. Most thirteen-year-olds probably knew little or nothing about court cases, but for months this one was at the center of my life. The name *Mount Laurel* became something of a slur—among the adults a metaphor for government overreach and oppression, among the kids a stand-in for generalized evil. Mount Laurel meant change and chaos and the destruction of everything you held dear.

Not long ago, at a conference in Minneapolis, I met someone from Mount Laurel, New Jersey, a suburb of Philadelphia an hour and a half south of Union Knoll. When she named her hometown I flinched, instinctively picturing a place of anger and strife and violent protest, and before I knew what I was doing, I said I was sorry to hear it. She looked at me strangely and said it was a lovely place to grow up, if a little stifling. She wished her own kids could have as peaceful a childhood as she'd had there.

The truth is, Mount Laurel was a town very much like Union Knoll. Upper middle class, overwhelmingly white, leaning Republican. Large single-family homes on sizeable lots, carefully maintained roads and parks, well-funded schools. What made it a straw man in my neighborhood was the fact that the NAACP had sued the township over zoning laws that made it nearly impossible for low-income families to find housing within its borders. Not once, but twice: first in 1975, and again in 1983. And both times the state Supreme Court sided with the plaintiff and called for remedies, one of which specified that builders could forgo high density zoning laws so long as they devoted a significant percentage of development to affordable housing.

All quite reasonable, I think now. A progressive decision but not a radical one. And yet, in Crescent Ridge, our neighborhood still under construction at the south end of Union Knoll, where the land rose steadily to a rocky shelf before dropping off, it was spoken of as if a new generation of Bolsheviks had seized all private property for public use.

Here's why: Two years after the second court decision, the owner of the last working farm in Union Knoll had a stroke while hoeing up weeds in a strawberry patch and was taken to a nursing home in Parsippany. His daughter, who no longer lived in the area, put the farm and the adjoining tract of woods up for sale, and a big developer in Chatwin quickly snatched it up. But no one paid much attention until he submitted his plans to the zoning commission. On twenty acres he proposed to build a hundred and eighty units, two-thirds to sell at market rate, the remainder reserved as low-income housing. The commission balked, and the developer threatened a lawsuit. The city council met for six hours behind closed doors, and when they came out—all visibly exhausted in the photo on the front page of the local paper, one whose eyes and nose were red—the plan had been approved. Within hours, half a dozen lawyers representing families in our neighborhood had filed injunction requests, and for more than a year the planned development had been tied up in the courts. But now there were only two or three more legal challenges to clear, and most people expected demolition to begin in the fall.

The property was known as Milburg Farm, though the man who'd owned it most recently wasn't named Milburg. No one remembered who'd owned it before him. The neighborhood hadn't existed long enough for such collective history. The oldest of our houses were built in the early '70s, and the newer residents had never seen the place without its bone-white sidewalks, its cul-de-sacs abutting the last significant tract of forest in the county, a steep slope of scarlet oak and birch scattered with granite boulders. The farm bordered the woods on the west flank of the ridge, and you couldn't see it from the road, only a long gravel driveway disappearing beneath a thick canopy of leaves.

I'd played in those woods all my life and passed that driveway hundreds of times as my father took the curves of Lenape Road over the top of the ridge and down to Chatwin, where, until my bar mitzvah, I went to Hebrew school three days a week. But I'd never thought much about where the driveway led. I knew, half-consciously, that there was a real farm tucked away behind the trees, but I had no idea what grew there or what sort of animals roamed its fields. I just took for granted that there was a quiet buffer between our neighborhood and the rowdy, vaguely sinister, semi-urban thicket of Chatwin beyond.

—◇—

It wasn't until a year after the sale that I visited the farm with Mike Piluso. He was finishing up the last of three big houses at the top of the ridge, and he looked a little sad when he told me he probably wouldn't be coming up this way again for a while. Most of the existing streets were filling in, and there wasn't much development left that wasn't already spoken for; his next few jobs were over in Lenape. "Too bad you can't be the one to do the Milburg property," I said, not because I really

wanted him to be involved with it, but only to have some way
to praise his work and to express how much I'd miss seeing
him most afternoons. "You're the only one who'd do it right."

"The Mill-who?" he asked. I told him about the planned
development and the distress it was causing in the neighborhood,
and he gave an odd little smirk, a mean-spirited one I'd never
seen on him before. "It's an idiotic plan," he said. "Still, you
gotta enjoy imagining how it makes these people squirm." He
laughed a short, hostile laugh, took off his hard hat, and ran a
hand through his bristly hair. "Should we go check it out?"

By then it was the late spring of 1987. I was in my last
stretch of junior high, a month shy of fourteen, and the approaching summer filled me with dread. I'd soon start my first
job, selling hot dogs and ice cream at the snack pavilion of a
community pool, and afterward I'd transfer to the big regional
high school at the other end of Union Knoll. I wasn't ready for
such momentous change—for what I believed even then to be
the end of childhood—and found myself wishing desperately
for time to slow down. I didn't want to give up anything, not
my teachers, my friends, my sports teams, my idle afternoons,
all of which I perceived as under threat. The anticipation of loss
I experienced physically, as an intense and unquenchable thirst.
It was as if the hair that had sprouted all over my body during
the past six months had sucked me dry. I guzzled three glasses
of orange juice at breakfast and two containers of milk at lunch.
I stopped at the water fountain between every class and had to
excuse myself to go to the lavatory five times a day, and still I
felt my insides withering from drought.

This was the anxiety I carried with me as Mike Piluso's
truck bumped down the gravel driveway, rutted with dry potholes
and covered in last year's leaves. And maybe it's also what
triggered the shock of astonishment when we came through

the screen of trees and Mike pumped the clutch and pulled the parking brake. I guess I'd never actually pictured what was back there, and even as I took it in I couldn't believe such a place had been so close, just out of sight, all this time. A meadow opened in front of us, surrounded by a silvered, split-log fence. The horses that must have grazed there were gone, as were the chickens that once roosted in the now-empty coop and whatever smaller animals—goats, maybe?—had lived in the pen beside the barn. But the fields beyond it were still scattered with crops that had reseeded themselves after the previous owner—Mr. Not-Milburg was how I thought of him—had his stroke. Tomato starts, knee-high corn, strawberries dangling green fruit, a variety of leafy vegetables I couldn't identify, all wild and unpruned and partially overtaken by weeds. And overlooking it all, a sturdy square farmhouse that looked as if it hadn't been touched for a hundred years, the small windows hung with yellowed curtains, the front porch covered in dust and pollen, a stack of split wood rotting in the shed beside it.

Even as I wandered around, I couldn't quite accept that the place was real. It was too vast to fit into this little forgotten corner of town, too out of step with everything around it. I kept thinking there was some trick of time or space that allowed it to appear in front of me, and as soon as I left it would vanish, and I'd never find my way back. So I quickly made distance from Mike, exploring the far reaches of the grounds, stumbling onto a little pond where frogs splashed from the bank into green shallows. I couldn't have put it into words at the time, but I was struck with the uneasy sensation that I'd found something I'd always wanted, though I hadn't known I was looking for it. And now, just as I decided how badly I needed it, someone or something—the developer, the state, the mysterious workings of the adult world—would snatch it away.

Mike caught up to me beside a narrow creek that ran along the edge of the woods. "Pretty nice spot," he said. "And these people—" He flung his mangled hand toward the edge of the ridge, in the direction of Chatwin. "They'll turn it into a scrapyard for a quick buck." If he had it, he said, he'd figure out how to make it pencil out at seventy units, nice places with good solid features, not these gaudy monstrosities with tissue-paper walls. "Maybe it's time for me to start thinking bigger," he said. And as we made our way back to the truck, he went on, "I should have raised the kids in a place like this. Maybe they would have turned out . . . I don't know, a little easier on themselves."

"You should buy it," I said. "Keep it a farm."

"Wouldn't pencil out now," he said. "Not once the vultures see a buck in it. Anyway, I do enough digging in the dirt as it is. Me, working a farm? I'd have stroke the first day."

"I wonder how Mr. Milburg—whatever his name is. I wonder how he's doing."

"Eggplant," Mike said. I thought he was identifying a vegetable in the field, and I followed his gaze, but he was looking at the old barn, silvered like the wooden fence and leaning hard to one side. "If he's anything like my old man after his." He pulled at his collar and squinted across the property once more. And then he sang, "I am the eggplant, they are the eggplant, I am the walnut, coo-coo, cachoo."

◄o►

My parents weren't the most outspoken members of the neighborhood association that had organized in the wake of the Milburg sale nor the most staunch in their opposition to the development, but they attended every meeting and continued debating over dinner—not the issue itself, but the appropriate method of resistance. "I won't have people attacking me just because I say what I think," my mother announced one evening.

"Emotions are high, that's all," my father said.

"They're acting like we're at war."

"Some of them see it that way. It's an assault on their entire way of being."

"That's melodramatic."

"I'm not saying I agree. Just that we've got to stay united."

"If someone accuses me again, I'm finished," my mother said.

"I'll talk to them," my father said. "I'll set everything straight."

"One more time," my mother said.

"I'll take care of it," my father said.

Even then I knew they were more conflicted about the situation than most of our neighbors. They were your standard Jewish liberals, had twice voted against Reagan, believed in the general principle of a government responsibility to help the poor. But they also felt the Milburg development was ill conceived, that there were more intelligent ways of going about creating affordable housing. Why put it right next to one of the most affluent neighborhoods in the county? Wasn't that asking for trouble?

The topic was particularly fraught for my father, who'd grown up in a part of Brooklyn that went through a major transformation in the 1960s with the construction of housing projects followed by an increase in crime and racial tension and ending in all the families of his childhood friends fleeing to Queens or Long Island or Westchester County. He understood the reasons for the Mount Laurel decision, even supported its implementation in the abstract, but he couldn't just sit back and suffer through Crown Heights all over again. He got misty-eyed whenever he talked about his old neighborhood, which he hadn't visited for more than twenty years, since his own parents had moved to Forest Hills. "It's a shame not to be able to show your kids where you're from," he told me. "I want this to be a place you can come back to."

My mother, on the other hand, had grown up in a multi-ethnic working-class neighborhood in New Haven, a fairly harmonious one, and her father was an immigrant who still spoke with a heavy Russian accent after fifty years in the country. She was more open to change than my father, though she, too, believed that the Milburg developer was taking advantage of the law to fill his pockets. There had to be a better solution, she said, but she also wasn't comfortable with the tone of the neighborhood association meetings, shaded as they were by anger and suspicion. At one of them she stood up and said, "Let's think about this rationally. We can't let our fears get the better of us." At another she suggested the association try to set up a meeting with the developer to come to an arrangement that would work for everyone. The first time she was ignored. The second she was accused of getting into bed with the enemy.

What struck me even then was how all the adults, including my parents, described the problems with the development and their potential impact on Crescent Ridge. They talked about an increase in traffic. They talked about extra wear on local roads and sewer systems. They talked about overcrowded school buses and classrooms. They never said the words *poor people* or *Black people* or *Hispanics*, never even mentioned the word *crime*. It was an amazing lesson in irony, even if I didn't recognize it then. I knew what increased traffic and a strain on policing meant without having to be told. I understood that my neighbors were picturing a teeming ghetto of dark-skinned criminals set loose to maraud their beautiful homes. But publicly they'd say only that they wanted to "preserve the character of the neighborhood."

All that's to say, I was aware of the irony, but I didn't question it or fight it or even call attention to it. I knew it was hypocritical for my parents to vote for Jimmy Carter and Walter Mondale, to support Peter Shapiro in his crushing loss to Governor Kean, at the same time they were working to block an affordable housing project. I had a sense that there was a lot of bullshit in the air, but I just accepted it as part of the world I lived in, and I, too, worried about the character of the neighborhood, though not necessarily in the same way. I wanted it to stay exactly as it was at that moment: the same roads, the same trees, the same houses mid-construction, the same builders running bulldozers, the same neglected farm tucked in the woods.

It troubles me to look back now and see how quickly my attitude would change. In just a few months, full-blown adolescence would arrive with indifference bordering on cynicism. By the time I graduated high school, I wouldn't have cared if the whole neighborhood burned down. Or the whole state, for that matter. But at the moment, anything less than a full stop I saw as a complete betrayal.

--<o>--

And that, I suppose, is why I volunteered to join a group of neighbors who'd organized a protest in Trenton one Friday in early June. There were about fifty of us, more kids than adults, holding up signs and chanting, "Oh, no, Mount Laurel must go!" My parents allowed me to skip school but declined to accompany us, claiming too many obligations at work. I rode with a family from higher up the ridge, the Hollahans, who had two girls, nine and eleven. Their names were Ashley and Leslie, but I can no longer remember which was which. The older one sat next to me in the back seat, and the whole hour and a half drive her sister kept shoving her into me and giggling. For a while I tried to maintain a serious demeanor, sitting stiffly and sipping from the water bottle I'd brought—this was important business after all, and I was now old enough to sell hot dogs at the Lenape Pool—but after twenty minutes or so I joined in the game, pushing the older sister back until she was in hysterics, pinballing between us, sometimes leaning against me to catch her breath.

When we arrived at the State House, however, and gathered beneath the two sets of columns stacked on top of each other, the gold dome and cupola rising above, she was the one to grow serious, almost grave, and her sister worked to match her expression. They both held signs that read *Hands Off My Neighborhood!* and waved them whenever anyone crossed the courtyard toward the front doors.

The legislature was in session, with a big budget vote set for early afternoon, and the organizers knew most assembly members would pass us on their way inside. Our own assemblyman, a stout Republican from Rockaway, made a brief speech for the benefit of a news crew from a local TV station, a few words about municipalities' right to self-determination. Others hurried past with their heads down. A pair of Black lawmakers gave us what I now recognize as looks of weary disappointment, though at the time I read them as disdainful and possibly tinged with fear. As they passed I held my sign higher—*Save Crescent Ridge!*—and chanted louder.

The TV reporter interviewed several of the adults, who talked about traffic and policing and property values. Then she spoke to a few of the children, including the two Hollahan girls, both lovely in long dresses and French braids, the younger swaying from foot to foot, the older standing perfectly straight and dignified. They both aped their parents and offered somber smiles that didn't fail to show their dimples. The reporter's enthusiasm flagged after hearing the same phrases repeated four or five times. I can imagine what she was thinking: *you bigots, just say what you really mean.*

Eventually she came to me. It's excruciating to think that somewhere in the archives of a Trenton TV station there may be a recording of me, almost fourteen years old, publicly spouting reactionary slogans. Even now I have the nagging feeling that it undermines all the causes I've supported since. My freshman year of college I joined a rally outside Jesse Helms's office in Raleigh, holding up a poster with reproductions of Robert Mapplethorpe photographs. Later I marched against the Iraq invasion. I volunteered for a homeless shelter and wrote for a street newspaper. I gave money to Middle-East peace organizations. Lately I've worked with a group lobbying for prison reform. A long list of progressive credentials, yet somehow none of it makes up for my standing outside the New Jersey State House shouting, "Our town, our rules, our town, our rules!" In the thirty years since, my branches have stretched far. But what does it matter, if my roots are rotten?

The reporter's question was open-ended. Something like, "So, young man, what brings you to Trenton today?" The vagueness of it flustered me, and I sputtered a few words about how much I loved Crescent Ridge the way it was, that I didn't want it to change, that the developer didn't care about the character of the neighborhood. My throat was dry, my water bottle empty. "They'll cut down all the woods," I said. "I've played there forever. And there's this old farm in the middle. It's beautiful. Fields and a horse meadow and a pond. It would be a shame to pave it all over for—"

I thought of Mike Piluso then, glancing over his shoulder as we drove away from the Milburg property, clucking his tongue and laughing again at the thought of all these rich people being overrun. His words were so close to my lips, I could feel them tingling there: *by a bunch of spades from the Bottoms.* And the reporter seemed to suspect it, her smile gleeful and nasty, her eyes flicking for a moment to the cameraman to make sure he was rolling. The adults from Crescent Ridge crowded around us, and I could sense them holding their breath. If I let the words out, it would all be over, their motivations exposed, the cause undermined by a little twerp with dark fuzz at the corners of his upper lip. And a part of me wanted to let loose, be done with it, quit bracing for change I couldn't halt. Behind the reporter, the younger Hollahan girl pinched her sister's side, and the older clapped a hand over her mouth to keep from crying out. But her eyes stayed fixed on me, the integrity of her words, of her lovely somber smile, mine to prop up or plow over.

I took a breath and said, "If they build all these houses, our school buses will be too crowded. And so will our classrooms. And the roads can't handle all the cars."

I don't remember if the reporter thanked me or just turned away in disgust.

—◦—

Our protest didn't generate any new legislation. But piled onto all the lawsuits, it must have brought the developer enough bad publicity that he finally decided the project wasn't worth the hassle. At dinner, about two weeks later, I learned from my parents that he'd sold the property to another builder who proposed ninety-four units, just within the zoning commission's density rules. As such, his plan wouldn't have to include low-income housing and invoke the Mount Laurel doctrine. My parents were clearly relieved by the news, though I could tell it also made them uneasy. They'd gotten what they'd wanted, but they didn't yet know how much of themselves they'd given up in the process.

"You did good work," they said, trying to sound encouraging even if they now regretted letting me participate in the rally. I stared at my food and didn't answer. They seemed to take my morose look as a sign that I, too, was uncomfortable with the outcome, that it challenged my notion of who I was and what I believed in, and they started justifying our stance, saying that if people only went about these things in a thoughtful way . . . But before they got very far I cut them off. Did they know who the builder was? "Local guy," my father said. "Piluso."

The next afternoon I found Mike in his trailer. The last of the three houses he'd been building was nearly finished. His crew was already on another job while he oversaw the final details, which, for a change, he'd decided to sub out: mudding walls, painting, tarring the driveway. He stood up and gave a big clap when I walked in, spread a grin beneath the thick brush of his mustache. "You ready to work for me?" he said. "Turns out I need more hands now."

I told him I'd heard.

"So you know I'll be hanging around this dump after all."

"I heard," I said again.

"Decided it was time," he said. "Try to go big. These guys," he said, waving south toward Chatwin, "they don't need to be the only ones making a buck. Not when they cut six corners on a square."

This time I didn't answer. My tongue stuck to the roof of my mouth. I tried not to glance behind him, to the mini fridge full of Cokes.

"I know what you're thinking," he said. "I told you I could do seventy units."

"And leave the woods alone," I said.

He was still smiling, but in a way that made his cheeks look weird, and he retreated to his folding table. Whatever he heard in my voice or saw in my face made him want to avert his eyes. He busied himself with some invoices, separating originals from carbon copies. "Seventy was just a guess. After a first look. But it didn't pencil out."

"You talked about buying the farm for your family. Moving your kids there."

"You know I wasn't serious," he said. "They're not quiet little guys like you. They don't want to live on a farm. They hardly even step in the yard. Plus, I gotta pay for college. You ever think about that?" He pulled another invoice apart, but this time the pink copy tore, and he slapped it down on the table. "Look. I know. You want the place to stay like it is. I get it. But it's not gonna happen. Nobody's buying a fucking farm. Not unless, you know, they're buying the farm," he said and jerked a thumb toward the ceiling. When I didn't laugh, he went on sternly, "You should be thanking me. I saved the place from getting run over by a bunch of—"

"You said no one should do more than five houses at a time. That you can't make a decent shed in less than a month."

"Yeah, well. This is the world we live in. You gotta go big if you want to survive. And you gotta make accommodations. You get a little older, you'll understand that." Again I didn't answer, and he finally glanced up at me. His expression was similar to my parents', seeking understanding, maybe acceptance. Much later I'd come to believe such a look always deserved my sympathy, but I didn't have any to offer then. "Anyway," he said, picking up his level and twirling it in a tight little circle next to his head. "I'll be around all summer. You can come up any time. Teach you how to drive the bulldozer if you want. And set a blasting cap."

"I've got a job," I said. "I start in two weeks."

"Well, just come around when you can," he said. And then, because the level was in his right hand, he started to raise his left for a shake. I might have given way then, might have decided his friendship was worth more than elusive desires I couldn't have named, but the sight of his stumps, the skin tight and purplish over the ends, the thought of them against my palm, sent a wave of revulsion through me, and I turned before the hand was all the way up. "Want a Coke before you go?" he asked. I don't know what I managed to answer. Another time, maybe, or no thanks, not today. "Good luck with the last week of school," he called as I left the trailer. "Stay tough. It'll be over soon."

The sun was bright outside, and I wanted only to get under the cool shade of the woods while I still had a chance. But on the way there, I passed the Hollahans' huge, brick-fronted house, the landscaping still new enough that you could see the seams of freshly laid sod, the little saplings at the curb braced with stakes. The girls, Ashley and Leslie, glimpsed me from one of the upstairs windows and called down. Did I want to come swim in their pool? The younger one giggled, but the older—almost as close to turning twelve as I was to turning fourteen—gave me that serious look, bordering on grave, and the hot dryness in my throat nearly made me cough.

"I'll go get my suit," I croaked, but the girls insisted I could borrow one of their dad's. Instead of heading for the woods that would soon be gone, I turned up their steep driveway and into the rest of my compromised life.

TRUST ME

◄○►

1.

Lewis doesn't want to turn on a lamp, though he needs more light. It's Monday morning, end of September, and the south-facing windows catch only the first dim flush of sunrise. Outside, the ground is wet from yesterday's rain, steaming between ferns washed free of dust. Beyond them the river, still low between its banks, carries sticks and the first downed leaves of fall. He waits for his eyes to adjust, and when they don't, searches with his hands, pawing the dining table, the cold stone of the mantel, the top of the shoe rack. He has the couch cushions flipped up, fingers running over crumbs beneath, when his daughter comes in from her bedroom.

"Lost them again," she says. A statement, not a question. She's dressed for school in a sweatshirt that's too baggy, jeans too tight, hair damp. Her name is Skye, but since she was an infant, he's called her Silly, or Sills for short.

"I didn't lose them. I just don't remember where they are."

"Last time they were in your jacket."

"I checked already." When she turns to scan the bookshelf, he hurries to the coat rack. Did he wear the leather jacket the night before? Or the fleece? He jams his hands into the pockets of both but comes up with nothing. She's watching him when he glances up. "I knew they weren't there," he says.

"Why don't you at least put the lights on?"

"I probably left them in the car," Lewis says. "Grab some breakfast. We're leaving as soon as I find them."

"Check on the path," Sills says. "You once dropped them on your way in."

She has one hand on her hip, head tilted to the left, so her hair falls across her neck. The way her braces push out her lips gives her mouth a permanent pout, made sour by the scrunching of her eyes. It's a disconcerting look, not only because it resembles the one Veronica turned on him so often in the last years of their marriage, when she was debating how long she could stay in it, but because it sits on Sills's face so naturally. Only twelve, and she doesn't have to work to make him squirm. Twelve and a half, that is. She reminds him every time he objects to her sitting in the car alone while he goes into a store or to her walking by herself to the diner on the highway, where, if he doesn't order a burger and salad for her, she'll eat nothing but a shake and fries. "I'm twelve and a half, for crying out loud," she'll say, and he'll reply, "Exactly," before walking with her to the diner though its food gives him cramps.

He takes the path slowly, shuffling his feet, hoping to hear the clink of keys without having to bend down to search. But the only sound is the crackle and whisper of skeletal weeds. He nudges some of the nearby ferns with his foot, but still nothing. The light has come up enough to splinter on the crack in his driver's-side window, but the river is still in shadow. To his relief, the car door is unlocked, but the keys aren't in the ignition as he hoped. Not on the floor, either, or between the seats. He pictures that disgruntled look on Sills's face, Veronica's look, and wonders again how long it will be before she tells him she can't come with him this weekend, she doesn't want to miss her soccer game or ballet recital or a trip to the mall with her friends. He feels the familiar panic again, along with a terrible urge to kick something and run. Why do even the smallest things have to be so difficult?

"Hey! Mr. Observant!"

She stands in the doorway, backlit by the kitchen window, her silhouette less like her mother's now than that of a stranger who's appeared without invitation in the cabin he bought so optimistically a year ago, when he still believed he could control the future by wishing it a certain way. A perfect little A-frame with a bedroom for Sills downstairs, a loft for Lewis and Veronica above, and a view of the river through a screen of fir and big-leaf maple. A Hail Mary, his therapist called it, which irritated him enough that he canceled his next two appointments.

"We can't take anything for granted," he said as he showed Veronica the listing two months into their first separation, when she agreed to give them another chance. "This is the only life we've got." At first she fretted over their finances and whether they could really afford a second mortgage, even a small one, and what about upkeep? But his words brought a flush to her cheeks that reminded him of their early days together, when they followed every whim—his, mostly—and couldn't be in a room together without touching, when they'd named an infant after an island they hoped one day to visit. With a familiar and comforting abandon, he picked up his phone, called the realtor, and made an offer.

But they spent only three weekends here over four months before Veronica decided their bond was frayed beyond repair. By then he was out of ideas to change her mind. All her claims against him were true. Yes, he was impulsive and forgetful. Yes, he was terrible with money. No, he didn't like to think about the future. "Don't we still have fun together?" he asked. She didn't answer.

Rather than take an apartment in town and unload the cabin, which his realtor assured him he could do at only a minor loss, he moved all his things out to the woods and made the long commute every weekday morning. On Fridays he picked Sills up after dance practice and sat in traffic, listening to her complain about being hungry and bored. "It'll be good for her to get out of the city, breathe some clean air," he told Veronica. But he knew that she took living in the cabin as one more example of his childishness, his refusal to grow up and participate in a world that didn't value his instinct for the impractical. His therapist told him getting rid of the place would be a positive step in his healing process, that he should focus instead on his daughter's needs. After that he stopped going to appointments altogether.

"Use your eyes much?" Sills calls now, her face still in shadow.

Then, in a sudden movement that makes him start, she swings the door closed.

2.

When she was at home in Salem, Skye was mostly sure she loved her mother more than her father. Even when they were fighting, usually over clothes Skye coveted that her mother didn't want to buy, she didn't question her feelings. Without thinking about it very consciously, she'd come to consider her mother an extension of herself, or maybe she an extension of her mother. Both were long limbed and sandy haired, with an appreciation for order and an attention to visual details, each obsessively rearranging objects: her mother the flowers in a vase on the dining room table, Skye the collection of feathers—

from a blue jay and a goldfinch, both murdered by a neighbor's cat—pinned to her bedroom wall. She never had to ask herself whether or not she loved her mother. The love was just there, an undercurrent to her drab days at school, her evenings of plodding through seventh-grade homework or watching TV or texting with her friends during the one hour her mother allowed her to use her phone.

It wasn't that she believed she needed to love one parent more than another, just that she did, naturally, because one was easier to love. Her mother was comfortably predictable, serious but affectionate, a setter of rules Skye could follow or flail against when necessary. When Skye related some drama among her friends—"Aliyah won't sit next to Kendall, because Kendall called her an attention whore"—she asked irritating mom-questions, like, "Can't you figure out a way to bring them together?" which of course was beside the point. What Skye wanted to talk about was whether Aliyah really was an attention whore or if Kendall was the one whoring for attention by saying so to the whole lunch table. So instead of answering the question, she said, "It must be boring to be old," which made her mother scowl pleasurably.

But staying at the cabin confused her, complicated her sense of order. For one, she still thought of the place as their family getaway rather than her father's house. When they drove the forty-five minutes out of town, snaking up the river until the woods closed around them for the weekend, she still in her ballet tights and leotard, it seemed to her that he was driving in the wrong direction, that he'd forgotten the way and was getting them lost. And then she asked silently, *Do I love him?* before answering, *Right now I do.* That loving him wasn't something she took for granted unnerved her, but the tenuousness also made the love more present. She couldn't just ignore it, as she did with her mother, because one day it might disappear.

So she found herself watching him as he went about his morning routine, muttering to himself, bumping into furniture until he'd had his first sips of coffee, then preparing something out of his range for breakfast—pancakes with fresh huckleberries they'd picked on a recent hike—only to realize after he'd mixed most of it in a bowl he didn't have some essential ingredient—baking powder, milk—and finally cooking it anyway and pretending to enjoy it while Skye took a single bite before switching to yogurt and store-bought fruit. In its wake a colossal mess would linger all weekend if she didn't clean it up.

Who was this person she spent sixty-three hours with every week? He looked nothing like her, with his dark curly hair and wide mouth and dimpled chin, his cheeks growing more shadowed as the weekend went on, until finally he scraped away the bristles before returning her to the world—usually late—on Monday morning. All they shared were long fingers and toes, bony wrists and ankles, crowded teeth, which her braces were now straightening. His, straightened decades ago, had since drifted into an overbite.

Almost everything he did seemed strange to her. He spent hours picking out hummingbird feeders and hanging them on the deck but then never remembered to check them. If she didn't fill them with sugar water, they would have stayed empty all summer. But when the birds came darting out of the woods, hovering over the plastic flowers, he'd watch them for an entire afternoon, mesmerized, their blurry wings holding his interest in a way little else did. It was that way with other things, too. One Sunday every month he labored over bills and his checkbook and then left the sealed envelopes, unstamped, on the shoe rack for weeks. He told Skye she was the most important thing in his life but then missed her most recent recital, in which she played one of Peter Pan's lost children, because he'd written down the wrong date on his calendar.

They did, of course, have some things in common, things they liked to do together. Swimming in the river on hot days. Building stone cairns on the bank. Laboring over jigsaw puzzles, the more challenging the better. They usually saved them for evenings, but today, because it was already raining and because her father's back hurt too much for him to stand in the river fishing, they pulled out a puzzle after breakfast, a big one he'd picked out on his last shopping trip in town. A thousand pieces that together would form the image of a peacock, its head and neck in the foreground, with a spread of feathers behind.

At the start it was slow going. The feathers were hard to distinguish from each other, and the neck was a solid stretch of blue with only a subtle shift in shade from top to bottom. But they worked well together, each with a different strategy: her father focused on edges while Skye sorted pieces by color before moving methodically from section to section. So far they had half the frame complete, plus the peacock's head, and it wasn't yet noon. At this pace, if it kept raining, they'd finish by dinner. There was evidence of their past success around them. Her father had figured out a way to glue the backs of puzzles onto newspaper and hang them, and here above the table was a jumble of brightly colored popsicles and over the couch a display of toy trains. More puzzles were in her bedroom: one of Cracker Jack boxes, another of tulips, a third of sleeping kittens.

She knew, too, that he spent a long time looking for them, picking only images she was sure to like, bypassing cut-up Cézanne paintings and photos of rivers and mountains. Why would you want something on the wall you could see out the window? Despite all her mother's complaints about his selfishness and inconsistency, he was considerate in this regard. But now his forehead was creased, and his whole body bent forward as he scoured the scattered pieces for flat sides, not paying attention when his head blocked the light and made it hard for her to see.

"Sure you don't have any edges in there?" he asked, running his fingers through one of her piles.

"Posture, Dad."

"I'm still missing two corners."

"You'll complain about your back all day tomorrow."

"I never complain. I just report."

He kept fishing around on her side until she pushed his arm away and told him to keep out of her bubble space, a concept she'd learned in kindergarten and had often used against him. Everyone's bubble space is different, she'd once told him at six or seven years old, deciding on that day, angry at him for reasons she could no longer remember, that hers took up the whole house. "Daddy," she'd said, "I'm afraid you'll have to go outside."

Now, when he backed out of her light, she tried out the gossip that had fallen flat with her mother. What did he think, was Aliyah the attention whore, or Kendall?

"It depends," he answered. "When Kendall said it, did she toss her head like this and make sure everyone was looking at her?"

"More like this," Skye said and flung her ponytail over a shoulder.

"Total attention whore."

"That's what I thought."

"I wouldn't sit next to her, either," her father said.

"Here's your corner."

She tossed it to him, a little blue wedge with which he connected the puzzle's left side to the bottom. Then he was fishing in her piles again and blocking the light, his head casting a shadow over the peacock's neck. "The other one's got to be here, too," he said, and as Skye leaned away to give him room, she found herself beginning to cry. Yes, right now, she loved him. But the problem was he expected her to, even if she didn't. The fragments of peacock blurred together into a puddle of shifting color.

She jabbed him with an elbow. "Out of my bubble," she said.

—◦—

By evening, when the rain hadn't let up and they both grew restless, her father wincing as he stood, then rolling shoulders and kneading a knot on his neck, Skye offered to teach him some yoga poses. She'd been taking a class once a week with her mom and had been badgering him to try it. Now, to her surprise, he agreed, even seemed to welcome the idea. He encouraged her further by groaning melodramatically as he crouched into Child's Pose. They both laughed when they compared their Standing Forward Bend, Skye putting both hands flat on the floor, her father unable to reach his shins.

"This one's my favorite," he said when she let him lie flat on his back in Shavasana. She told him to think about his breath, in through the nose, out through the mouth, and after a minute he dozed off and woke himself with a snort.

Afterward, she pulled chairs away from the dining table, scattered them around the front room, and told him to stand and close his eyes. He did. "Put out your finger," she said, and he did that, too. She linked her own finger with his and tugged. He resisted. "Come on," she said and explained that it was an exercise her instructor led at the end of every class. She tugged again, and this time he followed, slowly, shuffling his feet on the rug.

"What's this have to do with yoga?" he asked.

"It's about freeing your mind. Letting go."

"My mind isn't free," he said. "It's focused on not walking into a chair."

"You've got to trust," she said. "That's the whole point."

She pulled him to the left, and when his knee grazed the couch, he opened his eyes halfway. "Remember my back," he said. "If I fall, I might not get up again."

"No peeking," she said. "Or I'll have to blindfold you."

"I feel like I'm walking the plank."

"That's good," she said. "Picture sharks below. If you don't follow me exactly, you're lunch."

She pulled harder, and he let himself take longer strides. They turned figure-eights around the chairs, his foot occasionally bumping one of the legs, but now he managed to keep his eyes closed. In class she'd always loved the feeling of being guided around the room, of abandoning herself to someone else's sight, and she was glad to give him the experience, too. He'd soon start to become more conscious of sounds—the rain on the roof, the clicking of his knees, Skye's breath still phlegmy from a recent cold—and then his mind would drift. In another minute he wouldn't even remember he was walking around obstacles, that anything might stand in his way.

Lately her own thoughts during the exercise meandered to a boy in school. She hadn't really noticed him until he was assigned to play the judge in a mock trial they'd been acting out, as a way to learn about the legal system, her teacher had said, though if Skye, who'd played a juror, had learned anything other than how excruciatingly dull the legal system was, how little she cared whether the defendant had broken this or that statute, she couldn't have said what, except that the judge— Trayton Bush—was funnier than she'd realized, and cuter, with long eyelashes and a fan of soft bangs that swept across his forehead.

She thought of him again now, and immediately afterward she imagined her father's thoughts tracing similar paths. Not picturing a boy, of course. Who, then? Maybe an assistant in his office. Or a barista at the coffee shop where he often stopped on his way home from work; she'd seen a fresh cup in his car when he'd picked her up, late again, from ballet on Friday afternoon. One of those recent college graduates she always admired, with long arms and plucked eyebrows and a tattoo of a bird on her arm. A woman, that is, other than her mother.

The idea was so astonishing that she forgot for a moment that she was supposed to be watching out for him. She led him around the last chair too fast, and he didn't turn with her. His eyes were closed, lightly, his face relaxed as he headed straight for the bookshelf. She pulled hard, but it was too late. His nose hit first, then mouth and chin, and finally forehead, the raw wood corner striking right between his eyes. He bounced back in such a comical way Skye couldn't help letting out a horrified hoot of laughter.

"It's not funny," he said and yanked his finger from her. He touched his lip and came away with a spot of blood.

"Why didn't you follow me?"

"You walked me right into the shelf."

"I pulled this way. You kept going straight."

"I never would have done that to you," he said and went to the bathroom, where he splashed water onto his lip and dabbed it with a towel.

"You don't think I did it on purpose, do you?"

There was a red mark on his forehead, and along with the bags under his eyes and the gray hair over his temples, it made him look older than forty-six and tired.

"I didn't," she said. "I swear."

"Do you mind?" he said and lifted the toilet seat. "I need a minute."

"We can do it again," she said.

"I don't think so."

"You can do me this time."

"No more yoga for today," he said. "A little privacy please."

"I'll get you some ice," she called through the closed door. "It'll keep the swelling down, okay?" When he didn't answer, she pounded the wood with her fist. "Okay?"

—◦—

Late that night she woke to the sound of screaming and remembered once more that her family had fallen apart. In the dark, rising out of dreams, she believed she was still in Salem, in her bedroom facing a streetlamp only partially blocked by the leaves of an old oak. And her parents downstairs in the living room or kitchen, yelling at each other, though their words were indistinguishable, her mother's high-pitched, her father's garbled by growls. They'd never fought this way when they were still married. They'd just exchange angry whispers or sit in silence, her mother fuming, her father pretending nothing was wrong. Skye had often wished they'd just shout or throw things and get it over with. Why were they doing so now, when it was already too late, when her father had moved out for good?

The screams drew closer, louder. But they no longer sounded as if they were coming from two different people. Just her mother, then, venting all her frustration to the empty house. Or had someone broken in to rob and murder them? She was all the way awake now, and the window began to take shape, not the narrow one with wooden slats crossing the panes, framed by lavender curtains, but a stretch of glass as wide as her bed. The light wasn't from the streetlamp but the moon, nearly full, hazy behind thinning clouds and evergreen needles. Not in Salem, then. So not her mother screaming. Her father?

When she got out of bed and left her room, he was sitting quietly in the dark, stretched out on the couch beside the tall window. He was dressed in shorts and a T-shirt, his hair mussed in its usual way, his lower lip a little thicker than usual. She couldn't tell if he'd also been roused by the noise or if he'd still been up. How could she have imagined the screams coming from him? They were terrified and helpless, but not human. No one she knew could sound that way. But she didn't want to know what could, not yet.

"What time is it?" she asked instead.

"Don't know," her father said. "Late."

"You've been up?"

"I might have dozed a bit."

"You should quit drinking caffeine," she said. "Mom started taking melatonin."

He gestured at the window, through which she could spy tree trunks splitting a bright spot of river reflecting a broken moon. "Don't you want to see?"

"I guess."

"Right there. It keeps running from the driveway to the deck and back."

He didn't make room for her, so she knelt on the opposite end of the couch, just past his bare feet. At first she couldn't make out anything. But when the screams—no, she thought: shrieks—came close again she caught a flash of movement, a dark shape against the dark ground. On the next pass she saw it more clearly, a furry thing, the size of a dinner plate, tail trailing on the ground. It ran to the far side of the driveway, stopped and shrieked behind the car, and then ran back. Its frantic darting somehow made the sound more agonized. She wanted her father to make it stop, but he only gazed out placidly, hands behind his head, eyes sleepy and content.

"What is it?" she asked.

"Can't you see?"

"That sound is horrible."

"It's just scared. It'll be okay."

"What is it?" she asked again. But this time the creature passed through a stretch of moonlight, and when it came close she could make out the stripes on its tail, the pointed nose, the dark mask around the eyes. "Raccoon," she said. "Baby?"

"Got separated from the rest of the family," her father said. "I saw them earlier in the week. Mom and three little ones."

"We should help it," she said.

"It'll run off if we go out there. Then it might really get lost."

"I wish it would stop making that noise."

"I used to say the same thing when you were an infant. Screaming your lungs out every time we put you in the car."

The little raccoon ran across the yard again, but it was slower now, getting tired. This time after it shrieked, it stayed still at the edge of the driveway, hunched low, face tucked down between its paws.

"Can't we do anything?" she asked.

"Being scared isn't always a bad thing," he said.

"Try telling that to the raccoon."

"And anyway, it seems scarier than it really is. Look. It's already getting used to the idea of being on its own."

It shrieked again but stayed where it was. "Why isn't its mom coming?"

"She will."

In the woods, nothing moved. The baby raccoon lay there, silent and lost.

"Where the hell is she?" Skye whispered. She kicked her father's foot.

"She'll come," he said with confidence that only made her doubt him more. "She'll be here soon."

3.

The door slams shut. Lewis is left standing alone among the ferns, their fronds lush for the first time since early summer, spider webs strung between them jeweled with raindrops. Is she locking him out? Then he hears before he sees: a jingle coming from the door. The keys, still swinging beneath the knob.

He retrieves them and then his jacket—the leather one, though he can tell already it will be too warm by midday. He glances around for windows he needs to lock, for burners he needs to shut off for the eleven hours he'll be gone. On the coffee table is a nail polish stain—hot pink, a color Veronica hates—next to a plate with a mostly uneaten piece of cake.

Last night he tried to make a celebration. A year since they'd bought the cabin. "Our cabin," he said, bringing out the cake he'd picked up at Safeway a week earlier and hid at the back of the freezer. "Happy anniversary," Sills replied, took two bites of frosting, and then went to work on her nails. The word anniversary struck him as wrong, but he didn't come up with a different one. Had it really been a year since that hopeful call to the realtor?

If I can just make it through this first year, I'll be okay, he's been telling himself since moving out of the house, whenever he doesn't think he can make it through another day. And what's he supposed to tell himself when the year is past?

"You should always leave them there," Sills says, backpack over one shoulder, hands searching or arranging the contents of a black purse with silver embellishments, a pear tucked under her chin. "Never forget where they are that way."

"Is that all you're eating?"

"Not like anyone's gonna break in here."

"You'll be hungry in an hour."

"I mean, can you imagine? Dumbest burglar on the planet. Come out to the middle of nowhere looking for places to rob? What are they gonna steal, your fishing rod?"

She's found what she was looking for in the purse—a lipstick tube, which she runs over her mouth three times. The same hideous shade as her nails. Something else for Veronica to hold against him.

"I put a granola bar in your lunch. You can eat it on the way."

"That should be their reward. Drive all the way out here to rip us off, might as well have keys in the door. Come on in."

"This isn't the middle of nowhere," he says. "We're ten minutes from Mill City."

"Booming metropolis."

"Forty-five from the state capital."

"Likewise."

"And fly rods aren't cheap. A new one costs a thousand bucks."

"No wonder."

"What's that supposed to mean?"

"You didn't pay for my ballet class."

"I just forgot. How many times do I have to apologize?"

Sills mumbles something he doesn't catch.

"Forty-five minutes," he says and glances at his wrist. No watch. Who knows where it is? He has no time to look for it now. "We've got to go this instant."

She pushes past him, slinging the purse over her free shoulder and taking a bite from the pear. But once outside she doesn't head for the car. Instead she cuts off the path, passes the stack of wood that needs splitting, winds between the ferns and under the firs. For a moment he loses her in the shadows.

"Hey! I said right now!"

She ignores him. Her footsteps crunch through the underbrush, and then she appears again in a patch of sunlight just above the riverbank. But before he can shout again, she's climbing down to the gravel beach that stretches a dozen yards into the bend. He follows, cursing, the legs of his chinos quickly growing damp from the brush of wet ferns. The cuffs are sopping by the time he reaches her.

"What the hell don't you understand about now?" His voice sounds strained and thin, as if coming through a long pipe plugged at one end with mud.

She picks up a stone and tosses it into the water, which ripples here and there over mid-sized rocks. Past the bend it's still deep enough to form a pool even before the rains come in earnest next month. They swam in it all summer, and now he longs for those hot, languid days, even tinged as they were with grief. Will it really be a whole year before the heat returns? All those days and weeks and months?

She still says nothing, keeping her face angled away from him. She doesn't want him to see what's on it. This is far worse than her open stare. Veronica turned away from him, too, just before the end, to hide what she wasn't yet ready to say. The panic bubbles up once more. Isn't what he lost already enough?

In his mind, he's compromising with her: *if it's better for you, we can make it every other weekend . . .*

"I won't see the river again for five days," Sills says and sniffs hard.

"You can't be late again," he says.

"I always miss it when we leave."

Even as he's taking in what she says, he's speaking, out of instinct, and telling himself to shut up. "I can't have the school calling your mother—"

"It doesn't matter," she says. "She's gonna be mad at you either way."

"You always miss it?"

"So you might as well stop trying so hard."

"Did she tell you that?"

"It's obvious."

He almost laughs. "Jesus, Sills. Do you have to know so much? Can't you act your age?" He reaches out to ruffle her hair, but she bats his hand away.

"Quit messing with me, will you?"

He fingers the keys in his pocket, but the urgency to leave dwindles as the water brightens. She'll miss the river for the five days she won't see it. What else can he ask for? That she'll miss him, too? He knows better than to hope for more than he deserves. She tosses another stone, trying to reach the pool but falling short.

"I guess we'd better go," she says.

"Whenever you're ready."

They watch the leaves and sticks bob past, a few twirling in the eddies. Soon the light spills over the trees on the far bank and strikes the water, flashing on the ripples and turning the still parts clear all the way to the bottom.

BUTTERFLY AT REST

◄○►

He's been blacklisted four years already when the committee finally calls him to testify. Does that mean he has nothing to lose? There's always more they can take from you, even if your name is Zero. Dignity, conscience, honor. Maybe he can live without those things, *but they can't have my balls*, he tells his friends, *I don't care how sharp their knives are*. He's hardly worked since 1951 when Twentieth Century Fox canceled his contract and Columbia barred him from their lot, neither offering any explanation other than to say he was no longer welcome. It was another year before Martin Berkeley gave his name to HUAC, and by then he'd returned to New York, retreated to his painting studio, where he has spent more happy hours than any since his days at CCNY, when he took the same introductory art classes half a dozen times because no higher levels were offered.

This is his first love, moving paint across canvas, more than performing ever has been. More, too, than his first wife, who never understood why he needed to spend so much time alone, or worse, with his unkempt artist friends who clammed up as soon as she walked into the room. She left him after two years, and he was only mildly sorry to see her go.

His current wife, Kate, understands better. She loves art, takes painting classes from his friend Henry Kallem, but she, too, wishes he would let her spend more time with him in his studio on Twenty-eighth Street, in the middle of the Flower District, in what had been a junk heap of a loft before he signed the lease that allows him to rent it for almost nothing. Henry's studio is only a block away, and after her lessons, she makes unannounced appearances while he's working, though usually she knows better than to linger more than a few minutes before catching the subway back to their apartment on West Eighty-sixth. In general, she objects to his solitude less often than his first wife did, accepts discomfort as a condition of marriage. Perhaps because she's a gentile and wasn't trained, as his sisters were, to badger a husband into becoming the man you need him to be.

If only painting would pay the bills, he would be content. He need never step onto a stage or a set again. But he's exhausted most of the money he saved during his productive years, when he had two television programs broadcasting simultaneously: *Off the Record* on WABD and *Channel Zero* on WPIX. He can no longer recall the energy it must have taken to put in so many hours, and he supposes that had his good run continued, it would have already killed him. Now, at forty, he finds himself winded when climbing stairs. He's always been a big man, but he's put on weight at a new pace since doors started closing on him. Before 1955 is over, he fears he'll top 250 pounds. Those few booking agents who still call him to perform stand-up in downtown clubs or Catskills hotels—for a fraction of his former fee—refer to him to club owners as "the funny fat guy."

If Kate is in the room when he answers these calls, he always accepts the booking. Often, she answers and accepts on his behalf. But if she happens to be out of the apartment when the phone rings, he makes an excuse, says he's already booked for that night, and hangs up happy, ready to ride downtown and return to his newest painting. He works in figures, still, though they've become increasingly abstract, and most gallerists laugh when he shows them his work. What the more serious among them agree is that he has a feel for color, which he learned by repeatedly copying his favorite painting at the Met, John White Alexander's *Study in Black and Green*. "What's White and Black and Green all over?" he used to ask the museum guards, lifting those eyebrows he'd later use on screen for comic effect. "I am, obviously."

But a feel for color doesn't sell, the gallerists tell him, and so he drags himself once or twice a month to downtown clubs where no one cares if he's been accused of communist activities, so long as he makes them laugh. No one except the owners, who can use it as an excuse to hand him a check for half the agreed-upon fee, shrug, and say, "Take it or leave it," after he's already finished his set and it's too late for him to walk away.

—◦—

Kate resents his painting, he has no doubt, even if she keeps it mostly to herself. And he can't blame her for wishing things were different. She's had to go back to dancing to help make the rent, long-legged Kate who performed as a Rockette when they were first introduced. She's a talented actress, but few producers have ever paid her to do anything other than swing her feet in the air and let everyone get a good look at her thighs. Those thighs are still worth staring at, even after a pair of baby boys have squeezed out between them. The boys are now seven and nine, with appetites like their father's. They eat far more in a month than a handful of stand-up performances can feed them. So Kate teaches modern dance to uncoordinated housewives, stuffs cash into her dresser drawer, and gives him quick, bitter glances as he wipes the remains of breakfast from his mouth and sidles out the door.

He doesn't need to remind her that if not for painting, he would never have found his way into comedy, would never have met her after a show. It started when he was still an art student, earning a few dollars giving gallery talks in museums around the city as part of the WPA's Federal Art Project. He was nervous standing in front of so many people, talking about paintings he loved, and he worried he'd sweat through his suit. So to distract his audience, he cracked jokes about Picasso's underwear, about the warped glasses that made Monet see everything blurry.

Humor came naturally to him. Jokes were the only way to be heard in his family, with eight kids and two parents constantly shouting over each other. But in the museum galleries he felt something rising from deep within him, something he only vaguely recognized, and it took over his huge body, infused it with frantic gestures, made words come whipping out of his mouth before he'd thought to shape them. And he gathered larger and larger crowds, some members of which invited him to repeat his routine for private parties and charity events. Before long, he was performing weekly at the Café Society, and his brushes lay largely abandoned, though he never stopped hearing their call, never stopped telling himself that once he'd earned enough from the radio and television shows, from his film contracts, he'd take a long break and spend a year, two years, doing nothing but painting.

◄○►

Isn't it ironic, then, that it has taken a collection of fascists and collaborators to grant his wish? Nearly five years, and he's produced more artwork than he'd ever dreamed of making, even if no one wants to buy it. But this pace is soon to be interrupted. Over the summer he was cast in a play for the first time in several years, filling in for a vacationing Buddy Hackett in *Lunatics and Lovers*. It was a successful enough run that he's since been hired to take the lead in the West Coast production, three months in Los Angeles and San Francisco. Before leaving, he's desperate to finish one last painting, a self-portrait that's also a tribute to Chaplin, too-small bowler hat perched atop his thinning hair.

He's working on the eyes, trying to shift the somberness out of them, turn them playful, or at least sly, when Kate knocks on the studio door. He knows the sound of her knuckles, two tentative taps of her wedding ring followed by a more insistent thud. He never locks the door while he's inside, but usually she stays on the landing until he lumbers across the room and opens it for her. This time, however, she walks in without waiting for an answer. "It came," she says and hands him the letter. It was sent by registered mail, addressed to Sam Mostel, and the envelope is printed with the return address of the United States House of Representatives. He's to appear before the HUAC subcommittee in Hollywood on October 14. The letter advises him to bring legal counsel.

"They waited until they didn't have to pay for my flight," he says. "The cheapskates."

"I've already called Sam Jaffe, and he called the Ostrows. They found you a lawyer. Name's Gladstein."

"A pinko Jew to represent a pinko Jew. I'm sure the committee will love him."

"He's doing it for free," she says. "So don't complain." Then she hugs him quickly and steps back. Across her pale blue dress, from left shoulder to right breast, curves an elegant smudge of lavender paint.

"My masterpiece," he says.

"Don't you ever shut up?" she asks and weeps.

—◇—

Gladstein is a small man who wears suits too big for him, which only diminishes him more. This isn't his first time appearing before HUAC; his brother-in-law is also an actor, blacklisted for once attending a meeting of the IWW, while working for the Federal Theatre Project. He's generally dark and dour, and though Zero is grateful to him for taking on his case, especially pro bono, something about his demeanor brings out the worst in Zero. He spends the entire flight from San Francisco to Los Angeles trying to get a rise out of Gladstein by jiggling his chair and saying he's sure the plane is going down, any minute they'll be a smoking pile of twisted metal and liquefied organs, and thank God, he can forget about the hearing. Gladstein does what he can to mollify him, mutters what he must imagine to be comforting words, though after about twenty minutes it's clear that Zero's anxiety has infected him, his knuckles white on the arms of his seat.

The truth is, flying does genuinely terrify Zero. He believes every sound from the engine signals his impending death, and even before takeoff he's drenched in sweat, the wispy bangs plastered to his forehead, his thick mustache prickling his lip. But needling Gladstein calms him, and by the time they land, he thinks, *they can take everything from me, even my balls, as long as I can still paint.*

The hearing is in an office building only a mile from the Twentieth Century Fox lot, where he'd put in eighteen-hour work days for three years, only to have the studio executives cut him loose without a second thought. The tribunal is already seated when he's escorted inside, four stern men behind tables on an elevated platform staring down as Zero and Gladstein ease into folding chairs. A pair of congressmen, Doyle and Jackson, preside, and their interrogator, Tavenner, asks the initial questions. The fourth man, Wheeler, slim and nondescript, with a gray pallor to match his gray suit, stays quiet and scribbles.

Doyle, the chairman, flexes a hatchet face beneath stiff white hair and strokes his gavel, which he raps vigorously to open the proceedings. Tavenner has a mild Virginia accent, aristocratic, the voice of a man comfortable giving orders to servants, or perhaps in another era, slaves. He begins with straightforward questions about Zero's education and employment history, and when Zero says he worked in films, Tavenner's mouth forms an exaggerated expression of puzzled irritation. "Do you mean movies?" he asks.

Zero is aware of Gladstein beside him, his shoe—a scuffed wingtip, too cheap, Zero thinks, for a lawyer who wins his cases—nudging his heel. They agreed during the cab ride that Zero would take the Fifth on any question related to his political affiliations, that he should generally avoid saying too much. So for now he answers, "Yes, movies," and bites the inside of his cheek to keep from adding more.

For a while, all they want to know from him is where he was when shooting these movies, and what dates he'd been there. They are particularly interested in his activities in Hollywood. They ask about people he might have encountered and groups he might have joined. These questions he refuses to answer based on his constitutional rights.

Eventually they get to the point, naming the date of a particular party at the home of a Mr. Lionel Stander, to which Zero is able to respond definitively that he wasn't in California then and couldn't possibly have attended the party. When asked additional questions about whether he was a member of a Communist fraction in California in 1938, he again invokes his constitutional rights, and only then does Jackson speak up, a square-jawed former Marine colonel close to Zero's age, though with a full head of black hair, oiled and parted, and a look of disgust as he takes in the hulking Jew actor and his scrawny Jew lawyer. Zero can tell just by the way he holds his head that he believes the blacklist isn't enough for him, nor prison, either, and though he may be proud to have had a hand in toppling Hitler, there were certain things the man might have gotten right, especially now that Commies crawled out of every corner. Zero glances at Gladstein to see if he's thinking similar thoughts, but the lawyer only stares glumly at his notebook, scratching words Zero can't read.

What Jackson objects to is Zero having answered definitively that he wasn't in Los Angeles on the date of the Stander party and then invoking his rights when asked follow-up questions. Why refuse to answer, after already answering? If he wasn't in California at the time, a truthful answer about his affiliations couldn't possibly incriminate him. His logic is sound, but Zero holds firm, and Chairman Doyle, irritated, raps his gavel and moves on.

The longer the hearing lasts, the less Zero can control the feeling that used to creep up on him during his gallery talks, as if some small cackling animal were taking over his gestures and words. Though Gladstein occasionally nudges him with an elbow, he can't help letting out a quip about "Eighteenth Century Fox," or correcting Doyle when he quotes from a flyer advertising a meeting of the Voice of Freedom Committee. "Actually, sir," he says, holding up the photostatic copy, "it says here that the meeting began at 8:15 p.m., not 8."

Above all, they want him to name names, so each time they mention someone he once knew or half-remembered from a gathering a decade ago, he recites the name silently, over and over, until it becomes a collection of nonsense sounds unrelated to any person. It does unnerve him that they know so much about him, can track most of his movements for a dozen years. But they understand nothing about his painting. That is the one thing he can keep to himself, and while Tavenner and Doyle speak, he pictures his studio, the freshly stretched canvases, the half-used tubes of pigment, the smell of gesso and linseed, the stool he could hunch over for hours without noticing this big body that all by itself could make people laugh when he heaved it around a stage.

One of the things they do know is that he performed at a meeting organized by the editors of *Mainstream*, a tiny magazine hardly anyone who doesn't write for it reads. Did he know the magazine was an organ of the Communist Party? Doyle asks, to which Zero replies that he's a working entertainer, that he has to make a living, that he takes what jobs are offered to him, and that when he entertains he keeps his political beliefs to himself.

And that's when Jackson asserts himself again, leans across the high table and glares down at him, makes a speech about how the Communists benefit from such propaganda. By entertaining for them, he puts money into their coffers, and that is just as bad, Jackson insists, as plotting to overthrow the United States government. And though Gladstein puts a hand on his arm, here again Zero can't stop himself from answering. The cackling little animal has full possession of him now, though he ducks his head submissively before raising his eyes to meet Jackson's. "I appreciate your opinion very much," he tells the ex-Marine, who appears, when he isn't speaking, to be grinding his molars flat. "But I do want to say," Zero goes on, as impassively as he can manage, "if I appeared there, what if I did an imitation of a butterfly at rest?"

Wheeler, silent until now, coughs to cover a laugh. Jackson, red-faced, answers through his teeth. "If your interpretation of a butterfly at rest brought any money into the coffers of the Communist Party, you contributed directly to the propaganda effort of the Communist Party."

"Suppose," Zero says, misty-eyed now, rising and bending forward, arms stretching behind even as Gladstein hauls him back down into his seat. "Suppose I had the urge to do the butterfly at rest somewhere . . ."

"Please," Doyle interrupts, rapping his gavel harder now. "Don't have such an urge to put the butterfly at rest by putting some money in the Communist Party coffers. Put the bug to rest somewhere else next time."

Jackson, subdued now, leans back in his seat and says, "I suggest we put this hearing butterfly to rest."

Doyle moves to adjourn, and Gladstein, with no attempt to hide his relief, asks if the witness is excused. He tries to hustle Zero out of the room as quickly as possible. But the animal has been let loose now, and as he reaches the door, Zero glances over his shoulder with the half-mad smirk and dancing eyebrows that will one day be famous around the world, and calls out, "You remember what I said to you!"

It takes all his effort to keep from doing a little tap dance in the hallway, where cameras are waiting. "Ah, they're letting me back on television," he says. "First time in years." Then he lets Gladstein answer reporters' questions, soberly, saying his client has done nothing wrong, that the committee is relying on the testimony of a proven liar.

"You really don't want to work anymore, do you?" Gladstein says on their way outside, into that impossibly bright Hollywood October, the sky so blue it makes Zero think of sucking on a giant popsicle. He's suddenly famished, would eat a crust of bread if he saw one in the gutter, would fight off the pigeons for it, or eat them, too. There are breasts bulging out of dresses everywhere he looks and perfect ankles flashing under hems, and yes, he wants to work, wants to walk straight onto one of those movie sets just down the road and flutter his wings—bigger and more beautiful than he could have imagined—for everyone to see.

To Gladstein, he says, "I'm a happy pinko painter. What do I need any of this for?"

—◦—

On the plane ride home at the end of his run, he sits alone, the seat next to him empty, and he's alternately stricken and bored, his hands so sweaty on the armrests the palms are chafed when he lands in New York. Kate and the boys greet him, and when she asks, under her breath, if there've been any repercussions from the hearing—meaning, he supposes, will he go to prison—he says, "They gave me a medal of honor. I taught them everything they need to know about being patriotic."

The next morning, after breakfast, he rides the subway downtown, buys a bouquet of white zinnias from the first flower stall he passes, and carries it up to his studio. But even after he's settled in, he can't get the paint to behave as he wants, can't forget the bulk of his body, which hangs awkwardly over the stool, a twinge in his neck from leaning forward. And those goddamn wings on his back, flapping every time he stirs, nothing he can do to keep them still. The long remainder of his life stretches out before him, his usefulness cut short by the pittance he raised for the coffers of a handful of wild-eyed Jews who can't collectively agree on the placement of a comma, much less work together to overthrow the government and usher in a socialist utopia. Why does he have to be so much better at prancing across a stage or furrowing his brow or reciting lines from an overwrought script, than at moving brushes over canvas, the one thing he's always wanted to do more skillfully than anything else? What sort of dignity is there in being a permanent amateur, while his wife pays the bills teaching other women how to wag their asses in leotards?

For hours he doesn't lay a single brushstroke. He hardly even moves, just stares at the clownish self-portrait, the Chaplin hat sitting uncomfortably on the head that isn't Chaplinesque at all, far too bulbous and jowly, the mustache too wide. A head that's all his, a big Zero, atop a body not as adept as Chaplin's, perhaps, but one people would have paid good money to watch if not for the idiocy of small-minded men. He's suddenly sure it's wasted here, slumped alone in this loft full of fumes, but he has no idea what else to do with it.

This time, when Kate knocks, she waits for him to answer before entering. Her look is tender, sympathetic, and scared. "I'm on my way to Henry's," she says. "But before I left you got a phone call. Al from the Mulberry. He wants to book you for next week."

"That thief?" he says, trying not to show anything on his face, the wisps of hair flapping above his forehead in a breeze he can't otherwise feel. "After he swindled me last time I was there?"

"I didn't commit. Told him you'd get back to him."

"I suppose I should do it."

"You don't have to. You can wait for something else."

"We need the money."

"Word's gotten around," she says. "What you said at the committee."

"Gladstein. He must have talked to Sam."

"That you didn't give any names. That you made those congressmen look like fools."

"I sank us for good," he says.

"They think you're a hero. The blacklisters, anyway. Al said the club doesn't care if you're Lenin's first cousin. He wants to get you in regularly."

"For peanuts."

"I told him you'll only do it for the full fee. And that he has to pay you before your set."

"I'll think about it," he says, slowly, eyes shifting toward the canvas he's barely touched. "As soon as I'm done in here."

She steps forward and kisses him, and this time there's no paint on his smock to smudge her. Her blouse is as fresh and white as the zinnias when she backs away. He can't tell if there's pride or despair in the lines around her lovely eyes, this long-legged gentile who somehow followed him home and never left, though now she turns and hurries out, abandoning him to easels and pigments and oil. He cleans his brushes and puts them away. To Zero-as-Chaplin, he tips an imaginary hat. Then he puts a flower in his buttonhole and waddles across the studio, as if his shoes are three sizes too big.

The Depths

-◄○►-

Where the gravel road peters out in scrubby birch and oak woods, two boys and a girl spread a dirty blanket over dead leaves and pass a bottle of one-hundred-proof peppermint schnapps. It's dusk, early summer, and between tree trunks they can spy peach clouds reflected on the oily surface of Lenape Lake. Behind them is a 1974 GTO, burnt orange, with new tires, a broken headlight, a shaker scoop gaping like a toothless mouth in the middle of its waxed hood.

The car is older than all of them but one. Brent Shivas is eighteen, a big kid with soft brown hair pulled into a ponytail, a face that might look boyishly sweet if not for a chipped front tooth and a burst capillary in his left eye. The GTO belongs to him. He leaves the keys in the ignition, the engine rumbling, tape deck playing southern rock the girl, Danielle Schwartz, can't stand: either Lynyrd Skynyrd or the Allman Brothers or Molly Hatchet, she can never keep them straight. Dani likes music louder and faster and meaner, drums that pound her head and make her heart race. In her room she has a Bad Brains poster tacked over her bed. She's two years younger than Shivas, a heavyset girl with acne on her forehead and otherwise pretty features. If only she'd lose fifteen pounds, her mother often tells her, boys would call her for dates every week.

Instead, boys pull her aside in the hallway at school, make arrangements to get drunk and screw in the woods. But of course her mother doesn't know that. Her mother who talks about sock hops and soda fountains. She's been getting it from Shivas for the past two months, but her mother believes she spends Saturday nights at her friend Melanie's house, Melanie who hasn't spoken to her since spring break, when they came to the woods with a different pair of boys. Somehow every Sunday morning her mother fails to smell the alcohol and cigarette smoke and sweat, or else she ignores it, this watery-eyed woman thirty pounds heavier than Dani, who hasn't gone on a single date in the three years since Dani's father died of pneumonia, after shriveling up from cancer in his liver and then in his bones, and she certainly hasn't screwed anyone since, either. So maybe she knows what Dani does on Saturday nights after all, but doesn't care. Maybe she's envious.

Not that there's much to envy in screwing Shivas. He has a decent body, broad shoulders and cut chest muscles, but he's clumsy and boastful and insecure, and he takes any suggestion as criticism, in the face of which he gets cruel. While still inside her, he's called her *lard ass, porky, Jell-O mold*. He's pinched her side until it bruised. So she no longer tells him to slow down or speed up, go softer or harder, just keeps her mouth shut and accepts the limited pleasure he has to offer.

Tonight is the first night he's brought another boy along with them. She was surprised to see a dark figure sitting in the back of the GTO when she met them at the appointed corner, two blocks from home, halfway to Melanie's house. Even more surprised to realize who it was: Stefan DeMerea, a kid in her Spanish class, a year younger and quiet, though surly behind dark curls that fall in his face. He grunts when the teacher calls on him, mutters so you can hardly hear him. She's never seen him with Shivas, never knew they had anything to do with each other. "My neighbor," Shivas said by way of introduction, and then added, "Says he's not a virgin, but I don't buy it. Less he's talking about all the dick he sucks."

Stefan didn't answer, which Dani appreciated. When someone talks shit at her, she can never stop herself from opening her mouth, but she isn't quick enough to sound smart and instead garbles her comebacks or else just manages a pathetic, "Fuck you, asshole." Silence is more powerful, she knows. As he drove, Shivas worked his jaw, his little brain searching for more digs. Stefan said almost nothing on the way around the lake, except when she passed him the bottle and he muttered that the schnapps tasted like toothpaste mixed with snot.

Now, on the blanket, the bottle more than half empty, he mutters about the rich fuckers who own houses on the lake, leave their speedboats unlocked on their docks. "Someone should take them all out to the middle and fucking sink them." It's the most she's ever heard him say, and she's surprised less at his bitterness or its target—it's a tradition for the upper-middle-class kids of Union Knoll to sneer at the rich kids of Lenape—than at his willingness to voice it in front of her. She lives only three blocks from the lake, though across the town line, and the family of Melanie Nitkin, her best friend until three months ago, lives in one of the largest houses on the south shore. Even more, hatred of Lenape always carries other connotations. Most of the Jews in the county live there, while Union Knoll is largely Catholic, Irish and Italian. Kids often call her fat to her face, or ugly, or a slut, but if they ever call her a kike it's only behind her back.

Shivas isn't listening, in any case. He's already leaning into her, kissing her neck, sticking his hand down the back of her shorts. She thought he might leave her alone with someone

149

else along, but he clearly has no intention of doing so. Because she's already drunk, because she's already miserable, because everyone already calls her a whore, she lets him screw her in front of Stefan, who sits there watching for a minute before getting up and walking a little way into the trees. She sees him over Shivas's arm, slouching against the trunk of a spindly birch, hair half in his eyes, lips pursed in profile. The light is dwindling but there's still enough for him to glance over from time to time and get a view of Shivas's ass bouncing up and down above her. Shivas pulls at her T-shirt, working it up to her chest even though it's been her rule to keep it on—she doesn't like her belly exposed—and she tries instead to guide his hand underneath the wire of her bra and onto her nipples, if that's what he's after. But this only makes him wrestle harder, grabbing now at the neck of the shirt and ripping the collar.

"Asshole!" she shouts and tries to buck him off, but just then he goes stiff, grunts, and falls flat on her, pressing her spine into a rock beneath the blanket. "Off, you piece of shit," she says, but with his dick still hard and twitching inside her, he kisses her firmly, almost sweetly. This is her favorite thing about him, his lips and tongue after he's finished, as if he's thanking her for an unexpected gift.

Then he rolls off, and while she's pulling up her underwear and shorts, says, "Your turn, Stefanie."

"That's not up to you," she says, as Stefan turns back from the lake, flushed in the fading light. His glance makes her think of Melanie, skinny but beaky, with frizzy hair and a squinty smile. They've known each other since second grade, when they started Hebrew school together. Over the years they've talked about boys above all else, but Melanie doesn't get any more calls for dates than Dani does. Yet when Dani brought her out to the woods with a couple of Union Knoll boys over spring break, she pushed away the one who was willing to take her, slapped his hands when they tried to slip over her belt. Afterward she yelled at Dani for not helping her, and Dani yelled back that she needed to learn how to take care of herself. They haven't seen each other or talked on the phone since, but Dani has kept the argument going in her head all this time. How could she have helped, when she was on her back, arms pinned over her head? And as if to offer more proof that a person needs to take charge and decide things for herself, she asks Stefan, "Want to?"

"I guess," Stefan answers. "But not in front of him."

"You do whatever the fuck you want," Shivas says, lying on his back on the blanket, shirt off, shorts unbuttoned, head on hands. "I'm staying right here."

So she leads Stefan further into the woods, until they can just barely make out the GTO through the trees, like a second sunset though gaudier than the one over the lake. He doesn't say a word when she stops. Nor does he look at her. "Maybe we can use your shirt?" she says. "So I don't get scratched up?" His fingers shake as he fumbles with the buttons and slips it off, a long-sleeve black oxford with faint gray stripes, too hot for the day. Beneath is a ribbed white undershirt. He takes that off, too, lays them both on the ground. His shoulders are narrow, his chest bony and pale, with a few dark hairs in the middle and around his nipples. She tries to kiss him, but he flinches, and again she thinks of Melanie, holding her head and weeping after they got out of the woods, saying she never would have left Dani alone like that, and why didn't she answer when she called for her? "It's up to you, man," she says, more sharply than she intended. "We don't have to if you don't want."

"We can," he says. "I do."

She lies down on the oxford, balls up his undershirt for a pillow, strips off her shorts. But she makes him take off her underwear. He does so without touching her skin, not even letting his knuckles brush her thighs. Then he pulls off his jeans and briefs and kneels in front of her, comically hard, skinny dick jumping with every pulse. She forces herself not to laugh as he fumbles with a condom wrapper. "You better get me a little, you know, excited first," she says. He swipes two fingers between her legs and then returns to fumbling with the rubber. "Let me help with that," she says and has it rolled halfway down when he shudders and comes.

"Don't tell him."

"I'll say you were great," she says. "As long as you kiss me." He does as she asks, sloppily, but she doesn't mind. "And lie here for a few minutes."

She's glad to give instructions and have them followed. His lips are soft, and his neck smells of aftershave, his bony shoulder a better pillow than the undershirt. She takes his hand and lowers it between her legs, shows him how to rub in a way that doesn't hurt. She feels him getting hard again, but when she reaches to touch him, he jerks backward, as if she'll sting. "No," he says. "I don't want to . . . again."

"Okay. Then just kiss me some more."

He relaxes into it this time, holds the back of her head. The horrible twangy music has stopped. A warm breeze washes over her thighs, and birds squawk and clatter in the leaves overhead. For the first time when she's with a boy she closes her eyes. It gives her an odd, floating feeling, as if she could be anywhere, with anyone, and all that matters is the wetness of her tongue and the tingling of skin touching skin. Dizziness gives over to lassitude, and she thinks she might fall asleep this way, might stay in the woods all night. She feels her lips slowing, her head sinking toward Stefan's chest. And then comes Shivas's voice, loud and cross and pouty: "What the fuck's taking so long?"

◄○►

When they return, the GTO's engine is off. Shivas leans against its hood, holding up the empty bottle of schnapps. He waits for them to get close, then tosses it over their heads. Dani expects to hear it shatter, but all that follows is a thud and rustle of dry leaves. "So?" he says, leering at them with his bloody eye, the chipped tooth marring his smile. "Pretty good, right? Bigger the cushion?"

Stefan doesn't stop at the blanket but keeps walking toward the steep slope leading down to the lake. "It was okay," he says over his shoulder.

Okay. The word hits her like a slap. Pitiful little prick. "He blew before he got within five feet," she says. She thinks she sees him flinch, but it's too dark now to tell. He keeps moving, sideways down the hill.

Shivas hoots, laughs a fake laugh. "Of course he did. Stefanie the squirter."

"Where you going?" she calls, but Stefan doesn't answer, and soon his head disappears behind a ragged granite outcropping. She follows and, after a moment, hears Shivas coming up behind her. When she reaches the edge of the drop-off, she can make out Stefan below, hanging onto a root, then sliding, then catching himself against a trunk. She takes the slope sitting down, heels against dirt and ferns and rocks to keep from slipping. She's halfway down when Shivas comes bounding past her, taking huge leaps until he reaches bottom, where Stefan is already crouched low, approaching a short wooden fence. On its other side is one of the older lake homes, a modest bungalow with a concrete patio, a charcoal grill still smoking. Behind a sliding glass door and vertical blinds, bluish TV light flickers. Stefan waits for them to catch up. She shakes pebbles out of her shorts and whispers, "I wouldn't have told him if you—"

"Rich fuckers," Stefan says, though the people who live here aren't rich, nothing like Melanie and her family, her father an investment banker, her mother a frequent sunbather with wrecked skin and scars from suspicious moles she's had removed. Dani doesn't know where Stefan lives, exactly, but if it's near Shivas, then she's seen the neighborhood, which is dull but well-kept, a grid of ranches at the base of the knoll, bordered on one side by Route 10. Not poor by any standard. Why should he resent the lake dwellers so much? She waits for him to say *rich Jews*, and then she'll split, walk home if she has to. But he only hops out of his crouch, vaults the fence, creeps across the yard to a small wooden dock beyond. Shivas does the same, less gracefully. Dani struggles to get over the fence, catches a leg between the pointed boards. One foot on the ground, the other high in the air, the tendons in her groin straining, and she thinks this is where she'll stay all night if she doesn't split apart. But then Shivas comes back for her.

"Legs spread like usual," he says.

"If only I had something decent size to put in there."

She's pleased to have a comeback flash so quickly to the surface, and this time Shivas is the one who stays silent— insulted? angry?—as he helps her off the fence. They follow Stefan over the silvered boards of the dock, out to the end, where its posts disappear into brown water. Tied loosely to a rusted cleat, an aluminum canoe bobs on waves from a fresh breeze. Stefan's over the side and into the boat without a word, then Shivas. Dani eases herself into the middle, where there's no seat. Shivas is already unwinding the rope. Stefan pushes them off the dock. There are no paddles, so the boys lean out either side and run their hands through the water. Shivas laughs and hoots, and Dani shushes him, expecting at any moment that someone will come out of the little house and spot them.

But when she looks back, she sees that they are already surprisingly far from shore, the TV still flickering behind the curtains of a bay window. The sky has darkened all the way now. There is no moon. Stars begin to appear in her vision as if they're being poked out of the blackness as she watches. Crickets sound far away and content. The boys paddle toward the middle of the lake, the dark shapes of two small islands visible against a backdrop of houses on the far shore. One of them is Melanie's, but she doesn't want to figure out which one, not now. In this moment she's giddy with the warm air, the sound of water splashing against the sides of the boat, the smell of the two boys who've both wanted her, even if only briefly. She feels fearless and powerful, a sex goddess, and she gives a hoot of her own and yanks her torn shirt over her head. She doesn't care who sees the white belly, no matter how flabby, the breasts beneath a thin bra round and full and all her own. If Shivas or Stefan wants to screw her in the boat, if both of them do, she's ready.

But Stefan keeps paddling and doesn't glance behind. The boat jolts to one side, then back upright. Behind her Shivas has climbed up onto the seat, then puts a foot on each rail and rocks. "Quit it," she says, but he only rocks harder.

Now Stefan turns and says, "Pig fucker."

"What did you say?" Dani asks. Shivas only grunts and snorts.

"I wouldn't put my dick in that pig," Stefan says.

"That's because you only put it in hairy assholes," Shivas says. "Or squirt before you get close." She wishes she could hear his words as a defense of her but can't. When she looks behind again, he's unzipped his shorts and pulled out his dick, waving it at her. She doesn't know which of them to hate more, which to slap, so instead lurches against the side of the boat nearest her. Shivas goes sideways, flails his arms, then topples. His weight takes the rest of the boat over. She hears him cry out and then splash before she goes under. Stefan is silent as usual. The water is warmer than she expects, and she lets herself sink as far as her body will go before it floats to the surface. She wishes it would go all the way down to the muddy bottom and stay there, where she can be done with boys and their useless dicks, done with drunken head-spins and unwanted memories of Melanie's tears and Dani's father's sunken cheeks as he coughed and gasped.

But then her face reaches air, her lungs pull in a big breath, and she thinks about what her mother will say when Dani comes home sopping. And where has her shirt gone? She sees it floating a few yards away, swims to it, then back to the boat, which Stefan has managed to flip upright. He has no trouble hoisting himself up, but Dani struggles to get more than an arm over the side. Then she feels a hand on her ass, up the leg of her shorts, one finger slipping beneath the elastic of her underwear, and that's when she's had it. These boys who think they own her, can take whatever they want. Including Melanie, who did her best to fight off the one who eventually screwed her anyway, when Dani did nothing to help. She slaps the hand, and when it doesn't let go, gives a kick, hard, behind her. Her foot connects with something solid, and she kicks again. She thinks she hears a crack, and then the hand disappears from her ass, and Stefan pulls her up.

"What the hell did you do that for?" he asks, the loudest and clearest she's ever heard his voice. "He was trying to push you back in the boat."

"He's a selfish asshole," she breathes, as she lands in the canoe, which sloshes with four inches of lake. Then she sits up and scans the water around them, searching for him, ready to reach out her hand. But there's no sign of him. The breeze has dropped off, and the water goes calm. She whisper-shouts his name but hears nothing. "Where the fuck did he go?"

"You kicked him right in the face," Stefan says.

"Where is he?"

Now they both shout for him. Stefan calls him Brent, a name she's never heard anyone else use, though she supposes that's what his parents call him, and teachers. She's never had a class with him, and since he'll graduate in a few weeks, she never will. If he graduates, that is—if he gets out of this murky water still enough now to reflect a few stars, the whole lake silent except for the crickets and the sound of a distant car tearing up the curve of Lakeview Drive. She still feels the impact on her heel, which pulses inside her wet shoe. She's crying, or trying to, though right now she's more fascinated than scared or sad, imagining him down there in the dark space she can't see, deep enough he might never come up. When her father died, drowned in his own fluids, she sobbed for weeks, all the sorrow wrung out of her, or rather wrung to the surface, so that she became sorrow and nothing else. And so she has remained for three years, with no tears left to shed for her mother, for Melanie, for Shivas, for herself.

"We'll say he dove in," Stefan says, his voice shaky with panic, eyes wide under the shadows cast by his curls. "That his face hit the side of the boat. Jesus, we're fucked."

"You called me a pig," she says and flops down into the warm water, unexpectedly soothing, at the bottom of the boat. She wrings out her shirt and forces it over wet hair and shoulders.

"You said you wouldn't tell him what happened."

"What do you call a Jewish pig?" she asks.

"Don't you know how bad it is for me if that gets out?"

"No, wait. I forgot how it goes. Why don't Jews eat pigs?"

"I didn't mean it," Stefan says. He flaps his hand in the lake, turning the boat in circles. "I didn't even want to come with him. But he keeps telling people I'm a fag, and I thought if I tagged along and . . . I'm not, you know. And now . . ." He hits the water with his palm, splashing them both. "Fuck him. I hope he gets eaten by snapping turtles."

And then comes a cry from the nearer of the two islands. "Hey! Pussies!" She can make out Shivas's waving arms, or thinks she can, though they may be the branches of a sapling caught in a new upsurge of wind. She doesn't know if she's relieved or disappointed to hear him. It was so peaceful down in the water, where she didn't have to think or feel or breathe. Why face it all again, this filthy lake and these stupid bodies and their gross smells and the pleasure that never lasts long enough to make it worth the trouble? Next time she kicks him, she thinks, it'll be in the nuts. "Don't cry, babies," he calls. "You don't have to bury me yet."

Before Stefan can do anything, she's leaning over the side and paddling, not toward the island but back toward shore. Stefan leans over the other side and joins in. They move quickly. After a few minutes, Shivas calls again, "Not funny, assholes."

"Not funny at all," Stefan says and cackles.

She's shivering now as the breeze cuts across the wet shirt. She'll tell her mother she fell in Melanie's pool. And tomorrow she'll call Melanie and see what happens when she admits she was wrong and tries to apologize. Tonight, though, she's too tired to feel badly for being a shitty friend and a shitty daughter, for not caring about anything since watching her father sink into himself in his hospital bed, the morphine drip making his eyes foggy during the few minutes they were open, and listening to the strange conversation he tried to have with her the day he died—something about skiing, which they'd never done together, at a resort in the Rockies, or maybe the Alps, a mug of hot chocolate with marshmallows after a long day on the slopes. He kept repeating a number, two-eighty-one, and she had no idea what he was talking about until finally figuring out that was the number of their imaginary hotel room. Then she couldn't take it, hearing him picture them high up on a clear mountain when they were really down in the murk where he couldn't get any air. She walked out of the room half an hour before his breathing stopped.

Shivas shouts and curses as she and Stefan slide into the silt a dozen yards away from the dock, hop out, and kick the boat back into the water. It just bobs there, a few feet out from shore.

"What do you have against rich Jews anyway?" she asks.

"Only the ones who live on the lake," Stefan says.

"Not because we killed your Savior, I hope. Because you already got even for that. You know, Crusades, Inquisition."

"They ruined it with their fucking speed boats," Stefan says. "Used to be the best fishing in New Jersey. According to my dad, at least."

"Wait, I've got it. Why don't Jewish women eat pork? Because . . . Shit. I can't remember how it goes." They trudge back up the hill to the GTO. Shivas hollers once more, but she can't make out any words. "I'm too drunk to drive," she says.

"I don't know how," Stefan says. "Haven't got my permit yet."

She falls into the driver's seat. The key is still in the ignition. She turns it, and the horrible southern rock spills out of the speakers. She jacks up the volume as well as the heat. With the headlights on, the shaker scoop's open black mouth looks as if it might unfurl a tongue, lick the windshield or suck her out through it. She closes her eyes and hears Stefan drop into the seat beside her. "Touch me, and I'll tell everyone you screwed a pig in the ass."

"I dare you," he says, and after a few seconds his fingers slip between hers and squeeze.

PARENTAL PRIDE

◄○►

There was the cat—the one we called *Lady Luck* because we'd first found her, six weeks old, running through four lanes of traffic—jumping and prancing on the back lawn, tossing something into the air and leaping after it, back arched, tail stiff, claws bared. I caught sight of her from an upstairs window when I should have been getting dressed for work and stayed where I was, towel around my waist, underwear in hand. It was a mouse she'd tossed, I could see that now, and it was alive. Or rather, what I really saw was its movement as the cat let it wriggle away, the grass quivering in a curving line toward a flower bed, though it didn't get more than a few feet before she pounced, batting it down with both paws and holding it firm. Then she picked it up again by its skinny tail, bucked her head so that it flung over her back, and twirled so she could trap it as soon as it landed. I knew the mouse was suffering, terribly, but I couldn't help admiring Lady Luck's hunting skill and taking pleasure in her success. She'd always been a skittish cat, cowering whenever strangers came near, often getting attacked by one of the neighborhood strays, and even though I knew it was ridiculous to project human emotions onto her, I assumed that catching the mouse would provide a necessary boost to her self-confidence. I probably didn't think about it in quite those terms, but I did recall then, or maybe it was later, a fight I'd gotten into as a ten-year-old, the only one I'd ever instigated, though I'd been reluctantly drawn into plenty of others, usually by a sadistic neighbor who liked to beat me over the head with a rubber snake. This was a fight I'd asked for, challenging a kid who'd said something mildly insulting to me on the bus home from school. The kid was undersized like me, maybe a little smaller, a baby-faced redhead with big pink freckles everywhere, even on his lips and knuckles, and whatever insulting thing he'd said had sparked a cool rage I'd never felt before, an indignation that made me abandon the shy, shrinking self I'd always known and call out for everyone on the bus to hear: *Zeek Field, four o'clock. Be there.* It was one thing for the sadistic neighbor to beat me with a rubber snake or throw dog shit at me—I'd take that as a consequence of being small and badly dressed, an easy target—but I wouldn't let a word pass from the baby-faced redhead, who should have tried to make himself invisible to avoid being harassed, as I did, though it never seemed to do any good. After I told him to meet me at Zeek Field, he should have hidden himself away for a few days and hoped everyone forgot my challenge, but there he was when I arrived, in fresh shorts and T-shirt, bouncing on the balls of his feet as he must have seen boxers do on TV. Half the other kids from the bus had shown up, too, standing around the baseball diamond, already cheering us on as I laid my bike beside the backstop. It hadn't occurred to me to change clothes before coming. I'd just spent the last hour pacing from kitchen to living room, scarfing half a bag of Oreos, and now my mouth was dry, my school clothes stiff. I was probably wearing corduroys and a plaid shirt or else jeans my mother had ironed like slacks so a white line showed down the middle of each leg. No wonder I got picked on daily. The redhead kept bouncing as I approached, smiling to himself or laughing at something I hadn't heard, and the rest of the kids closed around us, calling out predictable things you'd always hear at a fight like this—*kick his ass, show him who's a pussy now*—and rooting half-heartedly for one or the other of us, since all they really wanted was blood and pain. Who it belonged to didn't matter. I'm guessing my sadistic neighbor was there, though I can't remember for sure, giddily pounding fist into palm. I knew nothing about fighting, how to throw a punch or block one, and at first all I could do was heave a few big roundhouses that nudged the redhead's shoulder and chest. The blows he landed weren't any firmer, and the crowd grew restless, their taunts menacing. If we didn't beat each other, I knew, they'd beat both of us worse. But then the redhead caught my nose with his forearm, hard, and I froze. There was a little trickle of blood onto my lips, and as I wiped it away, that cold rage growing colder, crystallizing, I could see in his face that he realized he'd made a mistake. All at once I knew exactly the right way to throw a punch, straight out from my chest to his jaw. He turned his face away, but I kept punching, the back of his head, his neck, until he went down on his knees. He was crying, I knew he was, but I jumped on him anyway, aware now that he was indeed smaller than I, quite a bit so, but that didn't stop me from shoving his face into the pitcher's mound, grinding cheek and nose into coarse dirt until other kids pulled me away. They carried me on their shoulders, howling in triumph, as if they'd been rooting for me all along. I'd given them more violence than they'd expected, they loved me for it, and if the sadistic neighbor was there, I want to believe I tossed him a look before getting on my bike and pedaling away, one that said, *You're next*. But my rage had already thawed or maybe evaporated; it was gone with the first punch, and on my way home I started sobbing. I wished I'd let the redhead's insult pass, wished I'd kept to my shy, shrinking ways, not because I regretted what I'd done, but because I knew news of the fight would soon reach my parents, which it did a day later. My mother called me aside after dinner to let me know what she'd heard from another boy's mother and ask if it was true that I'd started the fight. I probably relayed whatever insulting thing the redhead had said, blubbering, expecting her to scold me, which she did, but far more gently than I'd anticipated. She said predictable things about ignoring hurtful words, about defending myself only when absolutely necessary. But in her voice I could hear something other than chastisement and disapproval, and I could see it in the edges of her frown, too. There was a burgeoning pride in her undersized son who was so often getting beaten over the head with a rubber snake, whose school clothes were sometimes dotted with dog shit; yes, this little guy had finally found a way to stand up for himself, and not only had he challenged another kid to a fight over a trivial insult, but he'd beaten that baby-faced redhead nose down in the dirt until he was a weeping bundle of freckles begging for mercy. This was what she'd always wanted for her child, a confidence born of independence, of standing strong in a world that tried to knock him down, and if others had to fall for him to feel good about himself, so be it. Wasn't it what I wanted for my own daughter, now three, bossed around by older kids in her preschool class? When I dropped her off or picked her up, I could see already how she assumed the retreating manner of the smallest kid in the room, drifting to the edge of the story circle, the biggest and most aggressive of the others crowding forward and clamoring for the teacher's attention. And all I could do was hope that next year, when she was no longer the smallest, she'd find some new peanut of a child to boss around in turn, and though that other child's self-esteem might suffer, she'd just have to take it out on a kid who followed. As I watched my daughter through the window of her classroom, standing out of the way as bigger kids claimed the best toys and left her with nothing but an armless doll and a handful of faded letter blocks, I told myself that that other child was no concern of mine. And neither was the mouse, though it, of course, would have no such opportunity to take out its suffering on something else. Lady Luck carried it in her jaws now, gently, not wanting to crush it, not yet. She moved to the patio, a place she usually avoided because it was so open and exposed—evidence, I thought, that this game, however cruel, was good for her—and though I was too far away to see, I imagined the mouse's tiny frame trembling against her teeth. What power she must have felt, what fierce giddy unstoppable joy. How could I not want her to feel this way always? How could I not want to feel it myself? She dropped the mouse on the patio's concrete pad, and it scurried away, underneath a fern. For a moment it seemed that Lady Luck had lost sight of it, and I was already tugging on my underwear, ready to head out and pull aside the fern leaves to show her where it had gone. But her confusion was only a feint: soon enough, her paw shot out and dragged the mouse back into the open. And that was when I remembered, or maybe it was later—damn this associative mind, damn its love of patterns—an article I'd read in the previous Sunday's *Times*, about one of the recent gang rapes in India, a portrait of the perpetrators and the culture that had spawned them. The authors described the vast hopeless slums of Mumbai, the poverty and boredom and feelings of worthlessness that characterized the lives of men who did nothing but play cards and drink all day in concrete shacks with tin roofs, who dubbed young women *prey* and hunted them because they felt they deserved more than what they had and because they had nothing better to do. After the rape, one of the men had gone straight home and told his mother what he'd done, boastfully, as if he knew she'd want to hear it. The article quoted her at length, saying first that what he'd done was wrong, of course it was, but why was that girl here to begin with, everyone knew this part of the city was dangerous after dark, and wasn't she a harlot anyway, didn't she already have her knickers down for some other man, and what was her boy supposed to do when her legs were spread for all the world to see? Her defensiveness hardly masked pride in the son who'd wrestled with the cruel world that kept him on his knees, who'd found a way to make it his own. Why should she care about a girl in skimpy clothes? Remembering her words then or later, I had no doubt that if she'd been with her son in the abandoned factory where he and three other men repeatedly raped the woman, a photojournalist, while her coworker, tied up with her belt, listened from behind a partially crumbled wall, she would have held those legs apart so her son could squat between them, just as I would have pushed aside fern leaves to help Lady Luck find the mouse. But she didn't need my help now, because there in the middle of the patio, exposed to anyone who wanted to watch, she happily chewed the mouse's head loose from its body.

ENZO'S LAST STAND

◄O►

People had always told him he was funny. It didn't come to him naturally, or at least not without effort, but he'd culti-vated it, and making others laugh became something he craved. So when he got to college he gave stand-up a try. Open mics, mostly, with time for half a dozen jokes before he had to hustle off stage. Not long enough to get over the initial thrill of the MC calling out his name—"Next, all the way from smelly New Jersey, give it up for Ernie Schunkiewitz"—followed by claps and whistles from friends who'd already finished five-minute sets.

This was the early '90s, Chapel Hill. The music there got a lot of attention, but the comedy scene, though less well documented, was just as vibrant. Several of its members would go on to make names for themselves in the business. Reed Broadfoot became a successful agent and promoter. Lulu Vacek wrote for a short-lived sitcom featuring a former *Saturday Night Live* cast member. Jackson Ray, the most gifted of them all, worked the club circuit for a decade and scored his first major film role before downing a bottle of Xanax with a pint of bourbon and collapsing in the parking lot of the Helium in Buffalo, between a restored 1974 Corvette and a brand new Escalade, neither of which were his.

But long before all that, the three of them performed together in an improv troupe, and at the start of Ernie's senior year, they invited him to join. The troupe was called *Collected Hysteria*. They'd just landed a monthly gig at the Habit, a used bookstore and coffeehouse a block north of Franklin Street. Ernie couldn't quite keep up with the others, who specialized in a cerebral comedy out of his range. Even as a kid he'd silently rehearsed most jokes before delivering them, and his mind worked too methodically to pull off spontaneous riffs. So instead he played the clown. The others were all Southerners—Reed from Raleigh, Lulu from Virginia Beach, Jackson from some little hollow up on the Blue Ridge—and his accent provided counterpoint to theirs, as did his coarse features. With a clumsiness that came more naturally to him than wordplay, he disrupted sketches with sudden pratfalls, intentionally lousy impressions, outrageous characters.

One of them was called *Enzo the Magnificent*, a retired magician who carried a dead rabbit wherever he went and made rude Sicilian gestures behind audience members' backs. Another was called *Lord Wedgie*, who'd parade across the stage in nothing but boxers and pasted-on chest hair, and in a pouting, highbred British voice, cry out, "How unbecoming!"

For a while he became something of a campus celebrity. Kids would stop him as he went to class, mimicking Enzo's hand gestures, yanking on the back of their pants like Lord Wedgie. One of his professors, whom he'd invited to a show, took to writing, "How unbecoming!" in the margins of Ernie's essays whenever he misused *lay* and *lie*. That same professor told him about *How to Explain Pictures to a Dead Hare*, showed him photos in a fat book full of strange images he'd never seen before, and Ernie was unnerved by the black and white shots of the artist's head coated in honey and gold leaf, by the hare's vacant or bewildered expression as it received the whispered words. Who would ever think of such a thing, and why?

Still, he was flattered by the professor's attention and afterward named his rabbit Joseph Boyz. Over the course of the year, the size of their audience doubled, and when they passed the hat at the end of a set, they'd bring in two, three hundred dollars: enough to print T-shirts with their name on the front in heavy metal lettering, umlauts over every vowel, and a picture of Joseph Boyz on back, with Xs for eyes. The first batch sold out in a week.

—◦—

Nothing in Ernie's life had ever been as exhilarating as those months before graduation, when they were invited to play other nearby campuses and had gigs almost weekly. They even went to hated Duke, where in every skit they included jokes about rich carpetbaggers exploiting proud Southern traditions. Ernie came out dressed as Colonel Sanders, did a strip tease until he was down to G-string and bow tie, and was pelted with crumpled napkins. Afterward he drank a bottle of malt liquor and shared a tender kiss with Lulu, who'd been seeing Reed Broadfoot on and off since sophomore year. She was a small, spunky girl with short hair and big teeth, always wearing torn jeans and tight faded T-shirts that showed off her collarbones and slender shoulders. Ernie had been smitten for months, and he couldn't help silently cheering as she and Broadfoot fought in the days leading up to the Duke show. That first kiss crystallized all his hopes, until it was over. A second one never came. Instead Lulu spent the next three weeks dating a jackass horn player in a funk band.

Still, he felt part of something larger than himself. A family, he supposed, only entirely unlike the one he'd come to North Carolina to escape, free of judgment and expectation. When the year was coming to a close, he found himself growing nostalgic for things that were right in front of him: the musty shelves and burnt coffee smell at the Habit, the excited rustling of the audience after the lights went down, the sweaty tingle in his palms before he took the stage. Other friends worried about what they'd do after graduating, but that wasn't a problem for Ernie. He already had plans for the summer and the year following. For two months he'd travel around Scandinavia with a childhood friend before starting a job at an uncle's PR firm in Manhattan. He had no illusions about a career in comedy. He wasn't talented enough or driven enough. He didn't want to struggle.

But when Jackson Ray told him the group had an opportunity to keep performing after the end of the school year, that they'd gotten an offer from an Atlanta booking agent to set up a tour of colleges around the South, he hesitated. His first thought was that his uncle would surely let him start a year later. His second was that Lulu and Broadfoot were back together. His third, that they weren't likely to stay that way for long.

When he wasn't on stage, Jackson was a shy, amiable kid with a habit of snapping fingers and bouncing fists, one on top of the other, while he spoke. He'd grown up high in the mountains, somewhere between Boone and Blowing Rock, and he always seemed a little stunned to find himself on flat ground and surrounded by people instead of trees. Being funny must have been a necessity for him as it once had been for Ernie. What other means of survival did you have when you were small and weird-looking and constantly pushed around by sadistic dopes looking for victims? Jackson's accent was heavier than Broadfoot's or Lulu's, and already he worried about its impact on his future. He didn't know if he'd ever be able to play outside the South. In his act he could put on any accent he wanted, but when he tried to soften his own in ordinary speech, it sounded thin and tortured.

"I know you've got other plans," he said now in that strained voice, bouncing fists. "But think it over."

They were walking across campus under the big oaks near the Old Well. Spring had just broken, and people were sunning themselves on stretches of open lawn. It was that time of year when everyone just wanted to shed clothes and laugh and fuck, and Ernie was struck once more with the wistfulness that made him miss things before they were gone. "I will," he answered, but coolly, trying to hide how flattered he was to be asked. And then, in his usual fashion, he went on to say more than he meant to. "But you don't really need me. The three of you . . . You're the real show."

"We're stronger together. Everyone plays their part."

"I'm just the fool. You can find another one of those easy enough."

Jackson turned away a few degrees—looking west, Ernie thought, toward one of the old brick science buildings he'd never set foot in or more likely toward the far-off mountains he couldn't see. "You're lucky," he said, his voice richer, accent returning to full strength. "You're good at other things. You've got options."

Of course what Ernie wanted was for Jackson to say he was invaluable, that the troupe was finished without him—or at least that if he didn't stay they'd have to change their name. But now the thought of being replaced by some new clown who'd drop his pants and dance around the stage like a drunken monkey made him want to puke, and he said quickly, "I'll think about it."

Jackson's faraway look faded slowly, and then he opened the crazy smile that shifted every feature of his face, from chin to eyebrows—a smile you could imagine on a big screen, no matter his accent. "Man, oh man. We'd have us such a good time. You let me know soon, Enzo. I'm countin' on you."

—◇—

And he might have gone through with it, might have signed on to anything, if Reed Broadfoot didn't take him aside before their next show at the Habit. Broadfoot was tall and aloof, a cut-jawed strawberry blond with a posture that suggested an imminent shrug. Though Ernie wanted to believe he didn't understand what Lulu saw in him, the truth was, Ernie, too, found Broadfoot's indifference magnetic. You wanted to impress him because impressing him seemed so unlikely.

He'd always acted unofficially as the troupe's business manager. Until recently that had meant depositing the cash they collected into a checking account, paying for their T-shirts, and reminding the owner of the Habit to turn off his stereo during their set. But now that he'd negotiated with the booking agent, set the terms of their contract, fought for weekend dates rather than Tuesdays at four in the afternoon, he carried an air of authority that made Ernie nervous. They stood behind a bookshelf that served as backstage, jammed with used paperbacks that had never been organized, not by alphabet or genre. At eye level an Irwin Shaw novel rested perpendicularly across the spines of Carl Sagan's *Cosmos* and a guidebook to Bermuda.

"So," Broadfoot said in his breezy, who-gives-a-shit voice, the word coming from one corner of his mouth. "I hear you're sticking with us after all."

"Thinking about it."

"Tough decision. Vagabond or corporate shill."

"I'd hate to see you flop without me."

"Together we're always better," Broadfoot said, "than any of us could be on our own."

The words were similar to Jackson's, yet in Broadfoot's flattened tone they sounded tossed out, a scrap of language he'd tested and was now excising from his act. "I don't know," Ernie said. "I'm sure you'd manage fine without me."

"That's the thing," Broadfoot said, and now the casualness seemed forced, one hand fussing with the hair over his ear and then retreating behind his back. If he could have done so without calling attention, he might have snapped and bounced fists like Jackson. "Here, it's easy," he said and tilted his head toward the bookshelf, the audience on the other side. "People know us. They like what we do. We can afford to be a little sloppy. But on the road . . . We need to be tighter. More . . . purposeful."

They didn't want him to change what he did, Broadfoot went on, quickly now, his forehead creased and slick. Just tone it down a little, save easy laughs for the transitions and the finale. They were concerned he might distract from their bread-and-butter jokes, the subtlety of their sketches. "We're taking it up a notch," he added, peeking around the bookshelf—at the audience, maybe, or at Lulu and Jackson who were taking their time arranging props on the darkened stage. He didn't want to believe they were in on this. But every time Broadfoot said "we," he pictured Lulu in that moment after she'd pulled away from their kiss, her look of surprise giving way to one of amusement before she stopped him from leaning in again with a hand flat on his chest. "We want to go national," Broadfoot said. "We need to be pros."

Ernie didn't want to answer. Make the asshole squirm. But it was three minutes until showtime, and he'd already been planning to drop his jeans in the opening sketch, show off the wedgie he'd worked up high between his cheeks in the bathroom just before Broadfoot called him over. If he didn't go through with it, he had no idea what he'd do for the first ten minutes of the set. He didn't know if he could hold the fabric in his crack longer than that. If only Lulu had been the one to talk to him, he might have been able to live with it. Why hadn't Broadfoot sent her instead?

"I'll see what I can do," he said, and Broadfoot thanked him, a flash of relief crossing his smug, square-jawed face before he regained his impassive look and turned his back. For once Ernie didn't say any more than necessary. He skirted the bookshelf and made his way across the stage. He heard people calling out to him, or thought he did, but he ignored them as he headed straight down the center aisle. He was sure afterward that at least one person shouted, "How unbecoming!" as he pushed open the door, stepped onto the street, and hurried away. He was all the way back to his apartment before realizing he'd left Joseph Boyz behind.

–◇–

It was the right decision. He never doubted that in the years to follow. He had the summer of his life traveling in Sweden and Norway, watching the sun set at midnight and rise at two AM, falling in love with half a dozen women he'd never see again after a single night of drinking and laughing and flirting in the neutral, transitory spaces of youth hostels and campgrounds and pubs with a view of fjords. The job with his uncle's firm quickly turned into a career. Within three years he advanced from copywriter to account manager, and at thirty he was promoted to associate vice president. His uncle, childless, hinted at Ernie's taking over the business when he retired. Ernie cycled through a series of girlfriends before marrying a woman quick to laugh, and he delighted in entertaining his kids with goofy faces and ridiculous voices and exaggerated tumbles over furniture they purposely left in his path.

Collected Hysteria, on the other hand, lasted only a year on the road. They never made it north of DC or west of Austin, and though they did get some attention outside the region—David Letterman's people contacted them but then never followed up—they couldn't break out of the college campus circuit. Broadfoot and Lulu fought the whole time, eventually splitting up for good in Atlanta. That's where Lulu stayed, taking an internship at one of Ted Turner's TV stations and waiting tables to pay rent. Broadfoot returned to Raleigh, and to Ernie's surprise he turned out to be a loyal friend, never entirely dropping his superiority but always calling when he came up to New York to scout for talent, always complimenting Ernie on how well he'd done for himself as a shill.

Ernie didn't have regrets, though on occasion he'd slip an old videocassette into the VHS player in his home office, usually late at night, when his family was asleep. It was a recording from one of his early open mics, and he was always astonished to see the boyish face that appeared, high forehead shining under bad lighting, meaty lips hovering over a dented microphone, satellite dish ears flaring out beneath dense curls cut square as a hedge. A brief reminder of who he'd once been or wanted to be, a pang or an enticement or a caution, depending on his mood.

But mostly that time of his life had faded into the background. Every so often he'd get emails from other Chapel Hill friends, with subject lines like, *Jackson Fucking Ray!* or, *did you see jack on conan?* He drove to New Brunswick to catch Jackson's set at the Stress Factory, and afterward they had a drink together, Jackson gaunt and exhausted, nearly silent, his voice hoarse when he did speak. "I never needed a break so bad," he croaked. "Why don't you take one?" Ernie asked, and in response Jackson gave him the saddest smile he'd ever seen. "Enzo, you don't know how lucky you are." Three months later he was dead.

—◦—

In the days after walking out, however, Ernie wavered between rage and remorse. People stopped him as he crossed the brick courtyard beside the student union—the one they called the Pit—or the quad in front of Wilson Library. Was he coming back? they asked. Would they see Enzo again? They hoped to catch one more show before they started med school or moved to Charlotte to work in a bank. "Enzo's dead as his bunny," Ernie told them. "Stabbed in the back." But then came the temptation to break into character right there, to collect an audience in the middle of campus. It took all his willpower to maintain his somber face, thank them for their support, and continue on his way.

It was Jackson who reached out to him first. A phone call the night after the show, apologies on Broadfoot's behalf, and when Ernie refused to believe Broadfoot had initiated them, an admission that they were his idea. "You should know better than to listen to anything he says anyway," Jackson said. Was it true, Ernie asked, that all three of them had discussed toning down his act? "Just come on back, and we'll work everything out," Jackson said.

But Lulu was the one to come to his apartment two mornings later. He'd just gotten up and didn't have class for another few hours; it was spring, and hot, and after showering he'd put on boxers, nothing else. He told her to wait while he got dressed, but when he turned, something soft hit him in the back. Joseph Boyz dropped limp at his feet. "You forget how many times I've already seen your skinny bod?" she asked. "At least your ass is covered this time."

He shared an apartment with two other kids, one studying economics, the other planning to become a high-school chemistry teacher, both meticulous. Any mess in the place was his own, and there was little of it this morning: half a glass of orange juice on the coffee table, a damp towel hanging on the doorknob of his bedroom. It was too neat, he thought, too orderly, not suggestive enough of his wild and adventurous nature. Lulu slipped off her sneakers by the front door and stepped gingerly across the recently vacuumed carpet, sat upright on the edge of the stiff couch. This was the first time she'd been here, the first time any of them had been here, though he'd spent plenty of time at their places—Jackson's tiny studio, the massive and filthy Carrboro house where Broadfoot and Lulu lived with eight other people—rehearsing, relaxing before shows, drinking himself stupid after them.

"I know what you're going to tell me," he said as he took the chair across from her, careful to keep the slit of his boxers from yawning open. He set Joseph Boyz on the coffee table, beside the juice glass. Seeing that patchy, soiled, fake fur again pained him more than he could have imagined. "So don't bother."

"Oh yeah?" she said. "Then you already know you're an asshole. Good. I'm glad that's clear."

"*I'm* an asshole? When he's the one who tells me to kill my act?"

"No one told you to kill anything."

"You didn't hear the conversation. I don't know what he told—"

"I know what he said. It's what we all agreed on."

"All of you?"

He was up from the chair before she answered, stomping like a little kid to his bedroom. He punched the wall on the way, hard enough to hurt his knuckles but not to make a mark. What had he done to them, except grow their audience, give their fans a pleasure simple and pure? He wished he didn't feel so exposed with his hairless chest on display, his pale stick legs.

177

He pulled on the first T-shirt he found in his dresser and had his jeans halfway up when Lulu followed him in, carrying Joseph Boyz. "You don't have to get dressed for my sake," she said and lay down on his mattress, the sheets unmade and rumpled beneath her. She propped the rabbit on her chest, its pathetic dead eyes facing him, flaccid ears dangling above her belly. Her tank top didn't quite meet the top of her shorts, a slice of skin showing between two shades of black fabric. Her slender legs ended in ankle socks that turned little circles at the foot of his bed. His boxers bunched up under his jeans, and he turned away to pull them straight before closing the button and yanking up the zipper.

"This is bullshit," he said. "You want me to say it's okay, to make you all feel better. I'm not going to."

"It's comfortable in here," Lulu said. "How come you never invited me over before?"

He wanted to stay angry, but when he faced her again, her hands had gone behind her head. The soft pockets of her armpits, the bottom lip of her navel where the hem of the tank top rode up. He wished he hadn't pulled on his clothes so hastily. What harm would there have been in lingering in his underwear?

"I don't know what you want from me," he said. "I play it the only way I know how."

"We don't want you to do anything different," Lulu said.

"That's not—"

"We just want you to do it better."

"I—" he started, and then stopped. "Shit."

"He told you we need to be pros, right?"

"Yeah, but—"

"And that means not running out on a show right before it opens. Not even when some insecure member of your troupe picks the worst moment possible to have a talk about your act.

It means not being a fucking baby and just doing what you've got to do."

She said all this gently, with a sympathetic smile that intensified the sting. There was nowhere else to sit but the bed, so he eased himself down beside her feet. "If you were the one who asked me—"

"Then you would have said *yes, sure, I'll work on it*. But only because you want to kiss me again or get into my shorts. You wouldn't have meant it. You wouldn't have done it for the sake of the show."

"I never even thought about your shorts," he said, though now, the hems of them so close to his hands, high up on her smooth thighs, he pictured tugging them down over her hips, tossing them to the floor. He wanted to lick her kneecaps.

"Look," she said, more serious now, staring up at the ugly popcorn ceiling he'd have to live with for just less than a month longer. "You've got to understand how difficult it is for him to watch you every night, barely giving a shit, hopping out there on stage and wagging your ass and getting all those cheers. Don't you get it? He works so fucking hard. He puts all of himself into it. It's the only thing he cares about. He doesn't want to hurt your feelings, but it's his whole life, you know? It eats him up. In the middle of the night he wakes up crying."

"Him, cry? He didn't even blink when you were off screwing that horn player."

"Are you a moron?" she said. "This isn't about Reed. I'm talking about Jack."

For a moment he didn't say anything. He was still looking up the length of her legs. Joseph Boyz's dead white face blocked hers. "Wait a minute. Jackson?"

"Who else?"

"This was his idea?"

Lulu lifted one of Joseph Boyz's ears and said into it, "He's cute, but he ain't so bright."

"He could have just talked to me."

"No, he couldn't. You know that."

He did. Of course he did. But he was always so slow to recognize the things he knew.

"If it were just for us," Lulu went on, "Reed and I wouldn't have cared. We wouldn't have even tried to do a tour. It'll be hell on our relationship. We'll be lucky to make it through a week."

"You're doing it for Jack," Ernie said.

"He's the one with a real shot. We just want to help him make it."

Ernie stood. The boxers had inched up his thighs, a reminder of the fool he'd always been. He caught himself in the mirror on the back of his door, small and tidy and visionless, unable to see anything beyond whatever was right in front of him. "I could try," he said. "But honestly, I don't know. I'm just not that good to begin with. I don't think I'd get any better."

"Because you don't have to," Lulu said. She set Joseph Boyz on his pillow, slid her legs off the edge of the mattress until her feet found the floor. And then she was standing in front of him, just inches away. Her lovely shoulders, hair falling across one eye. His roommates gone for hours. If he stepped forward and kissed her again, she'd let him, he was sure of it. Maybe she even wanted him to. But here again was something he didn't know if he could do any better the second time around. Was it really just a matter of effort? What if you tried as hard as you could and still came up short? He stayed where he was until she backed a step away. "At least do the last show at the Habit," she said. "For Jack, okay? For me, too."

"Of course," he said, though he was mostly sure anything he'd ever done was only for himself. "Count me in."

—◁◦▷—

It was the night after the last day of finals. The Habit was full to capacity. People were still being turned away at the door. Behind the bookshelf, Jackson paced, snapping and bouncing fists, muttering to himself, and occasionally pulling a folded slip of paper from his back pocket to check his notes. On the other side, under the makeshift stage lights that threw long weird shadows from cardboard trees, Broadfoot and Lulu waited for the applause to die down so they could start the show.

A few hours earlier, Ernie had finished his last exam, one on the history of capitalism, and then stopped by a professor's office to pick up an essay. It was covered in pencil scratches and a circled C+, his lowest score of the semester. He tossed it in the air when he left the building, abandoned it on the path for people behind to step on. Heading home he passed all the bars on Franklin Street, already jammed, kids stumbling down the sidewalk, one retching in a shrub, though it was only three in the afternoon. How could he not miss all this when today rolled into tomorrow and the last day of the last semester would never come again? How could he not want to keep it going forever? A friend called to him from the doorway of one of the bars, but he only waved and kept going. In his apartment he spent all afternoon rehearsing in front of his mirror and wondered, if he had no choice, whether he could do this every day for the rest of his life. The thought alone wore him out.

Now he studied the bookshelf as the crowd's cheers and whistles dwindled to a few scattered shouts. There was Irwin Shaw resting across Carl Sagan, but the Bermuda book was gone, a slim gap where it had been, hardly wide enough to notice.

"Today we're driving down a country road," Lulu said into the microphone, in a put-on drawl twangier than Jackson's.

"What a glorious day," Broadfoot added.

181

"Sure is."

"What do you see?"

It was a sketch they'd done at least half a dozen times before, a favorite among the regulars. Horses, someone called. Scarecrow. Pickup trucks. A gun rack. Broadfoot wrote the items down on a flip pad, and when he'd reached ten, set it on an easel facing the crowd. Jackson quit bouncing fists, picked up his guitar, and strapped it around his neck. He gave Ernie that crazy full-tilt smile, as fragile as it was disarming—any wider and it might have cracked his whole face apart. "Enzo," he said. "I'm so glad you're back."

Ernie, cradling Joseph Boyz in one arm, flicked a thumb on the back of his top teeth and said, in his terrible Sicilian accent, "I live for this shit."

"That makes one of us," Jackson said.

And then he was striding onto stage, strumming the guitar and singing in a deep Merle Haggard voice: "I asked for horses to till my corn rows. You gave me nothing but dirt and scarecrows." Lulu and Broadfoot joined in with harmonies and a chorus: "Your love is a pickup without a gun rack. Conway Twitty without hair slicked back." The audience whooped and howled, and on the second chorus sang along. Ernie stroked Joseph Boyz—from nubby neck to threadbare belly—and thought, what smart, talented, funny people. What a beautiful, ridiculous, heartbreaking song. Then he adjusted his cape and stepped around the edge of the bookshelf, ready to fuck it all up one last time.

The Payout

◄◦►

The apartment building is in East Flatbush, brick, five stories, its stairwell windowless and dim. On the third-floor landing, a boy in a brown Ivy cap with a worn herringbone pattern leans against the railing to catch his breath. In his left hand, he clutches a thick folded envelope. His name is Abraham Nudler, and he has just turned fifteen. He's reluctant to continue climbing, not only because he's winded from riding his bicycle, but because he doesn't want to reach the door toward which he has been directed, doesn't want to knock and speak to the person who opens it, doesn't want to hand over the envelope to anyone inside.

It's mid-November, 1934, and like thousands of other men in Brooklyn, Abe's father is out of work. For a dozen years he ran a hobbing machine at the R. Hoe & Company factory on Grand Street, but now he spends his days lying on the sofa in their Troy Avenue apartment, covered in blankets. He's cold all the time, gripes that the super is trying to freeze them out of the building, though the radiators hiss every morning as usual. Three times he's sent Abe down to the basement to check that the boiler has really been fired, but each time Abe confirms it, he only shakes his head and mutters that he'll be lucky not to go stiff by lunchtime. He reads the newspaper on his back, holding it over his head as if he expects the ceiling to crumble and the rain to start falling on him. He sits up to eat but after a few bites complains of indigestion. Only in the evenings is he relatively content, listening to Sam Taub calling the boxing matches on WHN.

The change has been a shock to Abe, not only because there was no money to buy him new shoes at the start of the school year, but because until now the image he has carried of his father has remained clear, simple, and static. Short and stocky, with blunt powerful hands that lay out a stack of bills on the dining room table every Friday afternoon for his mother to use on food, clothes, birthday gifts. His voice, slightly accented—he left Minsk in 1903, at age six—has always been one of straightforward authority, not to be questioned. Before now he was always gone from the apartment before Abe woke in the morning, and three evenings a week he left again after dinner to go bowling with his five younger brothers. Twice a summer he'd take Abe to a Sunday game at Ebbets Field. The whole family went to services together every second or third Friday night, as well as to the movies once a year, on Christmas Eve. Otherwise, they saw each other only at meals. Though he's often heard him snoring through the wall that separates their bedrooms, Abe doesn't remember ever glimpsing the man lying down before now.

What he couldn't have anticipated was how different the apartment would feel with his father in it all the time. It used to be his mother's realm, the place where she spent all day cooking and talking on the telephone and reading magazines and hosting friends for endless games of canasta; and after school, his realm, too, where he'd sprawl on the living-room rug to do homework or flip through those magazines his mother had finished—*Woman and Home, Cosmopolitan, Silver Screen*—

looking at pictures of dark-haired girls with long necks exposed. But with his father on the sofa, his mother keeps her distance. She's a slender, vivacious woman, talkative with shopkeepers and hairdressers, but around her husband she's always been quieter and deferential, asking how he likes the food she makes, thanking him for the money he provides to keep the household running. Now she seems not only wary but afraid to be in his sights. She spends her days visiting friends and relatives elsewhere in Crown Heights, comes in to prepare dinner, and then retreats across the hall to a neighbor's. She and her father haven't argued since he lost his job, but neither have they spoken much, as far as Abe can tell, even when he presses his ear against their bedroom wall at night. If they've discussed any plans for the future, how they'll pay bills, how they'll buy food and survive, they haven't shared those plans with him.

He has never before thought of anybody but his father as responsible for the family's financial well-being, and he has certainly never imagined himself as a working man. He has his father's stature but his mother's long hands and bony fingers. He can't picture them running a drill press or lifting crates. But yesterday evening, not knowing how much longer he could take the sight of his father's immobile form on the sofa where his mother used to perch with a cup of tea and test his spelling, calling out whatever words entered her head and delighting herself when she came up with one that stumped him—he always confirmed his answers in the dictionary, because his mother's spelling was atrocious—he offered to go out and look for a job himself. He could work part-time until next year, he said, when he'd be able to drop out of school.

The truth was, he liked school and had no interest in dropping out. He hoped one day to become a chemist. The image of himself in a lab coat and goggles made him feel grown up despite his small frame. Plus the thought of spending his days mixing ingredients in a beaker reminded him of standing on a stool at the kitchen counter to help his mother cook when he was younger, and this made the idea of being on his own in the world less daunting. As soon as he let the words out, he regretted them, though he also experienced a quick flash of heroic self-regard, imagining his mother's gratitude when he saved the family from going broke.

But when he finished speaking, she only put hands on her hips, cocked her head, and asked, "You think it'll do any good to be ignorant as well as hungry?"

On the sofa, his father rustled the newspaper and muttered, "What makes him think there's a job for him when there's none for me?" Soon he switched on the radio to the listen to the fights, and his mother went across the hall. Abe snatched the most recent issue of *Cosmopolitan*—now more than three months old—and closed himself in his bedroom.

But the next afternoon, when he came home from school, his father called to him, and when he hesitated, waved him over. "I need you to do something for me," he said. "Something you can't tell your ma." He propped himself on an elbow, reached under his blankets, and pulled out an envelope. Abe peeked inside, saw the green bills. For a second his father seemed formidable again, a person in control, though he smelled of old sweat. "You want to be a big man?" he asked. "Here's your chance."

—◦—

Now, in the stairwell, Abe switches the envelope from his left hand, which has grown slick against the paper, to his right. He takes the rest of the steps slowly, turns the wrong way at the top, then backtracks and makes his way to the far end of the hall.

Number 408. He wishes he could have kept his mouth shut. He no longer has valiant aspirations or desire for glory, only wants his father's strength restored, his dominance confirmed, his body off the sofa and out of the apartment. He takes a big breath, holds it, taps a single knuckle on the door. Two locks snap on the other side. Then it opens halfway to reveal a woman's face. Squarish and big-lipped, heavily powdered. Dark hair to the shoulders, throat exposed by a low-cut neckline. It might have come straight out of one of his mother's magazines, except the eyes are a little too close together, the skin just below the collarbone a streaky red, as if recently scratched. Before he can speak, the woman says, "Every Jew in Brooklyn. Even the infants."

"I'm supposed to place a bet," he says.

"I bet you are."

"With . . . Puggy Borstein."

"You mean Mr. Irving Borstein?" she says with a smile that's loose and shows big teeth and a lot of gum.

"I've got the dough," he answers and holds up the envelope.

"The dough, huh?" The big teeth part and a rough laugh spills out. "You gonna bake us a cake?" She's younger than he first thought, too young for his mother's magazines—no more than a year or two older than Abe, three at most. Her tongue lingers at the front of her teeth. Without turning, she tilts her head and calls behind her, "It's just a kid. Should I let him in?"

He doesn't hear the answer, but she swings the door open wide enough for him to pass through but only by brushing against her bare arm on the way. Once he's inside, she slams it behind him. The room in front of him is no bigger than the living room in his own apartment, though here more doors lead away, all closed. But it's warmer than his apartment, and he wonders if his father might be right about the super after all. In the center, three men play cards around a table too small for them to sit without bumping elbows. Two smoke cigars, one small and pointy faced, wearing wire-rimmed glasses, the other hefty, a roll of fat cutting two seams into the hairline on the back of his neck.

The third, the only one wearing his suit jacket rather than draping it over the back of his chair, turns to Abe but says over his head to the girl, "He's no kid. He's a young man. Right, kid?" He's got a flat face, big forehead, black hair shiny with oil, thick lips like the girl's. Too much alike for her to be girlfriend or wife. Cousin, Abe guesses, or sister, surprised to find himself both relieved and hopeful. "Fanny tells me there's a kid at the door, I think she's talking about a six-year-old. And then in walks someone who doesn't look six to me. How old are you?" Abe tells him. "A man in my books. In the eyes of HaShem, too." His gaze shoots up to the girl. Fanny. "If he's got hair on his you-know-what, don't insult him by calling him a kid, okay?"

"Next time I'll check," Fanny says. She's standing so closely behind him Abe can't see her even in his periphery. He wonders if she's there to block him if he decides to turn and run away. He catches a whiff of her powder, or maybe perfume, a smell that makes him think of pink bubblegum, but then a drift of cigar smoke muddles it. "He asked for Puggy," she adds and laughs again, sounding more bored than amused. Her breath brushes across his ear and despite the warmth of the room, sends goose bumps down his arm.

"Is that right," Borstein says. He's still sitting, twisted around on his chair, legs crossed. His lips purse, and his brows dip. The other two men at the card table don't look up. The hefty one lays down chips and a pair of cards. "Do I look like a Puggy to you?"

"That's what—"

"Who told you to call me that?"

"Just my . . . some people I met."

"From this neighborhood?"

"Over in Crown Heights."

"Crown Heights," he says, slowly, as if he's chomping the words down. "That backwater. No wonder they're behind the times."

"I didn't mean—"

"It's no big deal," he says, and his face relaxes in an unnatural way, the lower half first, then the rest. "People used to call me that. Now I prefer Mr. Borstein."

"Sorry, Mr. Borstein."

"Like I said, it's fine. I don't mind." He turns to the table, picks up his cards, examines them for a moment, then folds them into a neat stack and lays them face down. "Listen to his voice," he says to Fanny. "It's shaking. I make him nervous. Nothing to be nervous about, kid."

"Okay, Mr.—"

"Now, tomorrow. When you're listening to the fight, then you can be nervous."

"Every Jew in the whole city," Fanny says.

"It's a big deal," Borstein says. "I keep telling her it is, but she doesn't care. Our two greatest fighters going head-to-head for the title. It's, what do you call it. Momentous. But to her, it doesn't mean anything."

"That's because she prefers the spades to her own kind," says the little man at the table, not taking his eyes from his cards.

"Shut the hell up, Herman," Fanny says without anger.

"You got every right to be nervous," Borstein says as if he hasn't heard. "Very exciting moment for our people. After all our struggles. We got tough for a reason. Learned to take some pain and dish it out, too. And now, whoever wins, he'll be our champion."

"Yes, Mr.—"

"Course to you it does matter who wins," he says, gesturing at the envelope. "Since you're purchasing futures. How big an investment you planning to make?" Abe tells him, and he whistles. The others at the table chuckle. It's more money than Abe has ever held before. He doesn't know how long it took for his father to squirrel away, only that he doesn't have much more left. "Eighty smackers, huh? Where's a . . . young man like you get that kind of—"

"Dough," Fanny says, nudging him with what feels like a fingernail in the middle of his spine. "He's planning to bake a cake."

She laughs her bored laugh, so languid now Abe thinks it might turn into a yawn. Borstein ignores her. "Where'd you get this much money?" Abe shrugs. "Good man. Keep your secrets. You don't have to tell anyone a goddamn thing. Except maybe your mother. Otherwise, it's between you and your maker. So, then. Who's this eighty mysterious dollars gonna ride on?" Abe opens his mouth to speak, but before anything comes out, Borstein continues. "Most people choose Rosenbloom. It's the obvious play. He's a great fighter. Has been for years. More bouts than any title holder since Jack Johnson. He's proven."

"That's what—"

"Course the payout's not great. Favored to win, seven to five. That'll turn your eighty bucks into, what?"

"Hundred thirty-seven and fourteen cents," says the hefty man, cigar clamped between his teeth.

"Not terrible, I guess," Borstein says, leaning back and adjusting the clip on his tie half an inch higher. "Fifty-seven bucks profit."

"And fourteen cents," Fanny says, with another nudge to Abe's back.

"Minus the five dollar processing fee," Borstein says.

"That's what I want—"

"It's a good safe bet, if maybe a little dull. Like Rosenbloom in the ring. Out of the ring, I hear he's a riot. Closes down a bar every night. Can out-drink even Fanny."

"I'd like to see him try," Fanny says.

Borstein's still fiddling with the tie clip, a look of dissatisfaction wrinkling his forehead. The room feels even hotter now, the envelope grown sticky in Abe's hand again, the paper softening under his fingertips. He just wants to get rid of it and considers handing it to Fanny while Borstein's attention is elsewhere. But when he tries to turn, his shoulder bumps into something soft. She's even closer than he realized.

"But as a fighter," Borstein goes on, "he's boring as it gets. Dances around, taps a guy on the jaw, scores a few points. Sure he can take a punch. But he doesn't hit hard. Slapsie Maxie, everyone calls him. Personally, I prefer a knockout. Big round-house. Uppercut. That was my specialty back in the club days. You know I used to box? That's where the name Puggy comes from. Pugilist. Nothing to do with a dog, like some people think."

"Hey, kid," says the little guy at the table, the one Fanny called Herman. "Why don't you take off your cap when you're talking to Mr. Borstein. You ain't in shul."

"Sure, this is shul," Fanny says. "We're giving praise to the almighty green—"

"As I was saying," Borstein says louder, with a little cough. He's done with the tie now, his eyes locked on Abe. "Maxie's a safe bet. But dull. Plus he's a Harlem Jew. Not downtown or Brooklyn. Probably roots for the Yankees."

"Bums!" cries the hefty man. He shows his hand to Herman and then sweeps the chips in the center of the table toward his belly.

"So there's also the question of loyalty," Borstein says. "Now, Olin, he's our hometown boy. Lives just on the other side of Utica Avenue. I met his mother once. Nice lady. Pays her bills on time. Plus, he grew up a tenement kid down on Orchard Street. Learned to fight at the Alliance. Same as me, back when I was your age. Course I moved on. Decided I preferred to fight dirty." He winks, and Abe, realizing he still hasn't removed his cap, does so now, stuffing the hand holding the envelope into it. "Olin. Won all his amateur fights, plus the Golden Gloves. Would have moved on, too, if it weren't for the crash. Did you know he worked on Wall Street until '29? Now he's just a guy down on his luck, trying to make a living. You gotta admire him for that. And he's got a good hard left, as many KOs as Maxie already, in a third the fights. Hometown hero, underdog. Hard not to root for him. Plus, the payout's better. Odds against him seven to five, which would make it, what?"

"Hundred ninety-two," the hefty man says, this time flipping a chip from his thumb as Herman begins to deal a new hand.

"More than double your money," Borstein says. "Minus the ten dollar broker's fee, of course."

"Bake a girl a pretty big cake with all that dough," Fanny says, stepping forward. She's next to Abe now, her hip an inch from his. Her dress tight across it, lime green, with pale blue flowers. He wants to smell that sweet powder smell again, but Herman has just lit a new cigar, and the smoke clouds around him, burning his eyes and making it momentarily difficult to see Borstein's face, which might be smiling or sneering.

"So you can make the safe choice, or you can take a little risk and go in for Brooklyn. Either way is fine by me. I'm just a neutral party. Objective. I'll respect you either way."

"So?" Fanny says and bumps his hip with hers, nudging him a step closer to Borstein. Her expression is serious now, or maybe stern, and she's holding a little pad of paper and a pen. "Who'll it be?"

He glances down at last year's shoes, tight on his toes and scuffed. He pictures his father on the sofa, blankets bunched at his waist, listens to him say, "on Rosenbloom," as he hands Abe the envelope. He hears his mother's quiet footsteps as she backs out the door, her glance at his father not fearful, Abe thinks, but contemptuous, maybe disgusted. If she's afraid of anything, it's only that his self-pity is contagious, that she'll catch his sulky gloom. What good is the man, now that he has nowhere to go during the day, no way to bring home the stack of bills they need? What does he know about boxing or about betting or about Borstein, whom he'd called Puggy? The envelope is Abe's now, his to do with as he sees fit. He raises his eyes, turns to face Fanny. She seems surprised by the bold way he looks at her, recoiling briefly before cocking her head and returning his stare. "Olin," he says and holds out the envelope. She snatches it, passes it to Borstein, who hands it off to Herman, who gives it to the hefty man. The last opens it and runs his fingers through the bills inside, mostly fives and ones.

"Ain't you ever heard of twenties, kid?"

"Where's a kid gonna get twenties?" Fanny says. "Knocking over the First National?" Into Abe's hand she shoves a slip of paper with tiny slanting handwriting. *B.O. $80.*

"You're a brave little man," Borstein says brightly, but with a little less enthusiasm, his eyes drifting back to the card game. "I admire people with guts. You gotta take risks, especially at a time like this. And you gotta be loyal to your people. What's your name, anyway?" Abe tells him and studies the paper Fanny handed him, the letters *B.O.* that should read *M.R.* Instead of Fanny's scent, he catches a hint of his own armpits, similar to his father's smell only fresher, and he knows it's too late to change his mind. The heat and the cigar smoke make him dizzy, and he has the strange feeling they also made him forget who he was or who he wanted to be. Without the envelope, he's drained. He wants to lie down and take a rest. "Nudler, huh?" Borstein says. "I'll call you Noodles. With a name like that, you could be part of this . . . esteemed organization. You'd fit right in."

"After this bet, he'll need the work," Fanny says, once more laughing her bored laugh. Then he feels the pressure of her hand on his back, prodding him toward the door.

—◦—

The fight is long and tedious, with hardly any action. Slapsie Maxie jogs around the ring, giving out frequent taps, while Olin chases, landing an occasional left. The only two exciting moments both come in the sixth round: first, when Olin commits a foul, wrestling Rosenbloom to the mat, and second when Rosenbloom accidentally knocks over the referee while standing up. Otherwise, it's nothing but drudgery. Over the radio, boos from the crowd of eight thousand at Madison Square Garden grow more sustained with each round. Even Sam Taub, calling the blow-by-blow as if every step the boxers take is the most crucial in history, sounds spent by the tenth.

For Abe, however, the tension is excruciating, especially as each round passes without Olin delivering anything close to a knockout punch. He paces into the bedroom, into the kitchen, and back into the living room, where his father lies on the sofa, not moving, staring up at the ceiling, every so often rolling his head from side to side. His mother left an hour before the fight started, and for the first time Abe wonders if it's really the neighbor she visits so often and for so long. After a while he even paces out of the apartment and into the hallway, listening for her laughter through the neighbor's door but hearing nothing. During the twelfth round his father says, "You can calm down already. I think he's winning," which only sets him pacing faster.

What he'll tell his father when the fight ends and he has to admit he put the money on Olin he has no idea. He imagines leaving the apartment as the announcer names Rosenbloom champion and never coming back. One less person to feed, clothe, and drag his parents into poverty. Destitution he can manage on his own. He won't be able to bear the moment when his father's eyes light up with hope for the first time in months, the moment before disappointment lays him flat again, along with the recognition of betrayal. Leave now, he tells himself, but stays put as the fourteenth round ends and the fifteenth begins. He sits now, elbows on knees, in an armchair beside the sofa, staring at a drooping philodendron his mother hasn't watered in weeks, hardly even registering the rush of Sam Taub's voice.

Then it's over. Taub describes the two fighters dropping their gloves, Olin heading back into his corner, Rosenbloom lingering near center-ring as the judges compile the scores. It's a tough call, Taub says, a close fight, but he believes the veteran from Harlem has the edge. Abe winces at the words. His father hasn't moved. In fact, he seems frozen, not even his chest rising and falling. For a second Abe thinks he's dead, his heart stopped during the last round, and before the thought quite crystallizes, he's relieved to think his father won't have to suffer the letdown that's coming. But then his father blinks, and Abe goes back to cringing as the announcer clears his throat into the microphone and recites the judges' scores. Abe wants to jab fingers in his ears. He squints, grinds his teeth. "And our new light-heavyweight champion," the announcer says. "Bob Olin!" Another resounding boo from the crowd, this one so loud it sounds as if it's coming not from the radio but from the street outside. Abe's father slowly closes his eyes.

Is it a mistake? Sam Taub asks. No, those are the scores, it's official. Abe can't believe it. Neither, it seems, can Bob Olin, whom Taub describes stumbling out of his corner to claim the belt. Abe is up off the chair. He wants to clap and shout, jump up and down, but something holds him back. Embarrassment, maybe. To celebrate now would mean admitting he ignored his father's instructions, done something reckless and foolish, even if it turned out to be lucky. But that's not all. Worse for his father than losing eighty dollars would be to discover his son respects him so little as to openly disregard him. Because that's the truth of it. He hasn't respected him for months. Neither has his mother, he guesses. All the power his father had once had, gone the moment he took to the sofa. It's an astonishing thing, one Abe can't quite comprehend. A person could loom so large in your mind one day and then mean almost nothing the next. It amazes him, but because he doesn't yet want to concede it entirely, he tells himself instead he'll surprise his father with the money later, when he'll be relieved enough to overlook how it came into their hands. Also, when his mother's nearby, so he'll have to keep any reproach to himself.

"It's not fair," Abe says. "He got robbed." He tries to imagine the family returning to its former routines, his father doling out bills, his mother expressing gratitude, Abe keeping a dutiful and awestruck distance. But no matter how hard he tries, he can't picture it that way, not ever again. "I might have a line on a job," he says. "I'll know more soon."

His father pulls a blanket over his chin and rolls to his side.

—◦—

This time, when he knocks on door 408 in the East Flatbush apartment building, it opens only a crack. Through it he glimpses an eye, half a nose partially blocked by a chain latch, a sliver of lips. He knows they belong to Fanny and not Borstein only because of the dark lipstick. Then they turn away, replaced by part of a cheek, unpowdered but even paler than on the previous visit, light veins visible near the temple. "Just another payout," she calls behind her. "That kid with the stutter."

"I don't stutter," he says, but she's already closed the door to unhook the chain. When she opens it again, she does so only wide enough for him to squeeze through sideways, and then quickly latches it behind him. Today it's colder in the apartment, and she wears a dark tweed dress that covers her arms and rises to her throat. But her hair is pinned up, which gives him a view of her neck and small ears ruddier than her face. There's no cigar smoke today, no men sitting around the table. Aside from Fanny, Borstein is alone, perched sideways on the radiator, looking out the window. He doesn't turn when Abe comes in.

"See?" Fanny says. "It's nobody." But Borstein keeps peering out, his gaze tracking slowly from one end of the street to the other.

Abe waited three days to return, in part because he was afraid of running into someone who might recognize him and report to his mother, but also because he doesn't quite believe he can stroll in and collect so much money, that he won't have to give up something significant in exchange. But today he has worked up the nerve, determined to finish what he started, and the sight of Borstein scanning the street, Fanny hurrying into the kitchen and coming back with a cup of coffee which she hands Borstein shakily, somehow gives him courage. "Do you need this?" he asks, holding out the slip of paper with Fanny's cramped handwriting. She takes it. Rather than raise the cup to his lips, Borstein leans down to it, as if he's afraid of spilling it onto his lap.

"I remember you just fine without it," he says. "What's your name again?"

"Noodles."

"Noodles, right," Borstein says, but this time he doesn't seem impressed by the name. "Lucky kid, just like the rest."

"I would have bet on Rosenbloom. If you didn't convince me."

"You and everyone else," Borstein says. His eyes suddenly quit moving, as if they've fixed on someone below. He sets the coffee cup on the windowsill, and his body goes rigid, except for a hand slipping into his jacket. He holds that way for a moment, and Fanny hurries over to get a look. Then he relaxes, says, "It's nobody," and picks up the cup, this time tilting it up until it's empty. "It's a gift I have. Persuasion, that is."

"He can talk someone into jumping off a bridge," Fanny says.

"Lotta good it does me now," Borstein says. "What's his payout?"

"One-ninety-two," Fanny says.

"Better get it. Don't want to keep the gentleman waiting."

This time Abe has taken off his cap without being asked. He tries to picture his father's expression when he hands over the money, but instead he can focus only on Fanny, who bends over a metal box, the dress tightening around her solid middle. She no longer looks like a woman from his mother's magazines, but he prefers this version of her, with a loose strand of hair hanging in front of her nose, one stocking twisted so the seam crosses just behind her ankle. She returns with a stack of bills no thicker than the one he brought four days earlier. But the bill that's visible behind her thumb is a twenty. Instead of bringing it straight to Abe, she takes the stack to Borstein, who counts the bills and slips one into his pocket. "Finder's fee," he says, and hands Abe the rest.

"How'd you know he'd win?" Abe asks.

"Not you, too," Borstein says, turning to him for the first time.

"Gets it from our mother," Fanny says. "She'd talk a baby out of a nipple."

"I didn't know," Borstein says. "Fact is, I didn't think he had a chance. Stock broker against Maxie? Course he'd lose. And he did, too, if the judges would've called it right."

"She would've made a fortune in sales if she spoke any English," Fanny says.

"And now everyone thinks I put a fix on it," Borstein says, his gaze returning to the window. "I didn't fix anything but myself. You know how much I lost on that fight? It was the Boxing Association. They're the ones that fixed it. Been trying to get rid of Maxie for years. He's a drag on ticket sales. People want punchers, knockouts. They got him out of the way, and now every hood in Brooklyn is after me."

"I'm sorry, Mr.—"

"Forget it. Enjoy your prize. And now clear out of here before someone . . . less easy to talk to comes knocking." Abe folds the bills and stuffs them into the front pocket of his pants, where he can feel them against his leg. "And take my sister with you. I been telling her to get lost all day."

"I'm not going anywhere," Fanny says.

"You think it's gonna do me any good, you being here?"

"I'm staying."

"You'll just get in the way."

"I'll make sure she's safe, Mr. Borstein," Abe says.

The words surprise him as much as they do Borstein, who cuts him a shallow smile. "See? Noodles'll look after you. And

I can look after myself." Fanny doesn't laugh, which surprises Abe even more. Instead she turns away and hides her face in her hands. Her shoulders shake, but no sound reaches him. Borstein's smile is strained and tired, but he winks and points to the door. This time Abe's the one to put a hand on Fanny's back and lead her out. She doesn't resist until they're in the hallway. Then she pulls against him, and he has to hold her tight around the waist while reaching for the door. She's strong enough to break away but oddly pliant when he maneuvers her away from the knob. "When you spent all that money, Noodles," Borstein calls from the window, visible now only as a small hunched silhouette, "you come talk to me about a job. If I'm still around, that is."

"Stop talking like a moron!" Fanny shouts at the door as Abe pulls it shut. Tears drench her face, and Abe does his best to comfort her, putting arms around her even as she flails against him. Her heel stomps his toe, her knee slams into his thigh, but he keeps a tight grip. This is the closest he's ever been to a woman other than his mother, who's bonier, less fleshy. The smell coming off her is salty and damp and musky, nothing like bubblegum. He manages to pull her to the stairs, and though she still struggles on their way down, she does so more cautiously, making sure to land a foot on each step. By the time they reach the third-floor landing, she's quit fighting and instead leans against him, her breath hiccupping in his ear. "He's the only brother I got," she whispers.

"He'll be fine," he says, though he doubts it's true. The look Borstein gave him was hopeless, the swagger in his voice paper-thin. "No one's getting in there."

He doesn't believe himself, and yet he feels only a grim resignation, strangely satisfying, and thinks, *That's the way it is.* He suspects Fanny doesn't believe him either, but she clings to him now, dragging him across the lobby to the street door. A steady breeze makes it hard to open, so he shoves it with his shoulder, then holds it for her to pass. As she does, her leg brushes his just below the pocket where the bills are folded. He claps a hand over it. Her face is blotchy, but she's done crying now, instead looking him over in a sober, scrutinizing way as he replaces his cap and steps in his too-tight shoes into the wind whipping down the sidewalk.

"What did you say you're gonna do with all that dough?" she asks.

He glances up toward the fourth floor, trying to determine which window Puggy Borstein looks down from, but with late-fall sunlight striking the glass, he can see only the reflection of the building opposite, part of a fire escape zigzagging uselessly across dirty bricks. He's already decided he won't give the money to his father, at least not all at once. He didn't realize he'd decided, but now that he's sure, he thinks he's known it all along. Instead he'll say he got a job, dish out a bill every Friday, and watch for his mother's meek, grateful smile. He waves toward the fourth-floor windows and lets Fanny take his arm.

"First thing I'm gonna do," he says with confidence undercut by his shaking voice, "is buy you a slice a cake."

She leans away to give him another curious look. "Make it an ice cream cone," she says and sniffles. The cold wind cuts through his cap, prickles his scalp, and leaves him shivering.

In Black and White

◄○►

Ian Malkin didn't want to go to Poland. If he had his choice, he would have finished his trip with a week in Italy or else stayed in the Austrian Alps, where he'd spent the past five days hiking to the nearest meadows and drinking strong beer in valley taverns. But his mother had made him promise to visit the camps, where some distant cousins—she didn't know how many—had been murdered during the war. Looking at gas chambers didn't rank high on his list of activities nor did he see the point. Those dead cousins wouldn't be any less dead for his effort. His mother had said all the predictable things about the importance of witnessing, the need for communal remembering and healing. He'd finally given in, but only because she'd paid his airfare and bought him a rail pass as a graduation present, three weeks of freedom before he started a job with his father's restaurant supply firm in Bloomfield. If he didn't go and lied about it, she would know—she was the one person who always knew—so he made himself skip out of a tavern for an hour to investigate train schedules.

Leaving Innsbruck was particularly disappointing, because while there he'd worked up a fling with an Australian nurse who'd recently lost a brother—to cancer, Ian supposed, though afterward he wasn't sure he'd ever learned the cause. Maybe it had been a motorcycle accident. In either case, she was letting loose after six months of solid grieving, she told him, though she still cried at least once every night they were together and then again when they parted at the station, she heading to meet friends in Milan, he to Vienna. "I can't believe I'll never see you again," she said and threw her arms around him, her heavy backpack knocking him off balance and nearly toppling him onto the tracks.

Why should it be so hard to believe, when she'd just spent three days frolicking naked with a complete stranger who'd forget her name within a week? There was a time when he might not have believed any of it was possible, back when he was in high school, short, scrawny, pimpled, and furious that girls didn't give him a second glance. But in college he'd filled out, lifted weights, discovered tanning beds and prescription acne medicine. More important, he learned that all it took was a bit of confidence and assertion, often aided by a few drinks, to improve his odds. His friends always marveled at how many women he slept with, but he was equally baffled by their failures. "All you've got to do is try," he told them.

Now, though balding at twenty-two, he found it perfectly natural for this Australian nurse—attractive if a little heavy—to wipe wet eyes and kiss him desperately on a train platform, though it also embarrassed him. Until three days ago, she hadn't known he existed. What was the big deal if he ceased to exist again? Still, as he extracted himself from her embrace, he told her to look him up if she ever made it to New Jersey, said their time together would help get him through his visit to the camps, which he knew would be traumatic and life altering. He pecked her cheek and boarded the train.

The trip was long, and the farther he got from her tears, the more they irritated him. He didn't want the image of her splotchy face to follow him all the way to Poland. Instead, he recalled the softness of her thighs, the wet sound of her breath in his ear, the way she gripped his buttocks as he emptied himself into the condom inside her, as if she were squeezing out the last drops. For a while he lost himself in these details, but on the final leg, from Brno to Kraków, a succession of conductors interrupted his reverie, asking to see his ticket and demanding a "supplementum" to the original fare. These conductors looked nearly identical in their boxy hats and uniforms with more buttons than seemed necessary, distinguishable only by the length of their mustaches. The first one managed to make clear that Ian had bought a ticket for a slow train but had boarded a fast one; the second that he'd paid for a rear-facing seat but was sitting in a forward-facing one. "Supplementum, supplementum," each muttered, holding out a hand and flicking fingers toward the palm.

When the third came around, he'd lost patience and spent five minutes arguing, showing receipts from the first two, and making outraged hand gestures. But the conductor only barked more insistently. A family gawked at him from across the aisle, parents in ill-fitting clothes blinking moronically, a little girl cowering in the corner, and a big-eared boy of ten who translated for him: "He says you paid Czech supplementum. Now you pay Polskie." All Ian had left in his wallet were schillings and dollars. Seeing the latter, the conductor waived the final supplementum—he'd paid for an aisle seat but was sitting beside a window—in exchange for a single crinkled greenback.

Ian handed it over and tried to return to visions of his Australian nurse with her legs spread, but instead kept hearing her sniffles and seeing her reddened nose and upper lip, wet streaks exacerbating the start of a second chin. From the picture she'd shown him, he knew he looked nothing like her brother, who was slim and square-jawed, with masses of wavy hair hanging to his shoulders, and there was no reason Ian should have called him to mind. Otherwise, he'd done nothing more than give her a few hours of distraction. So why in the world should she cry over him? Why should anyone?

—◄○►—

By the time the train finally pulled into the Kraków station, his back was sore from the uncomfortable seat, and the thought of visiting death camps depressed him even more than before. He'd planned to stay only two nights and then book it to Amsterdam for the last few days before returning home and beginning the long next stage of his life, selling grill tops and sinks and sprayers. He'd wanted—expected—to start in management, but his father said he needed to earn the respect of the staff first, show he wasn't just the boss's kid. So by midsummer he'd be driving to kitchens all over Essex and Bergen counties, making pitches to chefs in greasy hats or to their staff who'd jabber at him in Spanish. No matter what he did, he knew he'd still be the boss's kid, resented until the boss retired or kicked off, after which he'd take over. He'd resigned himself to a period of drudgery, which these three weeks were meant to counter, if only briefly. It was pure selfishness on his mother's part to spoil them with a visit to crematoria.

He wouldn't go to the camps tomorrow, he decided as he checked into the youth hostel, a squat building of thickly painted concrete blocks smelling of chlorine, though as far as he could discover, there was no pool on the premises. He needed more time to get his bearings, adjust to the strangeness of this place— behind what had still been the Iron Curtain just six years earlier—where suddenly the money in his pocket seemed to stretch infinitely. A meal for less than a dollar, a beer for pennies. Who could have imagined? After several tries, he figured out how to use the pay phone in the hostel lobby and called the airline to push his flight back a week, paying the penalty with his mother's credit-card number, which he knew by heart.

The hostel itself, however, was a disappointment, crowded largely with other young American Jews here only for Auschwitz. He missed the bustling air of adventure he'd encountered in other hostels, the scent of booze and socks and bodies fresh from showers. In his dormitory, he found half a dozen people lying somberly on their bunks, some with headphones on, none talking. He slept badly and spent the next morning drinking Turkish coffee at an outdoor café on the old market square, watching women in sundresses and wedge heels crossing the cobbles to the brick basilica. Later he toured the castle. He hoped to find some more Australians to pal around with, those cheerful globe-trotters with tousled hair who were always up for a good time, even if they'd wandered through concentration camps earlier in the day or if their brothers had recently died. But he only managed to make the acquaintance of a couple from Leipzig, who'd stopped off on their way to a beach on the Baltic Sea. They exchanged nervous glances when he announced that several of his relatives had perished at the hands of their countrymen, that he was waiting until he was ready, emotionally, to visit the camps—tomorrow, perhaps, or the next day. They politely begged off when he suggested they join him.

That night he drank alone in a bar near the station, looking out for other solo travelers, and then, encountering none, staggered back to the hostel. Another couple lay in the bunk across from his—they were everywhere, these couples, smug and superior, looking down on people who just wanted to enjoy themselves—the girl facing the wall, weeping quietly, her boyfriend stiff on his back, staring at the coils of rusty springs overhead. "It was so much worse than I imagined," the latter said. "My mother's Jewish, father's German. I'm fucked up coming and going."

Who knows how many times Ian had heard that phrase, but only now did it strike him as absurd, the boyfriend so still as he said it, not coming or going anywhere, hands linked behind his head, glasses steamed so Ian couldn't see his eyes. "It hurts, but it's important to see it for ourselves," Ian said, imagining what his mother might have told them. "I'd go tomorrow, but I'm waiting for a friend to get here. I don't think I could handle it by myself." In response, the girl sobbed harder but with even less sound, her ribs shaking violently beneath the thin fabric of her tank top. The boyfriend didn't move at all.

Their sullenness threatened to nudge his buzz toward a headache, so he wandered to the kitchen down the hall, hoping someone had left unmarked food in the fridge. And there, he came upon a young woman in shorts and flip-flops and a University of Michigan T-shirt, dark hair held back from her forehead with a pink headband. She sat at a folding table drinking tea. A journal was open in front of her, pen resting across the pages, a single line of illegible writing visible. She was the type he usually avoided at home, wholesome and matronly, with a long face and downturned mouth and wide hips that suggested she'd one day be hefty. Now, though, she was still fairly slender, and the sight of her bare legs, smooth and shapely even above the knees, revived his spirits. He asked cheerfully, before thinking it through, if she'd enjoyed her day. Then, catching her surprise, he checked himself, put on a serious look, and said, "You went to the camps."

"Not yet," she said. "I'm planning to go tomorrow. But I'm nervous."

"Me, too," he said.

"I would have gone today, but I needed some time to prepare. Plus I wasn't sure about going alone."

"I'm with you," he said.

Her name was Michelle, she told him, but her friends called her Shelly. She was from Westchester County, and she'd just graduated from Tufts. The Michigan T-shirt came from an ex-boyfriend, a basketball fan. He was supposed to have come with her on this trip, but they broke up just before she left. He turned out to be even more childish than she'd realized. When she suggested they get an apartment together after graduation, he freaked out, said she was pressuring him, that they should take the summer to see other people. "He didn't object when I got an IUD," she said. "No problem moving in down here." She waved a hand toward her lap. Her voice was low and raspy, and he couldn't decide if her tone was crass or simply frank. "But an apartment, forget it. He went running for the hills."

So instead of staying in Boston, she'd move back to New York when she got home, look for a job in the city—she'd studied economics—and live with her parents until she'd saved up enough to get her own place. After the IUD comment, little of what she said interested him, and hoping to steer her back toward compelling topics, he repeated what he'd said to the German couple, about relatives lost to the ovens. This time he gave a number and added a few imagined details—about ages and occupations—though what he knew of his ancestors was sketchy at best. His father's family had emigrated from Lithuania before the turn of the century, his mother's from some town near Minsk in 1905. Who among them had stayed behind he had no idea. He'd never heard any names or details of how they'd lived their lives. But mentioning them returned the anxious, vulnerable look to Shelly's face, and she uncrossed and recrossed those smooth legs, the toenails unpainted but neatly clipped, the shorts riding high enough to expose dimples on her upper thighs. He wished he had another beer on hand to keep the buzz going. Feeling it fade filled him with impatience.

"That's the thing," she said. "I've heard about it my whole life. My grandparents' aunts and uncles, all their kids. At least five babies. But it was always so far away. I'm not sure if I can handle seeing it up close. I don't know, I just want to go back to my blissfully blind life and forget about this place." She whipped her cheeks with thick hair. "So selfish."

While she spoke he managed to slide his chair around the table, and now he was right next to her, where he could put a hand on her back and run it from one shoulder blade to the other, his fingers catching on what he guessed was a mole near her spine or maybe a small scab. "We'll go together," he said. "It won't make it any easier, but at least we'll know we don't have to deal with it on our own."

She thanked him, said she felt lucky to have bumped into him and lucky, too, that her ex had dumped her before the trip—"he would have chickened out for sure"—and then just as her eyes were filling with tears, she gave an abrupt snort of laughter. "The first night we slept together? He was so scared he wet the bed. I'm not kidding. Pissed all over me while I was asleep. I don't know why I stayed with him after that. What was I thinking?"

She suggested they meet by the front desk in the morning, but Ian said he liked to get a run in first thing, so it would be better if they met at the bus station, and if for some reason they missed each other there, then at the main entrance to the camp. He walked her back to her dorm, still cradling a shoulder blade, and at the door gave her a hug. When it lasted long enough, he added a kiss, too, sliding a hand up the back of her head so she couldn't pull away, tasting the woody tea on her breath.

When he let go, she smiled a surprised smile, maybe confused, and he said he was sorry, he was just overcome with emotion; it was the intensity of being here, he supposed. "But I just felt really close to you."

"No, it's okay," she said. "I did, too." Then she kissed him again, quickly, said goodnight, and slipped behind the door.

◄○►

In the morning, he heard people clearing out of their bunks. Light seeped around the heavy curtains. The watch his mother had given him in high school, so he'd no longer have an excuse to miss his curfew, was tucked in his backpack under the bed. *Up,* he told himself, but then pictured the grimy bathroom, where he'd have to wait for an open shower, mirror splattered with toothpaste, sulfur smells drifting from the toilets. He pulled the blanket over his head and went back to sleep.

When he woke again, it was past ten. He showered slowly, dressed, and returned to the outdoor café, where he enjoyed the view of the cobbled square, surrounded by arched doorways and baroque facades in various shades of yellow and brown, in its center a statue of a man draped in robes, high on a pedestal, with bronze women and children sitting at his feet. He didn't know who the man was and didn't particularly care. The day was warm, another group of women in sunglasses and short skirts coming out of the Town Hall Tower, and he felt languid as he sipped the thick, bitter coffee and ate sausage he expected to be spicy but which turned out to be surprisingly sweet. His mood was a product of last night's success, which he kept playing over in his mind, the ease with which he slipped an arm around Shelly's waist, the slight resistance quickly giving way, her breasts firm beneath the ex-boyfriend's T-shirt.

There was no point in ruining such a mood by going to the camps, and in any case, Shelly would have been there for hours already. So instead he visited the old Jewish quarter, where a synagogue and a few ancient residences had been converted into museums. Once there, he decided to see everything in black and white, as it had been filmed in *Schindler's List*, and experienced a pleasant nostalgia, not for the dismal shtetl life of his forebears, but for his junior year at Rutgers, when he'd seen the movie a month into its original release with a flat-chested blonde whose thighs were muscled from modern dance. Afterward she'd wept and clung to him and didn't notice when her shirt rode up in back and his fingers slipped beneath the elastic of her underwear. Her emotion seemed overblown to him—her family was Irish and Norwegian, after all—but he didn't mind that it left her trembling in his arms. "I can't believe anyone could do such things," she said. He added, "To my people," redirecting her sympathy, which she then offered in abundance.

He was thinking about that blonde, whose name he'd forgotten, and Shelly with her shorts and smooth crossed legs as he toured the rooms of what had once been the home of a family not much different, he supposed, from those of his great-grandfather's cousins. It didn't look like much, just wooden floors and plaster walls and an iron-frame bed, upon which he could imagine a married couple from earlier in the century screwing silently so the children wouldn't hear, the wife's teeth clamped on the husband's knuckles, his knees jammed up under her thighs. The image distracted him, and he lost track of what the dowdy tour guide was saying in her tortured English. When she finished, he declined to give her a tip.

The synagogue was small and musty, nothing like the grand sanctuary where he'd celebrated his bar mitzvah. Why anyone had stayed here, when they could have enjoyed the benefits and opportunities of a new continent, he had no idea. True, his great-grandfather had died poor, after two decades of inhaling fumes at a paint factory, but his children had thrived, and his grand-children owned beach houses and went skiing in Vermont for a week every winter. And the offspring of those cousins he'd left behind? Ashes. Their grandchildren had never even been born.

Despite the gloom, Ian spent some time taking photographs of the vaulted ceiling and the wrought iron bimah that looked more like a birdcage than a place from which to lead prayers. He knew his parents would enjoy flipping through them, would exclaim over how independent he'd become, how brave he was to visit such exotic places on his own. They'd never ventured anywhere past Paris, Rome, or London, the last of which was their favorite because they didn't have to struggle with the language. By then his mother would have forgotten she'd bullied him into coming. He wished he'd brought black and white film for his camera, so they could see the place the way he wanted to, without the bright sun shining through the high windows, little arches of blue sky marring the drab white walls. It was sad being there, he'd tell them, knowing how few members of the congregation had survived. A haunting experience, he'd say, one he'd never get over. And then he'd ask his father if he could put off his start date for another week, so he could settle into his new apartment and reflect on all he'd seen while away.

—◦—

This time he did meet some Australians, in the café of the National Museum, and they were happy enough to join him for an afternoon beer. He emerged hours later from the third of three bars, finishing off a kielbasa wrapped in foil. All evening he'd raved about the joys of Polish sausage. What made it so good? he'd asked, and one of the Australians answered, "It's pure hog dick, mate. Didn't you know?"

Crossing the market square, alone, he gave the finger to all the lit windows he could see and shouted, "The Krauts killed my people. What did you do? Stand by and cheer?"

It was just after ten o'clock when he lurched back into the hostel. In the bathroom he rubbed his eyes until they were red, laughed at himself in the mirror, and then forced his mouth into a frown. He cleaned a spot of grease from his chin, but another on his shirt only smeared when he swiped at it. A belch brought the smell of sausage and more laughter. It took another minute to get under control.

He found Shelly in the kitchen as he expected, puffy-eyed and unappealing in sweatpants, but also sweetly fragile, chin crinkled in a way that made him want to cup it in his palm. "Where were you?" he asked, with a touch of exasperation. "I looked everywhere." He'd gotten to the bus station at eight, he said, after a long vigorous jog, and then hung around the main gate for an hour. He hadn't wanted to leave her, but then he thought she wasn't coming after all. So he'd gone in on his own.

"I don't know how I missed you," she said. "I couldn't have gotten there much past nine."

"Maybe it was better this way," he said, settling beside her and pulling his chair close. "To go through alone. More honest."

"I was thinking the same thing," she said. "It made sense somehow."

"But I'm glad you're here now," he said and took one of her hands into both of his.

"It was so awful, wasn't it? That pond where they dumped the ashes. And those drawings on the walls inside the barracks."

"And the guard towers," he said, recalling images from *Schindler's List*.

214

"I don't know how I'll get on a train tomorrow and go back to the regular world," she said and hugged herself.

"We'll never forget," he said. "But we'll figure out how to move on."

"I'm so devastated," she said, eyes brimming. "All I want to do is lie down."

They did so, together, on her bed, a top bunk in the center of her dorm. The room was dark, people sleeping or grieving on either side. For a while she cried into his shoulder, and he stroked her hair until she calmed. Then he stroked her side, down her ribs to her hip, then back up and around to her breast. Her breath sped up again, and when it turned to a gasp, he pressed his mouth against hers. She stopped his hand when it slipped between her thighs, but he whispered that no one would hear, they'd be super quiet, and rolled on top of her. The sweatpants pushed away easily enough. She kept her jaw clamped, no need to bite down on his hand. They were as quiet as he promised, and he expected the sorrow to disappear from her eyes, leaving her only with a blissful look—or maybe a grateful one—as he pressed his weight into her. For a short while, she could forget about the things she'd seen, forget the people gassed and burned. He'd return her to the world of the living.

But if there were any change, she looked only sadder now, though her eyes were dry as she bucked her pelvis upward to meet his. He tried of focus his gaze on the spot where their bodies came together, but she yanked the hair at the back of his head until he faced her again. She was trying to drag him there, he thought, to those barracks with drawings on the walls, the pond full of ashes. Couldn't she just let it go, pretend none of it had happened, the world she knew now the only one that ever existed? He lowered his forehead to hers, and she grabbed him by both ears, thrust hard, and let out a guttural burst of sobs that was sure to wake one of their neighbors. He closed his eyes, pictured the nurse in Innsbruck yanking down his shorts, and then he went rigid, shuddered, and dropped to her chest.

"Feel better now?" he asked.

She didn't answer. He rolled to one side and pulled up his pants. When he sat straight, she gripped his arm, hard, just below the elbow. "Stay, asshole," she said. He lay back down, but as soon as she released him, he kissed her, said he needed the bathroom, and lowered himself off the bunk. In the hallway, he hesitated, dizzy under the humming greenish lights, a little nauseated, unable to remember which direction would take him to his dorm. But he wasn't ready for his narrow bed nor for the sound of snoring in the dank, overcrowded room. Someone was banging pans in the kitchen, but he didn't want to go there, either. He had the feeling that any way he turned he'd find another door he'd prefer not to pass through. So instead, he left the hostel again and returned to the bar, relieved to find the Australians still gathered around a scratched and wet wooden table, joined now by some young Poles, red-faced and clinking glasses. He elbowed his way in, lifted the beer he'd abandoned not quite an hour ago, and drank. "Long piss break," said the Australian who'd teased him about the sausage, flipping a swoop of surfer hair out of his eyes. "Get lost on the way?"

"Had to make a call," Ian replied, but no one was listening, and soon he found himself bumping hips with a drunken Polish girl wearing combat boots and black leather wristbands, who laughed at everything and playfully threatened to stab him with a steak knife when he put an arm around her back.

⊷◦⊶

The next day he woke close to noon, hung over but pleasantly so, his body hollowed out and ready for the day. The hostel was empty except for the stout woman behind the desk, who giggled when he blew her a kiss. Shelly's train would have left by now, and a new crop of visitors would soon arrive. The air was crisp when he walked to the market square, pigeons swirling around the statue in its center. At the café, the waiter brought him coffee before he'd ordered. Tourists snapped pictures of everything, including him. He'd become part of the scenery, and he imagined himself, too, in black and white, though his sunglasses were tinted brownish-orange.

This should have been his first full day in Amsterdam, where he'd long planned to visit the red light district. Most of the money from his graduation gifts he'd saved for that purpose. But he knew he couldn't leave yet, not until he'd done what he'd come for, and at least here nothing was costing him much. He could go on for another month and still have what he needed. Even more, he felt perfectly at home in this place where he might have lived a century ago, or a place like it, only free of the fear he might have experienced then, the threat of being rounded up and shipped off to his death. He'd been born at the right time. The world was entirely open to him, regardless of history, or maybe because of it. After whatever his family had suffered, he deserved to indulge in pleasure wherever he could find it.

Today he couldn't possibly stand on a train platform where cattle cars had stopped and unloaded, not when the sky was so clear, the air so refreshing, a breeze rustling the dresses of all the women who passed through the square. He'd seen that platform already—in books, in *Schindler's List*, in a slideshow full of tangled corpses with which his Hebrew school teacher had traumatized him when he was only ten years old—and each time he told himself that was plenty, he never needed to see it again. For now he wanted only to sip his coffee and enjoy a world free of horrors. It was easy enough to imagine it had always been this way. All you had to do was look around and hold the picture in your mind. When the buses brought people back from Auschwitz this evening, he'd return to the hostel, and maybe there he'd find a grief-stricken girl who could use some comfort. Wasn't that more productive than walking through buildings where terrible things had happened to people he'd never met?

A narrow cloud passed overhead, briefly blocking the sun and turning the breeze uncomfortably cool. With it came the image of his mother, that pained expression on her face as she talked about the cousins who'd died, similar to the squint of concern she gave whenever she knew he wasn't telling the truth. It made her lovely, that look, though old, and the moment it appeared he wished he could do something to wipe it away. Why did she always have to care so much about where he was going, what he was doing, who he was with, and when he'd come home? The thought of her brought distracting questions about bus schedules, and to shake them off he swigged the dregs of coffee in his cup and swallowed with difficulty.

The sun returned, and then warmth. He signaled to the waiter for another cup, which he sipped more carefully, swishing liquid over his teeth. But it did no good. For the rest of the afternoon, jagged grounds stuck between his molars, gritty every time he closed his mouth.

Last Bus Home

<o>

My grandfather had died after a sudden diagnosis and quick decline, but I couldn't afford to fly across the country for the funeral. Instead I carried around the only photograph I had of him, a black and white portrait, two inches square, taken during his last days in what was then Leningrad, just before he crossed the ocean to join his father, who'd already settled in New Haven. In the photo, shot in 1929, he was seventeen, dapper though unsmiling, with oiled hair, a strong jaw, imposing eyebrows.

I kept it just behind my New Jersey driver's license, another relic from the past. Though by then—the early spring of 2000—I'd lived in Oregon for several years, I hadn't yet updated it. I told myself I'd hung onto it because I didn't know how long I'd stay here, and why should I take a number and sit for an hour at the DMV office if I didn't have to. Plus, I didn't drive much in Portland, usually riding the bus to my job downtown instead of paying for parking. My real reasons for keeping it are murky to me even now: a reluctance to let go of the life I'd mostly abandoned, perhaps, or a fear of losing some essential part of my identity. The image in the corner of the license showed me also at seventeen, though without anything close to my grandfather's poise. My hair was long and bushy, a few dark wisps visible at the edges of my lips. A patch of acne marred my forehead, and stray pimples dotted my nose and chin. The smile I wore was half-cocked, a smirk at best, as if I knew the very night after I got the license I'd drink five cans of Meister Bräu and back my father's Plymouth into a telephone pole.

Now, at twenty-six, I kept my hair short. The only remaining signs of acne were a few faint scars on my left temple. Even when I shaved every day, a distinct shadow rose up my cheeks. I liked to think I was finally coming to look like my grandfather, had earned some of the toughened dignity he'd found so early, though by this age he was a father twice over, ran a business, owned a house and a beach cottage, while I was single and living in a rented basement, with two part-time jobs and hefty credit-card debt.

The funeral was on a Sunday. Both my mother and my cousin Nina left me tearful messages afterward, saying they wished I could have been there, that it was so hard to say goodbye. "I miss him already," Nina said on the tape of my old answering machine, her voice shaky and distorted. "He was such a good man, Chickle."

I missed him, too, but hearing her call him *good* only irritated me. He'd often been imperious and brash; he'd had a temper; he'd belittled people for his own amusement. He'd been especially hard on Nina as an adolescent, picking on her when she gained weight, calling her lazy when she didn't help her mother in the kitchen, telling her she'd never find a husband. Now she was married to a stock analyst, had recently given birth to her second child, spent every morning at the gym, all this in addition to working full-time as a speech therapist. And yet the last time I'd spoken to my grandfather on the phone he'd gone out of his way to criticize her for not knowing how to keep a house, for letting her older child make messes everywhere he went, for forcing her husband to help fold laundry. Nina was the only person who still called me Chickle, a nickname derived from *boychikul,* my grandfather's pet name for me. I'd never heard him call her anything but *Nina.*

To describe him as good was to dismiss him, I thought, to kill him a second time by denying the person he'd been. I was determined to keep him alive in my memory in all his complexity—ugliness included—and after listening to the messages on the day of his funeral I decided to honor him by taking a bus to a downtown bar I frequented, where I ordered a double scotch, though he'd always favored bourbon. In fact, I spent most Sunday afternoons and evenings at this bar, an upscale place with a long polished counter, brass fixtures, frosted glass separating booths, first drinking coffee, then switching to beer with dinner, while grading student essays. One of my part-time jobs was teaching composition classes at a nearby community college, and all week I put off reading student work until the looming prospect of having to collect more papers and add to my overstuffed folders forced me to start. I worked more efficiently at the bar, I thought, and I was also smitten with a certain cocktail waitress who tapped her pen on my shoulder—affectionately, I hoped—every time she finished taking my order.

The first time I'd come in, the waitress, petite and gregarious, with cat-eye glasses and a silver stud in her lower lip, had laughed after she'd asked for ID and I'd shown her my old driver's license, which would finally expire in another year. "You really need to get a new picture," she'd said. "You're much better looking than this now." I took that as a good sign, as well as her friendly questions about the papers I was grading. I read her some of my students' tortured sentences and pointed out their most egregious spelling errors—one of them wrote about pulling on "a pear of pants"—and she laughed again and tapped my shoulder with her pen. I usually stayed later than I meant to, despite my early class on Monday morning, and drank enough that I struggled to stay awake on the bus ride home.

This afternoon when I ordered the scotch, the waitress—whose name, if I remember correctly, was Renée—asked what I was celebrating. "Last papers of the term?" I reached for my wallet to show her the photo of my grandfather, but before I got it all the way out of my pocket, she waved it off, saying, "I know how old you are. And I never need to see that picture of you trying to look like, what? Early Freddie Mercury? I'll happily never look at that again." She left the scotch and walked off before I had a chance to tell her about the funeral I'd missed. She had a sassy, hip-swinging walk that usually enticed me, but now I found it arrogant and self-indulgent, and I wondered what I'd ever seen in her. The cat-eye glasses were pretentious, the stud in her lip looking like a bit of food had dribbled out of her mouth. Her nose was too small, I decided, her hair oily in its high bun. When she came around to ask if I was ready for another, I muttered, "Not yet," without glancing up at her, and pretended to be deeply immersed in a student's essay arguing, without evidence, that we shouldn't feel sorry for homeless veterans because most of the dirt-encrusted men holding signs at freeway exit ramps were neither homeless nor veterans but rather con artists who collected fifty grand a year and drove away in souped-up Honda Civics parked at nearby strip malls.

Still, I lingered until closing time, drinking more than usual and finishing only half the essays in my folder before turning instead to a Russian novel in translation—Platonov's *The Foundation Pit*, I think—and trying to connect with my grandfather's history as a young Soviet worker who'd painted factories before being called away by his family and, by luck, avoiding Stalin's purges. When Renée brought my bill, she said she hoped I'd keep coming in even after the term was over, and this time when she tapped my shoulder, her pen slid down my upper arm. My earlier spite vanished instantly, and I left her an enormous tip, nearly half the amount of the bill. "I wasn't trying to look like Freddie Mercury," I called, louder than I'd meant to, with a smile that hurt my face. "I was going for Joey Ramone, but my hair wouldn't sit flat."

"If you say so." She laughed a mean-spirited laugh as she cleared away glasses from a table across the room and then bumped sideways through the door into the kitchen, swinging her hips away from me. I wanted to tell her more—that my grandfather, to my surprise, had liked my hair long, said it made me look regal, though he'd complained bitterly when Nina cut hers short. I wanted to ask what other nights she worked, and maybe what nights she was free, but the bus was due in a few minutes, and I couldn't wait for her to come out of the kitchen.

As it was, I had to run to the stop and got there just as the bus was pulling to the curb. It was the last one of the night, the number 15 from downtown across the Morrison Bridge and east on Belmont Street. It was a little past midnight, Monday morning now, and in a few hours I'd have to get up and drive to campus. Going to teach was the only time I used my car, which also still had New Jersey license plates. I preferred the bus, where I could let my thoughts drift, though on Sunday nights to keep from falling asleep I always had to listen to up-tempo music on headphones—the Stranglers, Sonny Rollins, Rachmaninoff—but even then I often found my eyelids growing heavy and falling shut, my head bobbing. Once I nodded off and rode all the way to Sixtieth Avenue and had to walk the thirty blocks back to my apartment.

Tonight it was cold for early April, and it had begun to drizzle. I wanted to walk as little as possible so turned up the volume loud on my portable disc player. I remember what I was listening to: the Ramones' first album, which not only refreshed my anger at Renée but made me nostalgic for a particular stretch of adolescence when Nina and I had played punks together, sneaking out of the house to drink and smoke cigarettes in the woods, riding the bus into the city to thrash around in mosh pits in all-ages clubs. This before she went off to Brandeis to become the upstanding girl my grandfather had always wanted her to be, and I grew less and less eager to return her phone calls.

I didn't think I'd disturb anyone if the sound leaked out of my headphones. There weren't many people on the bus. Just behind the driver, an old guy clutching a black plastic garbage bag to his chest. A group of college kids or recent graduates who didn't care that it was Sunday night, or rather early Monday morning, drunk and talking raucously near the back, their hoots of laughter sometimes penetrating the flood of music in my ears. And a few seats in front of me a couple whose heads leaned together for a moment and then suddenly pulled apart.

I found myself watching these last two, maybe because there was nothing else to look at besides my reflection in the bus window, or beyond it, the dark warehouses on the east side of the bridge, or maybe because their movement had struck me as odd. They'd seemed to be heading toward a kiss before jerking away, or rather being pushed, involuntarily, it seemed, like the ends of two magnets with identical charge. Now their heads were a good foot and a half apart, the man's bald on top and obviously shaved around the sides, the stubble just beginning to assert itself beneath the ruddy skin of his scalp. What I could see of his neck above the collar of a black wool coat was thick, the same width as his skull, so that from behind he appeared to have neither neck nor head but just a domed cylinder atop his shoulders, a lone horizontal wrinkle marring its smooth surface. His ears were small and flat and hardly noticeable. He kept his gaze fixed firmly forward.

The young woman's head now rested against the window, occasionally jolted by bumps but then returning to the glass. All I could really see of her at this point was hair—long and black and straight, except at the ends, where it must have been curled with an iron, a style that seemed out of date, as did the fur collar of her coat—faux fur, maybe—which I noticed when the bus rolled over a big pothole and jolted her upright again. This had been a hard winter on the roads, and on me, too, and watching the girl bounce against the window while listening to the Ramones and remembering my grandfather, I found myself longing for spring to come in earnest, with brighter days and sunshine and trees sporting full leaves instead of the puny new growth on most of those we passed. The boisterous music in my ears urged on new, reckless beginnings. If the woman had been in the seat beside me, I wouldn't have leaned away. I would have wanted that dark lush hair as close to me as possible.

But then her head swiveled slightly, the hair fell out of her face, and I realized my mistake. She wasn't a young woman but a girl, maybe fifteen, with very pale skin, a sharp nose, lots of makeup around her eyes and pink gloss on her full lips. I felt ashamed of my longing, which was so pervasive it would have attached itself to anything that entered my sight, though for now I mostly blamed Renée, who tortured me by wavering so unpredictably between flirtation and indifference.

So not a couple, I thought, but perhaps father and daughter. This made more sense of their yanking away from each other. Why a father would have his fifteen-year-old daughter on a bus after midnight I didn't know, but I was still absorbing the information and didn't yet pause to wonder.

The bus stopped at Twelfth Avenue, and the college kids or graduates lurched forward, jostling each other as they tumbled out the rear door, which was just behind me. In my ears the Ramones were shouting about a Vietnam vet turned hustler on Fifty-third and Third, and any noise the kids made on the way out was garbled and lost beneath the hard-driving chords. But they must have shouted something, because the thick-necked father turned abruptly to watch them leave. And then I caught sight of his face, which was flat, pug-like, forehead and chin more prominent than nose or mouth, the latter of which was surrounded by a fringe of light bristles. I couldn't tell if they were blond or gray. His eyes were small and blue and set deep in their sockets, and under the left was a square bandage that covered most of his cheek, a translucent one showing something dark beneath. If there was any resemblance between him and the girl, I couldn't see it, and I changed my mind again. He wasn't her father, though he was clearly over forty. He wasn't anyone's father, I thought. That is, he might have produced offspring, but he'd never acted fatherly toward anyone. I don't know how I could have guessed such a thing, except that his face showed no hint of nurturing or affection. It was an aggressive, selfish face, a type I'd seen before, though I was sure I'd never laid eyes on this particular iteration until now.

I looked away, but not before his gaze passed over mine as he turned back to the girl. It lingered just briefly, but long enough, I thought, to fix my image in his mind. The door closed and the raucous kids disappeared down Twelfth Avenue. The bus jerked forward. I was wide awake now. I wished the man hadn't noticed me and then told myself it didn't matter. What was I to him? The old guy clutching the garbage bag had fallen asleep. I tried to catch the driver's eye in the rearview mirror, perhaps to share my concern about this couple, particularly about the girl with too much makeup out late with a man I doubted was her father. I'd ridden with this driver a dozen times by then, most Sunday nights for the past four months, and I felt I could trust him, though we'd never spoken more than a few words in greeting or wishing each other good night. He was in late middle age, Black, with sleepy eyes and a belly that came close to touching the steering wheel, and on a couple of occasions I'd been tempted to strike up a conversation with him but had never quite worked up the courage or figured out what to talk about. Jazz, maybe? I could have shown him the CDs in my backpack, asked if he was a fan of McCoy Tyner, who was scheduled to play at the jazz festival in town next month. But then why should I assume he liked jazz just because he was Black and middle-aged? Tonight, as on every Sunday night, I'd simply said, "Evening," while showing my bus pass, and he'd replied, "Morning, now."

In the rearview mirror I could see only his shoulder and part of his neck. I didn't know how to get his attention short of calling to him, and what could he do anyway from up there at the front of the bus? He had to keep driving. He could have called something in on his radio, but there was nothing specific to report. Nothing specific to be concerned about, either, except a vague hunch that the girl was in trouble, that she needed help, a hunch I only partly believed. It might just as easily have been my imagination, worked up by exhaustion and alcohol and grief, by nostalgia and the Ramones and the message from Nina, whom I'd comforted more than once after our grandfather had made her cry, including on her fourteenth birthday, when he'd joked about her newly sprouted breasts matching the pimples on her chin. *Relax*, I told myself, and let my gaze return to the man and girl, expecting to see them as they'd been, the one sitting stiffly erect, face forward, the other slumped against the window, content despite the sudden jolts, all of it perfectly normal, or at least normal enough.

But that's not what I saw. The man inclined toward the girl now, his face in profile, the bandage visible, and the black marks of what must have been stitches underneath. The girl seemed to cower beneath him, her hair tucked over an ear so I could see her wide animal eyes made raccoonish by so much dark eye shadow around them. The man's lips moved, but the song was still playing, drowning out all other sound with the angry lament of a conflicted male prostitute. I could have taken my headphones off but decided I didn't want to hear what he was saying. It was no business of mine, and I didn't want to imagine what he'd do if he thought I were eavesdropping. And just as I made the decision the song cut off in the abrupt way Ramones songs always did, startling me so completely that for a moment I forgot the couple and thought instead about what had made the Ramones so radical, not the songs themselves but the way they started and stopped.

But then in the brief silence before the impossibly fast drum beats revved up again, I did catch the sound of the man's voice, which wasn't as deep as I'd expected, more nasal, though still as aggressive as his expression. I didn't catch any words, maybe because they were muffled by my headphones, or maybe because they weren't in English. The sound of them, like his face, was vaguely familiar. Of course I was already thinking about my grandfather, so it makes sense that I'd hear the inflection as Russian. Now I can't be sure. At the time, though, suspicion quickly slid into certainty.

And then curiosity made me bold or perhaps careless. I pulled off the headphones so I could hear more. But by the time I did, he'd stopped speaking. A meaty hand rose up above the girl's head, and I thought he was getting ready to strike her.

But he only pulled the cord over the window to signal the driver to stop. The girl retreated back under her hair. The bus kept chugging along for another block before reaching the next stop at Twenty-sixth Avenue. But the man stood while it was still moving, brushed the front of his coat with both hands, and gestured at the girl, who seemed reluctant to leave her seat. Again I glanced up at the rearview mirror, trying to catch the driver's eye, but he was focused on pulling over, hands turning the big wheel above his belly.

The doors opened, and the bus's hydraulics hissed, tilting us toward the curb. Only then did the girl get up, shoulders slouched, sulky, I thought, the way any teenager would be around her dad. The man stood behind the seat, waiting for her to go ahead of him. But just before she did, she glanced back at me, and I caught sight of those raccoon eyes once more. Were they always so wide? Or was this a sign of terror, a plea for help?

Before I could decide, the eyes disappeared again behind hair, and then the man's body blocked most of her skinny frame. All I could see of her now was the outmoded coat with fur collar. They made their way to the front door, though the back was closer. And when they reached it, I saw that the driver was finally looking up at me, his eyes in the mirror troubled, maybe, or simply puzzled, though I was too far away to see for sure. The glance we exchanged seemed urgent, in any case, and before I'd thought it all the way through I grabbed my backpack and slipped out the back door, though my stop was four blocks farther east.

The feeling I carried with me off the bus was the same one I'd experienced after hearing Nina's message: that the world was far more complicated than most people wanted to acknowledge. It was a prideful feeling, maybe an arrogant one, though it remained buried under a layer of caution. I was mostly conscious of the need to keep the man and girl from noticing me. Man and girl. That's how I thought of them now. Not father and daughter. Not couple. I stayed near the bus's back door as it shut and the hydraulics hissed again, the frame straightening on its axles. The man and girl had their back to me, walking east on Belmont Street. The bus pulled away, empty except for the old guy and his garbage bag. I hung back in the shadow of a medium-sized maple whose roots had already begun to buckle the sidewalk. Beside me was a squat rectangular building, glass-fronted, dark inside. It housed a methadone clinic, I'd learned after passing it a few days a week for most of a month. During the day there was often a crowd out front, scruffy men and haggard women waiting to get in or just having come out, most of them smoking. They were always there when I rode downtown to my second part-time job as an administrative assistant at a solar-power company, the bus packed then, the driver a stout, sour-faced woman who liked to shout out the stops along the way. The gathering outside the clinic had the air of a reunion, not quite celebratory, but not entirely somber, either—more like the tail end of a reception following a memorial service, after everyone had visited the drinks table more than once and the talk became equally wistful and optimistic, new life sprouting from loss. I imagined that's how it was at the reception after my grandfather's service, my mother and Nina crying together, saying they couldn't believe he was gone, but that his spirit would live on in their memory, that they'd carry him with them always, and wasn't the rabbi's sermon just lovely, weren't the flowers beautiful, wouldn't my grandfather have loved it, and let's make sure to keep the family closer together from now on, we'll gather the next time Chickle comes east, but let's not tell him in advance so he doesn't back out at the last minute.

Now the sidewalk in front of the clinic was deserted. A few cars passed, then a bicycle. Half a block ahead a bar was still open, its neon sign reading *VERN*. Some years earlier a tall truck had smashed into it, crumpling the first two letters. Beneath it were a couple of picnic tables, but this was back when you could still smoke inside, and it was too cold for anyone to stay out. Too cold for me, also. My jacket was thick enough, but not waterproof, and already the drizzle was seeping through the shoulders. I could have gone into the bar—dingier and cheaper than the one where Renée worked—gotten a beer or a scotch, played video poker, and then walked the rest of the way to SE Thirtieth Avenue, and then another five blocks north to my apartment across Stark Street. How easy it would have been to retreat, to let the man and girl disappear from view, delete Nina's message, continue with the routines of work and shallow friendships and frustrating romantic longings that kept me distracted enough most days to forget about the complicated or sinister workings of the world.

Instead I waited until the man and girl had passed the bar, reached the intersection of Belmont and Twenty-seventh Avenue, and turned right. Then I followed, crossing to the other side of Twenty-seventh and making my way south, far enough behind that they'd have to search hard in the dimness to find me. All the lamp posts were on their side of the street, and every half block they'd emerge from the shadows into a misty cone of orange light. Then I could see the girl hunched down into her fur collar, the curled hair looking wet even from a distance. A father would have held an umbrella over her, I thought, though I knew not all fathers were kind or thoughtful or caring. Hadn't my grandfather refused to let my mother attend any college of her choice, insisting instead that she enroll in an all-girls school within an hour's drive of New Haven, where she had to wear

231

ankle-length skirts and white gloves whenever she left her residence hall?

The man kept a hand on the girl's arm closest to him, just below her armpit. The houses on either side were mostly dark, but the occasional flickering of a TV lit up a closed curtain or lowered blinds. If the girl were really in trouble, she could have screamed, and someone would have come out to see what was wrong. This was a respectable neighborhood, still affordable at the time, and populated by a mix of families and professionals and young people in rock bands who lived ten to a house. She should have felt safe here, even if the man threatened to do her harm.

They walked three blocks, then turned right on Salmon Street. I jogged to catch up, afraid I'd lose them. But they stopped at the second house in, a red-brick ranch that seemed out of place among Craftsman bungalows and a two-story Queen Anne with a wraparound porch on the corner. The trees in front were young and left the man and girl exposed to the lamp overhead. From my new spot across the street I had a clear view of them. The girl's coat looked definitively like an artifact of an earlier time, something my grandmother would have worn in the '30s. The girl might have bought it in a vintage store, and on a woman ten years older perhaps it would have been stylish. Below the collar it was a dark greenish-brown wool, belted at the waist, and it came down to mid-calf. Below the hem the girl's legs were bare, feet in red shoes with high heels. She wobbled on them as she climbed the two steps to the walkway, and then another two steps to the front door. Maybe the man's hand was on her arm to keep her from falling, but whether she needed the support or not, she leaned away from it.

The man rang the doorbell, then knocked. A minute passed, maybe more. No lights came on in any of the windows. While they waited, a new idea occurred to me: the man was a cop, he'd caught the girl doing something illegal, hanging around with unsavory people, and now he was bringing her home to her parents, letting her off with a warning. This was my favorite explanation yet, and as soon as I thought of it, relief made me loosen my clenched jaw and let out a breath I hadn't been aware of holding. I didn't know if it was relief at the idea that the girl might be safe after all or at being absolved of the responsibility to help her.

The large fist lifted again, but this time before landing, the door opened. Still no lights had come on. A figure appeared in the doorway, but I couldn't make out any features before it withdrew, leaving a black empty space. The girl stepped into it. Whether or not the man pushed her I couldn't tell, but when she crossed into the darkness he released her arm. If any words passed between them, I didn't hear. The girl teetered forward on her red heels. I caught one more glimpse of her face as she turned back, but from where I stood it was just a white blur with dark smudges, framed by that mass of black hair. Then the door closed.

That was it, I told myself. I could go home now. I tried to hang on to the narrative of a cop bringing the girl to her parents, though in my mind it had already begun to collapse. Why would a cop have ridden the bus? It didn't make sense. Nor did his action after the girl disappeared into the house. He lingered on the concrete landing, fiddled with something on his wrist. A watch, I guessed. Then he backtracked down the walkway. When he reached the sidewalk he turned and headed down Salmon Street, but only until he came to a bigger tree, an ornamental plum that had leafed out earlier than the others around, its young purple foliage thick enough to keep most of the rain off him. I was right across the street from him now, just a narrow stretch of pavement between us. I ducked behind a white pickup parked at the curb. If he glanced over he might have seen the top of my head sticking above the bed, but I couldn't stop myself from peeking.

In any case, he faced away from me now. He leaned against the tree trunk, watching the house, and occasionally checked his watch. I didn't wear a watch so could only guess how much time passed. Seven minutes. Ten. At what I thought might have been fifteen, he reached into his coat and pulled out a cell phone. Its style, too, was out-of-date even then, bulky, with a long antenna. His hand went back in, and out came a little notebook, smaller than the cell. He flipped through some pages, stopped on one, squinted at it closely, then pressed buttons on the phone. He held it to his ear and waited what seemed a long time, though the colder I got the slower everything felt. Eventually he spoke, and for the first time I heard not only the sound of his voice—nasal and weary—but also clear words. "Yes. Ready? Salmon and Twenty-seventh. No, Southeast."

English, yes, and accented, but I couldn't be sure it was Russian, or even Slavic, though I did have a flash of my grandfather's condo in Fort Lauderdale, the screened-in porch overlooking a canal full of alligators, and someone—my grandmother, my mother, my aunt, Nina?—scrambling to bring him an item he'd called out for, a cup of tea, or the newspaper, or a toothpick to dig a poppy seed out from between two molars. But as soon as I thought I'd locked on to it, the voice cut off, the phone disappeared back into his coat. The man went back to leaning against the tree trunk, glancing at his watch. Behind the pickup, my shivering went from sporadic to steady. Rain dripped down my back, into my underwear. My hair was flat on my forehead, and I kept having to push it out of my eyes.

Another ten minutes passed, maybe more. My knees and ankles ached from crouching.

And then a sound came to me from across the street, a fast electronic beeping, three pulses at a time. The timer on his watch. It wasn't loud, but it cut through all the other sounds of the empty nighttime street—the buzz of the streetlamp overhead, light raindrops on the truck's cab, my shallow breath. He let it beep for half a minute before switching it off and starting back to the house. His steps were slow. Tired, it seemed, or else reluctant to reach their destination.

He was halfway up the concrete path when the front door opened, and the girl came out. Still no lights on in the house, no sign of the figure who'd been in the doorway. The man stopped where he was and waited for her. I couldn't see her face, only the too-tall shoes that made her wobble on her way to him, and one sleeve of her old-fashioned coat. He took her arm again, gently, I thought, maybe even tenderly, and this time she did seem to lean on him, though only to keep her balance. They turned down the path, facing me directly, and I knew I ought to duck behind the pickup to keep them from seeing me. But I couldn't look away. There were the raccoon eyes, the dark lips. If she'd been affected by whatever had happened in the house, it didn't show. The carefully curled hair swept across her pale forehead and blended in with the fur collar.

I told myself I should do something, but I didn't know what. I was half the size of the man, and even if I managed to surprise and overpower him, then what? Take the girl to a police station? Or a hospital? On foot? I might have brought her back to my apartment or knocked on the door of some other house in the neighborhood, rousing a sympathetic mother and hoping she'd be willing to help. I imagined doing all manner of things, but what I actually did was watch without moving as the two of them made their way to the sidewalk.

And just as they reached it, a car came rolling slowly down Twenty-seventh. Its headlights lit up the raindrops, which were falling harder now, and then blinded me for a moment as it turned onto Salmon Street. It pulled past the brick ranch, rolled under the shadow of the purple-leafed plum. Then it stopped. I don't know if the driver put it into park or just kept his foot on the brake. In either case, the engine kept running. The big man with the bandage on his cheek—except now I'd stopped thinking of him as *the man*, or *the father*, or *the cop*, but rather as *the Russian*—opened the passenger door, leaned down, and spoke. No words reached me this time, only the aggrieved nasal hum of his voice.

The car was nondescript, a dark gray sedan, or maybe dark green. A Nissan or a Toyota. A little mud-splattered above the tires, but otherwise well maintained, at least on the surface. The windows weren't tinted, but under the shadow of the tree, all I could make out of the driver was the back of a head, both hands on the steering wheel. The Russian straightened, stepped aside, and the girl climbed into the passenger seat in an odd, childish way, crawling on hands and knees before swinging her feet forward and sitting upright. The driver faced forward now, and I could see a fleshy profile through the window, a lumpy nose, maybe glasses. The Russian leaned down again, pulled the seatbelt across the girl and buckled it for her as if she were a toddler and couldn't do it for herself. Again I told myself it was time to act, that this was my last chance, but I only continued to crouch behind the truck as the Russian closed the door and the car eased away from the curb.

It rolled away slowly enough that I caught a glimpse of a sticker on its back window. Some kind of parking pass, a purple rectangle with letters and numbers. I strained so hard to read it that I forgot to look at the license plate until it was too late. The car picked up speed. It continued east on Salmon through two or three intersections and then turned south towards Hawthorne Boulevard. I watched until its taillights disappeared behind a two-story apartment complex.

And when I turned back, the Russian was hurrying away, faster than I'd seen him move thus far. He'd already rounded the corner onto Twenty-seventh and was heading back toward Belmont, his wide torso tilted forward. I left the cover of the pickup but stayed hunched as I followed on the opposite side of the street. After a few steps I jogged to catch up. My feet were numb inside waterlogged canvas sneakers. The backpack made soft squelching sounds as it bounced against my shoulder blades. I worried about the paper sleeves inside the CD covers, the song titles that would smear, and even more about the Discman I needed so badly to keep me awake on Sunday night bus rides home.

The thought of it, along with an image of Renée laughing at me as she dropped a drink at my table, distracted me for a moment, and I didn't notice when, a block shy of Belmont, the Russian began crossing the street in my direction. He was halfway across before I realized what was happening, and I froze in place, right in the middle of the sidewalk. *This is it*, I thought, though what "it" was exactly I didn't know. A violent confrontation? Confirmation that I'd just witnessed something I shouldn't have? He reached into his coat again, not an inside pocket this time, but one at his hip. I couldn't see what came out, but my imagination conjured snub-nosed pistols and switchblades.

When he reached my side of the street, he didn't come up onto the sidewalk but stopped instead at a black Jeep Cherokee.

In his hand were keys. Just keys. His eyes passed over me but didn't pause. I was part of the landscape, no different from a nearby tree trunk or fence post. He opened the door and let out a weary little groan, or maybe a grunt of pain, as he settled behind the wheel. And then, more distinctly, an abrupt shout, an exhale of rage or frustration, as he pulled the door shut. This surprised me more than anything else I'd seen. I didn't know what to make of it. As soon as he turned the ignition, a blast of music reverberated through the closed windows, heavy bass and drums I could feel in my chest. Unlike the sedan, the Jeep tore away from the curb, squealing, and sped forward.

This time I remembered to read the plates. I recited the string of letters and numbers to myself as the Jeep reached Belmont Street. The brake lights blinked on for just a second before it shot out across the eastbound lane and careened left, back toward downtown. By the time I made it to the corner, it was already out of sight, and the street was empty in both directions. I was shivering, though whether from cold or distress I didn't know. The remaining letters on the tavern's sign had gone dark, but I tried the door anyway. It opened. Warm air hit me, along with the smell of disinfectant, but before I could take a step inside, a voice—female and smoke-scratched, whose owner I couldn't see—called out, "Closed, hun. Come back tomorrow."

I ran the ten blocks to my apartment in the basement of a big old Craftsman on SE Thirtieth, the high squat windows looking out on the concrete slab of a driveway and a boxy garage my landlord used to store construction materials. The place looked more drab than usual, with its mismatched secondhand couch and armchair—the former blue, the latter burnt-orange—fold-out table, shelves for CDs and books built out of cinder blocks and one-by-fours. I stripped and toweled off and wrapped myself in blankets. A huge yawn rippled through me. I considered calling the police, reporting the Russian's license plate, the address of the brick ranch, but the conversation I imagined having with the dispatcher never got very far. Had I witnessed a crime? Did I know for sure the girl was in trouble? I thought I could make up a story, claim the Jeep had sideswiped me on my bike, a hit and run, and hope they'd find evidence of other wrongdoing. But instead of picturing the Russian in jail, I saw only myself dragged off in handcuffs for giving false testimony.

Instead I replayed Nina's message. "I miss him already. He was such a good man, Chickle." Now I heard something different in her voice. An urgency I hadn't noticed before. Her words were less statement than argument, one she expected me to resist. Was she telling me to forget what I knew, to erase the memory of her crying on my shoulder one night after we rode the bus back from an all-ages club in Hoboken, Nina wearing ripped jeans and a Fugazi T-shirt, my grandfather telling her how disappointed he was, how she was supposed to set an example for me? Or was she saying he was a good man despite how he'd treated her? I took out the picture of him from Leningrad, when he'd been living on his own, apart from his family, doing who knew what to survive, and took out my old license, too, the seventeen-year-old me looking not like Freddie Mercury or Joey Ramone but a pampered and sloppy child playing a streetwise hood.

It's time to let it go, I told myself, though I wasn't sure if I meant the license or the photo or both. The message kept playing after Nina's last word. There was no click of the phone hanging up, just the sound of her breath trailing off into tape hiss before a cruel beep signaled its end.

THE CAKE

━◦━

The night before being arrested and sent to the prison from which he'll never emerge, the playwright David Gronfein has a long and bitter quarrel with his mistress, Natalya Ivanovna Kalmykov. It's a quarrel they've had before, many times. Natalya wants to marry. Gronfein is already married. His wife, long estranged, lives abroad. To travel to France with divorce papers would require permission from the authorities here in Moscow. Such a request would likely be ignored. Worse, it might provide a bored official evidence to accuse him of spying for Western powers.

"This is pointless," he says. "The whole topic is a waste of time."

"For you, maybe. But if you haven't noticed, I am not yet old and used up. I have a life ahead of me."

They go to bed hurt and angry, undressing in the dark and lying with backs to each other. In the morning, as usual, they both wake contrite, though pride keeps them from showing it. Gronfein knows the argument isn't pointless, not if read for subtext, something he should understand professionally if not personally. It might, after all, have been a scene from one of his own plays, back when he could still write them. How else can

Natalya express her longing for a future they both know he doesn't have? How else can she fight off despair?

It's May, 1938. Many of his friends have already disappeared. The only reason he still lives free is because for so long he has produced so little. To denounce his work as subversive now would be to admit having overlooked it for years. Yet he knows it's only a matter of time before the police come for him. Eventually they'll run out of more threatening figures and find him an acceptable stand-in for an actual counter-revolutionary, even at fifty-six and wrung dry of words, abandoned by wife and daughter, suffering from a kidney ailment, living with a twenty-nine-year-old engineer who is as much nurse as lover.

What else can she do but occasionally rage against the inevitable, blame him in advance for the pain she is sure one day to suffer?

If not the feeling itself, the memory of insult lingers so that they do not speak over breakfast in the small kitchen they share with an electrician and his wife, both of whom have finished eating and retreated to their rooms on the apartment's lower floor. But Gronfein has already decided he will stop at the market in the afternoon, to purchase fresh herbs. For his wife he would have bought flowers, but Natalya prefers practical gifts, those she can wear or eat rather than simply gaze at in passing. She is an efficient woman who speaks only as many words as she needs, and when it comes to pleasure, she wants multiple senses engaged. He already imagines their silent reconciliation, the fragrance of dill and parsley filling the kitchen while she cooks and he prepares their tea.

And he's relieved to find he's not alone in imagining it. Natalya, too, anticipates the coming dissipation of hard feelings. Before leaving for work, she sets on the sideboard a plate bearing three small eggs. He notices only after she's shut the door, and seeing them looses a flood of affection that nearly propels him out of his chair, makes him chase after her to call apologies and endearments down the stairs, beg her to return so he can embrace her and cover her neck with kisses. But with the pain in his kidney, he cannot rise quickly and run. In any case, such a display would likely embarrass her. So instead he remains sitting, sipping the last of his coffee, contemplating the scene of a play he guesses he'll never write.

He understands what the eggs mean. This evening, when she returns from her office at the Metroproekt, where she designs underground rail tunnels and station platforms, she will make Medovik, the honey cake that was her favorite as a child. She will present it to him as an appeasement, though he knows she makes it only when she's feeling most in need of comfort. And he will do his best to act both surprised and touched, assuring her that they will indeed one day be married, he will find a way, he promises. What's the harm in a bit of fantasy, if it gives her an hour's solace, a day's hope? How lucky he is to share a bed with this handsome young woman—brilliant and intrepid daughter of Siberian peasants, model of the proletariat, symbol of progress—even if only for a short time.

And thinking of their bed, he finds himself aroused for the first time in weeks, the desire that has been suppressed by pain and fear seeping to the surface like warm air through a narrow vent. If only he can maintain it for the rest of the day, then after they have eaten the Medovik he will lead her to the bed, remind her that there is vitality in him still, this small, paunchy Jew who fought White Cossacks in Kuban, who was once considered the standard-bearer of the new Yiddish literature, though now he is mostly forgotten. He'll sweep her into his arms, ignoring the pain in his side, and for one more night at least give her the passion she deserves.

243

In the meantime, he will channel the feeling into words, which have eluded him for much of the past decade. He returns to the desk he avoids most days, opens his notebook to a draft of the play at which he has been hammering for longer than he cares to remember. It is meant to be about the early days of the revolution, the period of famine that followed, the resilience of those who believed in the dream they enacted, the dignity that accompanied suffering. He, too, once believed in this dream—in its purest form, he still does—but for too long he has been writing with censors in mind, those who would weigh each word for the appropriate amount of patriotic fervor. As a result, the characters have become wooden, their lines spoken as if from a podium, even in scenes set in a blighted field.

Today, though, he manages to abandon himself to these people he once felt he knew so well, allows them to argue and say hurtful things masking feelings they cannot name. For the first time in many months, he envisions the stage from which the actors will project their lines, and on it conjures a sideboard, a plate with three puny eggs, a sign of hope amid misery and strife. He has written four pages—more than in the last six weeks—and is still scribbling, sweat gathering under his arms, when there comes a knock on the door. He wants to ignore it, to let the words continue pouring onto the page. They seem to arrive now almost without his effort, and he is afraid that once he releases the pen, they will never again come so easily or with such assurance.

But the knock sounds a second time, followed by a voice— male and officious—calling out his name. He pushes back his chair and rises with difficulty. His kidney aches. The desire he experienced two hours ago has cleared like smoke in a soft but steady breeze. He will have nothing left to give Natalya when she returns. So maybe it is for the best that they have come for him today. And yet his hand shakes as he turns the lock. He has imagined this moment so often but now struggles to recall how he is meant to act. Stoic and dignified or incensed and defiant?

He opens the door to three officers of the People's Commissariat, whom he welcomes inside with a smile that pushes strangely against his cheeks, as if it has formed without his consent. They are polite even as one reads the warrant for his arrest. Two wear soldiers' uniforms: hats, heavy belts, and high black boots. One is round-faced and boyish, with blond fuzz on his upper lip, the other creased and haggard, with kind eyes staring down at his shoes while he listens to the charges. The third, who reads them, seems uneasy in a light gray suit whose jacket is too big for him across the shoulders, an unsuccessful attempt to make them look broader. He's hatless, with a sharp widow's peak, hardly taller than Gronfein and much younger—too young to have fought in the war, still just a child when Lenin died.

Despite all the time Gronfein has spent anticipating this scene, there are so many details he has failed to picture. The discomfort on the officers' faces as they carry out their task, or, for that matter, the presence of faces at all. He has never really considered the people with whom he would share his lines, and he has certainly never envisioned the carefully clipped fingernails of the officer in the suit, nor the crumbs on the young soldier's jacket, nor the bitter smell of coffee on the older one's breath. They have eaten breakfast together before coming to him, he guesses. If only he could have listened in on their conversation and written it down. Their exchange would have been far more interesting than the words he hears now, written by a bureaucrat who likely never set foot in a theater, at least not one without film projector and screen. The short officer finishes reading, and Gronfein offers them tea. They decline.

Instead they search the two rooms he and Natalya occupy, along with the shared kitchen. They gather his papers, including the open notebook, the ink still wet enough that it may smear when they close it. These four pages, he knows, will reappear at his trial. They will serve as proof of his decadence, his promotion of capitalist ideals, his crimes against the state. They are the best thing he has written in years, and they will doom him, even if he was doomed long before getting them down.

It is, then, as it should be. He has always wanted his words to have power, and finally they have the power to destroy him. But now he begins to suspect that those four pages are thin and contrived compared to the conversation of these three officers over breakfast, a conversation he imagines as he watches them empty his desk. He thinks they would have discussed women, which would have provided necessary distraction. Not wives or girlfriends, but women they've seen in passing and admired. Maybe just one woman, glimpsed from a distance as they ate. The three of them watched her cross the street. Dark hair, pale neck. They argued over who would go speak to her. The squabble began with teasing but soon grew fierce, full of insult. Maybe they even threatened blows. All this as a way to keep from saying what they really felt about the day that lay ahead. In the end, none of them approached the woman or said a word as she walked near.

"It must be difficult," he says from the doorway, surprising himself. He seems to have as little control over his voice as he did his smile when they entered. "To carry out unpleasant tasks day after day. But I understand. Orders are orders. The most important thing is to support your comrades. Don't let the pressure undermine your good will toward each other."

The officers don't respond. They finish their work, and he accompanies them out the door, the one in the suit carrying his papers, the notebook with the unfinished play, tightly against his jacket. When they reach the landing, the two in uniform grip his arms, though he has shown no intention of resisting. He is ready, he is tired of waiting, listening for the knock he has always known would come. That it did when he was too preoccupied to expect it is an irony he finds quite satisfying. Stepping out of the cramped rooms where he has experienced such constant apprehension, he is relieved, almost joyful, and a surge of fellowship makes him wish he could reach out and brush the crumbs from the boyish soldier's lapel.

Instead he tries joking with them, asking if it isn't a lovely day for an interrogation. None laugh. The one in the suit nudges him in the back, just above the kidney, as if to show that he knows Gronfein's weak point. Gronfein in turn lets out a groan, and the officers seem gratified. They all have their roles to play, and a jubilant prisoner does not suit the demands of the drama. He stiffens his arms against them so as not to seem overly compliant.

But when they near the stairs he experiences a twinge of regret at being taken before he can write down the breakfast conversation he has imagined, and even more, before he and Natalya have had a chance to make up following their quarrel. If only he could have set aside his pride and acknowledged the eggs, acknowledged the subtext of their argument. If only he'd told her their time together was the most precious thing in the world to him, no matter how short; that he wished daily they'd met a few years earlier, before the state tightened divorce laws to strengthen the Soviet family; that he was far more deeply wedded to her—a thousand times so—than to the woman who'd left him for the safety and indulgence of the capitalist West. He says over his shoulder to the officer in the suit, "Before we go. May I please leave a note for my . . . my wife?"

This, however, only makes them pull him more forcefully toward the top step. He imagines Natalya arriving home to find him gone, his desk cleared. She might think he has driven to his villa in Peredelkino, the writers' village thirty-five miles away, where he claims to work more effectively, with less distraction, but where, in truth, he drinks and naps and chats with the few remaining friends not yet replaced with propagandists and hacks. She might even be pleased at first, given the time to make her honey cake in secret, preparing to surprise him with it when he returns. As she mixes the batter, she will feel sweetly nostalgic, thinking of her childhood. She might even imagine passing on the recipe to a child they would have together, married or not. If only he'd given her one when he had the chance.

"Please," he says. "It will take just a moment. A quick note so she won't have to worry."

Shouldn't the officers understand such a request, they who might have talked about women to keep from voicing misgivings about their jobs? Yet they say nothing. He plants his feet on the second step and shifts his weight to his heels. He pictures Natalya pulling the baked dough from the oven, layering it with sweetened cream. For a short time she will lose herself in the work, forgetting the fears that dominate their lives. She will be living, ever so briefly, in the utopia they have all worked so hard to create, the utopia for which they have struggled and sacrificed only to have it poisoned by those who can't accept its nuances, who refuse to embrace the complexities of desire. The boyish soldier shoves his foot with a boot, forcing it down to the next step.

"She's going to bake a cake," he says. "I have to tell her I won't be home to eat it."

But already he is picturing the cake sitting on the sideboard, Natalya at the small table where this morning they avoided each other's eyes. Her lighthearted mood will begin to fade with the spring light outside the window. Her thoughts will return to their quarrel, to their bitter words, and she'll wonder if this time they penetrated more deeply than in the past, if they hit a new mark and caused sharper pain. She'll wonder if she has finally pushed him away, as she has always feared she might, as she once feared she'd pushed away her father, loving him so much and scolding him so often for his excesses that he drank himself to death in the snow. For a while—an hour, a whole evening?—she might believe he has willingly deserted her as his wife deserted him, without a word, without so much as a note, all his previous claims of devotion exposed as lies. He wants to spare her this pain, even if short-lived, knowing he can't spare her any other.

"I won't go," he says, "not without a sign," and grabs the railing, an old wooden one worn smooth by many hands, slick under his palm. The officer in the suit, still behind him, shifts notebook and papers to his left hand. With his right, he punches Gronfein in the bad kidney. The pain makes him release the railing. Release his bladder, too, which looses a dribble down his leg. Of course they know about his ailment. They know everything about him—that he wants to leave a note not for his wife but his mistress, that he has long been washed-up as a playwright. They have been watching him, for months, probably, or maybe years, perhaps waiting until the day he finally added to his notebook some new subversive lines for which they can crucify him. But how could they have known this was the day? It's as if they've been in his head all along, looking out through his eyes, reading the words as he writes them. David Gronfein spying on himself. And what did he discover? Until today, only laziness, resignation, forsaken ideals. The haggard soldier, whose eyes still look kind, kicks his shin hard enough to crack it, he thinks, the pain vibrating all the way up his spine. Afterward they drag him without trouble, his feet clunking on each step.

He reasons, with what reason remains, that it will not take long for Natalya to realize what has happened. Yes, she might believe he has left her, but only for a moment. Then she will notice that his desk drawers have been emptied, she will know his fate is the one he has expected all along. He tries to comfort himself with this knowledge, tries to believe that a note would make little difference. But then he pictures the cake again, eight thin, moist layers with cream seeping out the sides. He sees it sitting on the sideboard, perfect and uneaten, a symbol not of hope but of all that has been wasted, and he feels his mouth filling with saliva, not from hunger exactly but some other need, more diffuse yet all-encompassing. All the desire left to him, desire that might have spread among his remaining years, now concentrated in a single moment as the officers pull him upright at the bottom of the stairs and straighten his collar. Desire for pleasures of the body, yes, of all the senses—the smell of Natalya's hair, the first taste of her honey cake on his tongue, the sounds of birds along the Svislach in Minsk where he spent his childhood, a failed yeshiva boy often punished by his teacher—and of the mind, too, of language, of the words emerging from people's mouths, implying everything they could never actually say.

He is sick with desire, it makes him cough and retch, and then out of anger or obligation the officer in the too-big suit punches him once more in the kidney, making him spit onto the floor. And he sees that it hasn't been saliva in his mouth after all. Blood, yes, of course, just blood, the medium of desire that pumped through his body for fifty-six years now spilling from his lips into the apartment's downstairs hallway, a dim space with wood-paneled walls and no windows. To his left, a door behind which the electrician Tupolev and his wife live in two rooms as small as his own. Tupolev is sure to be at work, but his wife, Klavdiya, seven months pregnant, must be inside. He makes a noise, or tries to, hoping to rouse her. He wants only for her to open the door and see what is happening, so that she can assure Natalya he did not leave of his own accord. But even as he thinks it he knows she will not open the door even if she does hear, will not say a word to Natalya for fear of retribution. He is now quite certain she hears everything, that she is standing just behind the door, listening as he spits blood onto the tiles, telling herself she must never say a word.

So he hopes instead that Natalya will linger just long enough in the hallway to notice the blood and understand what has taken place before climbing to the rooms above. That's the crucial thing, that she knows before she makes the cake. She can save it for another time, when she has recovered from this blow and is open once again to the comforts of sweetness and recollected childhood.

But of course the officers will return to clean up the blood, or else they will send others to do so, as well as to scour the apartment for any papers they missed. By the time Natalya returns, all will be put back to order, as if they have never been here. As if Gronfein has never been here, either, not just in the apartment but in the city, on the stage, in the pages of any newspaper or book. They will remove all trace of him from the public record, his works will disappear from libraries, no one will be able to read or hear a word he has ever written.

The two officers in uniform lift him again, and the third brushes the front of Gronfein's shirt with a handkerchief. But there is a spot of blood on the front, one they won't be able to scrub away, and for that he is thankful. It's the last lingering hint of him, something they will have to hide from passersby as they walk him out of the building into their waiting car. Still, there will be nothing to keep Natalya from making her cake. He accepts that now, the beautiful Medovik uneaten on the sideboard, waiting for someone who will never appear. This, too, is one of the nuances of longing, a part of the true utopian dream, and now all he can do is mourn it and hope that one day another playwright conjures it before an audience when they are too entranced to look away.

The boyish officer kicks open the door to the street. The sunlight is dazzling. Gronfein finds enough strength in it to pull against the hands on his arms, not enough to break away but to make them wrestle with him as they haul him outside. This is what the officers expect in their line of work, what they have come to crave, and who is he to deprive them? To his surprise, he manages to yank one arm free. It flails, half closes into a fist, lands on the ear of the short officer in the suit, hard enough to make him flinch. It's a gift he gives this dutiful defender of the state, whose loyalty is matched only by his cruelty, a little smile on his thin lips as his comrade—the one with creased cheeks and gentle eyes—grips both Gronfein's arms behind his back so the other can land blow after blow on the ribs. Gronfein coughs up more blood onto his shirt. There is no hiding it now, and he is pleased. Everything in plain sight.

But in front of the apartment building, Brestskaya Street is empty of pedestrians, and before anyone sees, he is shoved headfirst into the back of a car whose seat smells of ammonia. The officers settle in with satisfied grunts, the boyish one beside him, crumbs still visible on his jacket, the others up front. The little one takes the driver's seat and pushes a hat onto his head.

Unlike the suit, it is too small, sitting lightly atop his widow's peak, perhaps to make him appear taller. All three light cigarettes. They have played their parts well. They deserve applause, then drinks to celebrate a successful performance. What Gronfein experiences as pain is nothing more than the fulfillment of their studious and disciplined training.

The more compelling scene, however, is the one that will follow, the conversation they'll have over breakfast tomorrow morning, before visiting another tired revolutionary who has outlived his usefulness. But he no longer has the concentration to imagine such an exchange, doubts he imagined it correctly before. They wouldn't discuss a woman, not a stranger or a wife or a mistress, wouldn't need distraction from their unsavory duties. How absurd to believe he could have understood them. What hubris to think they needed his encouragement or reassurance. Whatever passes between them is beyond the reach of his comprehension or fancy, it always has been, and instead all he can access is the thick metallic taste of blood filling his mouth. To spite them, he leans forward over his knees and lets some of it seep onto the floor of the car. But as soon as it's gone, more replaces it. He can no longer recall the taste of anything else. The little officer starts the engine.

Knowing this is his last chance, Gronfein tries again to say what he must. The blood makes speaking difficult, his words garbled, and he has to repeat himself three times to be heard. But even when he's sure he's made himself clear, the officers don't respond.

"My wife," he sputters once more, as the car pulls into the street.

CUT LOOSE

◄○►

Claudia Silver, a member of Actors' Equity and part-time assistant kindergarten teacher at All My Friends Montessori in Livingston, New Jersey, waited for the next step to take shape before easing onto the escalator. She wore a floor-length cotton dress, and all day she'd had to concentrate to keep from tripping. Now it was a relief to stand still as she descended from the second to the first floor. Over one shoulder she carried a large leather purse, scuffed on the straps and bottom, its silver clasp tarnished. In the opposite hand was a dainty bag of thick paper, shiny pink, with twine handles. Inside, a bottle of perfume, a scent she'd never worn before, with a French name she couldn't translate beyond the first two words. Water of what?

At the cosmetics counter, she'd asked for something that smelled of gardenias, and this was what the clerk brought her, a vial the size of her pinky, priced one penny short of a hundred dollars. She'd never spent so much on perfume. In fact, she'd hardly worn perfume since high school, when she'd douse herself every morning with her mother's Obsession. When she'd gotten to the mall she'd debated between Macy's and Lord & Taylor, settling on the latter because what she found there was likely to be more expensive and therefore classier. This was an investment after all, with the promise—or at least the hope—of dividends down the road. She agreed with the clerk that the fragrance was lovely, mild but sweet, though whether it had anything to do with gardenias she didn't know. She couldn't recall how gardenias smelled, or, for that matter, how they looked. She knew only that they were supposed to be tasteful and distinguished.

The dress she'd bought a few weeks before. Not from Lord & Taylor. That she couldn't begin to afford. Not even from Macy's, but from a discount website that shipped directly from Cambodia. It was two inches too long, and even with platform sandals it sometimes caught underfoot. She should have taken the time to hem it, but she was a lousy seamstress, and if she asked her mother to do it for her, questions would have followed: Another audition? Or maybe a date? Are you going to let us meet him for a change?

Still, it was the most flattering garment she owned that wasn't frayed at the cuffs, showing off her slender shoulders and long arms, hiding the weight she carried in her thighs. White- and navy-striped, sleeveless and fitted to the waist, falling straight from the hips. Her lead teacher had remarked on it this morning, and so had several of her students. "You look pretty today, Miss Claudia," one girl said, and another, jealous, piped up, "My mom's a size two." Even one of the better-looking dads eyed her during drop-off, and as usual, what struck her was how little it took to get noticed in the ordinary world. Something as insignificant as pinning her hair behind her ears or clipping a chain with an amethyst pendant around her neck, and people who'd taken her presence for granted— men, especially—turned her way with surprise, as if they didn't quite recognize her. Why was it so much harder on a stage, facing a director and producers hidden in the shadows of an otherwise empty theater?

Today, though, instead of welcoming the attention, she wanted only to fend it off. Riding the escalator from the second to the first floor of Lord & Taylor in the Livingston Mall, she was sure everyone could see more than just the dress, more even than the outline of her underwear showing through. If they got close enough, she thought as she neared bottom, they'd sniff out her desperation, the rankness of her deceit. It would have taken a whole vial of perfume to cover it.

In front of her, the moving stairs flattened. She took a step forward, wobbled on a heel, recovered. Then she felt a tug from behind, and before she could process what was happening, she pictured the little hands of her kindergarteners grabbing onto her hem—*Don't leave us, Miss Claudia, oh, please don't!*—or the larger ones of the actors and directors she'd worked with over the past ten years, the teachers and coaches who'd mentored her before that, all of them begging her not to leave behind what she'd worked so very hard to achieve. And thinking, spitefully, that no amount of work had ever done any good since no one had worked as hard on her behalf, she swiped at the back of the dress to snatch it out of their clutching fingers.

But the tugging continued, harder now, stretching the neckline when she twisted her body to look behind. And only then did she realize the hem was caught in the escalator's blunt metal teeth, the end disappearing under the floor. She jerked hard, but it didn't come free. Her astonishment was so great she couldn't even call out, and the dress kept going under, dragging her down. She was afraid it would rip, or worse, get pulled off and leave her standing in bra and panties—both blue lace and sheer, the only lingerie she owned—so she bent her knees to give it slack. Only when she crouched nearly to the ground did she hear someone above her give a cry, and then footsteps running toward her. There were grinding sounds, a hint of smoke. With effort, she managed to turn her head to see a woman punching a button beside the moving railing, and then the whole thing shuddered to a stop.

Before shock toppled into embarrassment, first she experienced only impatience. She didn't have time for this. Not today, of all days. Normally after school she drove home to West Caldwell—her childhood home, not a permanent one—where she helped her mother with groceries and dinner and tidying. It was her way of contributing to the household without paying rent, which her parents refused and which she couldn't have afforded in any case. "You should be saving up," they told her, "so you can buy your own place when the time comes." With her earnings, even if she spent nothing, it would take ten years to do so, and then at best she might be able to put a down payment on a one-room condo in Totowa. But she knew her parents were hoping for a quicker alternative: that some man might take pity on her and pluck her out of their lives. "Any divorced families in your school?" her mother asked in a theatrically off-hand way, as if her daughter couldn't spot bad acting from a single gesture. "Must be tough to be a single father. What you'd want is a mature woman who could step right in and take care of the kids."

Claudia had just turned thirty-three. She'd moved back in the fall, after ten years in Brooklyn, during which time she'd cycled through eight apartments, each one smaller and farther from Manhattan. She'd gone through nearly twice as many boyfriends, only a few of whom had lasted long enough to come to dinner with her parents on the rare occasions they drove into the city, though they lived only half an hour away. She'd given everything she had to the career, never taking a permanent job in order to leave her schedule open for auditions. She made most of her money as a nanny and a substitute teacher and tore up credit card bills as soon as they arrived.

A decade of sweat and sacrifice and sleepless nights. And what did she have to show for it? One season at the Beckett Theatre. A month as understudy for Beth in *Little Women*. Two summers with a company in Milford, Pennsylvania, doing *Annie* and *Our Town*. Her only regular gig—Tuesdays and Wednesdays for the past six years—as a garment worker at the Tenement Museum, she who couldn't sew. Then her rent went up again. The only place she could find in her price range was in Canarsie, a ten-minute walk to the nearest subway. Commuting from New Jersey was no less arduous. She called her mother and made a proposal.

But all it took was half a year of living with her parents, pretending to ignore her father's silent judgment and her mother's loud dismay—the hardest acting job of her life—to make her want to give it all up. She couldn't take another month. The sacrifices no longer seemed worth the cost, so she'd started sending out applications to jobs for which she wasn't qualified, inventing experience on her résumé and begging friends, most of whom worked with her in the Tenement Museum sweatshop, to serve as fake references. And this afternoon she had her first interview scheduled with a law firm in East Hanover. She'd spent the past two days learning what a legal secretary did, getting down the lingo, memorizing the difference between a motion and an appeal. It wasn't much different than preparing for auditions, during which she'd taken on any number of professions. Over the years she'd been nurses and prostitutes and cops and fairies. How hard could it be to stuff papers into appropriate files?

What she lacked in experience, she'd make up for with enthusiasm and style. Having looked up the lawyer who was interviewing her and discovered from the firm's website that he was a heavy-jawed man of maybe forty-five, with the first silver streaks in his wavy hair, she decided the dress and perfume would cover any shortcomings in her performance. Yet all morning, with the dress swishing around her, she'd felt cheap and slutty, as if she were about to cheat on a boyfriend or sleep with a married man—both of which she'd done previously without having felt either. Who was she betraying but herself?

Sure, her friends at the museum would be sorry to see her go. But they'd replace her an hour after she quit. A number of kids at All My Friends told her they loved her, but she suspected it was mostly because during her three morning shifts she diverted them from their normal independent learning—their "jobs," in the Montessori parlance—and instead directed them in skits or gave dramatic readings from *Curious George* and *Madeline*. And she'd already gotten hints from her lead teacher that she likely wouldn't be hired back next year. No one would really miss her, and as she crouched at the bottom of the escalator, she experienced a dizzying sadness, which she tried to allay by picturing the dress freed and settling around her as she swept into the chair across from the lawyer, the scent of gardenias wafting toward him as she crossed her legs and rearranged the fabric over her knees.

But by now a crowd had gathered, and it was hard to envision herself anywhere else. The woman who'd turned off the escalator, older and elegant in slacks and blazer, spoke to her kindly, with reassurance, while a pair of kids from Verona High School, a girl with stick legs poking out of a skirt that ended just below her buttocks, a boy in a letterman jacket though it was far too heavy for the warm spring day, stood giggling off to one side. Three young mothers with babies in strollers circled her, as if in judgment, cataloguing her failures: not married, childless, barely employed, broke, living with her parents, giving up on her dreams. Several people tried to yank her free with no success, including a store manager who said, "Not the first time it's happened since I've worked here, if you can believe it. Just never quite so jammed before."

"I'm in a hurry," she said. "I can't be late."

"I called maintenance. They're on the way."

The dress was tight against her left side, showing too much breast and hip and thigh, and the tarty platform sandals were exposed along with a blue bra strap. No one watching would have guessed she was on her way to an interview. Neither would she, if she'd seen herself. She should have dressed like the kindly elegant woman, in professional attire she didn't own. And maybe she would have if the job were something she'd really wanted. But studying the lawyer's photo, she'd already taken flight into fantasies that had nothing to do with working. Whether he was married or not didn't really matter, not when he saw her glide into his office with the dress fluttering behind her, when he caught a trace of her scent. Yes, he'd hire her as his secretary, but only for a short while, and then he'd set her up—as wife or mistress, either would be fine—so she could return to her acting career, because of course she couldn't give it up, it was in her blood, it was the only thing she lived for . . .

The boy in the letterman jacket stepped forward, and without asking, grabbed hold of the dress. On his shoulder, his school's ridiculous team name was stitched in maroon and white: Verona Hillbillies, with a picture of a sleeping bearded man, wearing a hat and cut-offs, pipe in his mouth, rifle propped on bare feet, a jug with three Xs under his arm. Whose idea was it to represent a high-school football team with the image of a drunken lout? And what did hillbillies have to do with a town in the middle of flat, suburban Essex County? It was the clearest evidence yet that she needed to get out of here, back to the city, no matter how small her apartment, no matter how long a walk to the subway. The boy set his feet and pulled, his face straining, his knee brushing against her backside. For a moment the dress seemed to give way, but then came a tearing sound, and he let go.

"If he can't do it, it's in there for good," said the girl in the short skirt with a prideful flip of curls over her shoulder. The boy returned to her, put an arm around her waist, and together they went back to snapping gum and gawking.

"I've really got to go," Claudia said, helplessly. She wasn't wearing a watch, but she knew it must be close to two by now, and the interview was scheduled for two-thirty. East Hanover was at least a twenty-minute drive away. Coming to the mall had already been pushing her time, though she'd reasoned it wouldn't hurt to show up five minutes late—as she did for most auditions, as well as all dates—to make the lawyer wonder, just briefly, if she'd backed out. A little pang to sweeten the sight of her when she finally floated in.

"Maintenance should be here any minute," the manager said. Then he walked away. So did the mothers with their sleeping infants, and the elegant woman who'd stopped the escalator from swallowing the entire dress. The latter offered one final bit of encouragement before she left: "Make them pay for it." Only the teenagers hung around, not close enough to keep her company, instead carrying on a private flirtation beside a rack of oxford shirts. What were they doing out of school before two on a Wednesday? And in a Lord & Taylor, where any single ensemble cost more than everything Claudia owned?

"Broke my machine, did you?"

She'd been crouching long enough for her knees to ache, the dress cutting into the flesh of her neck, and she was in no mood for jokes. The janitor was a young guy with sleep-mussed hair, red faced, wearing overalls the color of leather chaps. More cowboy than hillbilly, she thought, though either way she didn't want to smell his sweat.

"Let's take a look at the damage," he said cheerfully and clicked his tongue. She held her breath as he maneuvered around her to unscrew a metal plate in the floor, but no matter how she shifted her body, she was always in the way, and he kept apologizing for bumping her. When she could no longer keep the air in, she breathed through her mouth. As he worked, he scolded the escalator: "Why'd you have to eat this nice lady's dress? Don't I feed you enough?"

"How long will this take?" she asked. "I'm already late for . . . an important audition."

Her phone was in her purse, and she could have looked up the lawyer's number, but what would she say? That the inappropriate dress she shouldn't have worn to an interview was stuck in an escalator, to which a big amiable janitor named Patrick—she read the embossed letters on his chest—was muttering as if to a pet? Nothing she imagined saying would maintain the vision fixed in her mind of the lawyer's breathless surprise when she first stepped through his door. She couldn't bring herself to call.

Only when Patrick finally had all the screws out did he realize he couldn't take the plate off with her standing on it. "Could you slide up a step?" he asked, but she couldn't without also sliding out of the dress. "Looks like we'll have to cut you out, sorry to say."

"Fine. Just get it over with."

He rummaged in his toolbox, but all he could come up with was a pair of wire cutters. A little steel PAC-MAN, its mouth an inch long. "Might take a while with this," he said. "I can go look for scissors."

The high school kids, she noticed, had their phones out now, pointing them at her, and then tapping furiously with their thumbs. She'd worked so hard to get her image into the world, and by this evening it would be all over the internet.

"No," she said. "Don't leave me here alone."

"Okay, then. Here goes."

He snipped an opening at the front of the hem, and then made his way higher, the PAC-MAN slowly munching a ragged slit up her right leg. The kids came close again to get a better look. Someone had to bear witness, she supposed: to her humiliation, to her dashed hopes, to her descent into the mundane life she'd tried so hard to abandon. Patrick worked slowly but carefully, muttering now to the wire cutters: "That's it, a good clean cut, you're doing just fine." When he reached high enough, he turned the blade horizontally and cut across the front panel, the fabric dropping away to reveal a wedge of pale thigh. Then he turned to the teenagers, who were getting their phones ready, and said in a voice surprisingly sharp, "How about giving the lady some privacy."

The girl giggled again, and the boy did something with his arms that made the jacket jump higher on his shoulders. Then the two of them strutted off, bumping hips, and Patrick went back to cutting. He tried to keep his eyes averted as he uncovered more of her, but Claudia was afraid he'd nick her leg with the blade. "It's okay to look," she said. "Just pretend you're a doctor."

"My patients are usually made out of metal," he said, but then faced forward, with a hard, serious squint, and she did her best to keep her knees together. But soon she forgot to breathe through her mouth, and she took in his smell, which wasn't ripe so much as tangy, a little on the sweet side. And what about hers? Surely he'd caught a whiff already. She wished she'd dabbed the perfume behind her ears at the counter rather than waiting until she made it to her car. Her mother's car, that was, which she borrowed on the days she worked at All My Friends, making her mother ride the bus. "Shame to ruin such a pretty dress," Patrick said, quietly, as if they were alone in a small, snug room and not under high fluorescent lights interspersed among white ceiling panels, invisible speakers spilling out pop songs stripped of voices and played on too many strings.

"I have others," she said.

When he reached the far side of her left thigh, he apologized again, his red face going redder. "I've got to go around the back," he said. "I'm afraid I'll have to have you—"

"It's okay," she replied and dropped forward onto hands and knees. If anyone was watching now, she didn't want to know. She closed her eyes and focused on the snip of the wire cutters, on the sound of Patrick's breath.

"I sure wasn't expecting this when I left the house," he said. "Be ready for anything, they told me when I took the job. But who ever is? It's a stupid thing to say. Anything? Am I supposed to be ready for an attack of giant scorpions next?"

When his knuckle brushed the back of her thigh, a shiver went through her, and she drew in a quick pull of air. Another brush of knuckles, a little higher up, and the air stuttered out of her. "It's okay," she said again, though this time he hadn't apologized.

"Just a little bit more," he said. "You're a patient patient."

Fabric fell away from her leg, and cool air rushed against the exposed skin. His warm breath followed, and she heard herself make a strange noise, one she couldn't have repeated on cue if she'd tried.

Still, she imagined giving it to her character at the Tenement Museum, a woman named Frieda Levine. She was forty-two years old in 1904, bent-backed, gravelly-voiced, the mother of six children, two of whom had died in infancy. She showed visitors the perfect seam she'd stitched into a pair of black trousers and told them about a rail-yard accident that had left her husband an invalid. Claudia never had more than five minutes with a tour group, but in order to connect with the character she'd invented a secret backstory for Frieda, and it made her performances richer, she was sure of it. A former sweetheart, left behind in the old country, had recently arrived in New York. One evening he appeared beneath a streetlamp when she came out of the sweatshop. Under the pylons of the brand-new Williamsburg Bridge, they rekindled their romance with a passionate embrace. But Frieda wouldn't sleep with him; her loyalty to her husband was too strong. She was a woman of principle, unwilling to compromise her dignity for fleeting desires of the heart. And yet her heart was vigorous, too, and it wasn't impossible to imagine Frieda ending up on hands and knees, her old lover crouched behind, her dress rising up over her thighs. She waited for him to touch her again.

"That's it," Patrick said. "Surgery's done. You're free."

She opened her eyes. No one was watching, except for a bald mannequin in peach capris and a hideous floral blouse, its impossibly long fingers splayed as if they'd just dropped garbage onto the floor for someone else to pick up. Patrick faced away from her, stowing his tools, snapping his box closed. When she stood the dress was nearly as short as the high school girl's skirt, at least in spots, hanging to the knee on one side and rising up almost to the line of her underwear on the other. Here were the chunky thighs she'd meant to hide, too white, veins close to the surface. Bits of dirt stuck to her dimpled knees.

"Almost forgot," Patrick said, reopening the toolbox. "Still have dental work to do."

The manager reappeared, said how terribly sorry he was, and suggested that next time she might want to lift up her hem if she wore a dress that was too long for her. "We'll give you credit to replace this one," he said. "And here, I should add, tailoring is always complimentary." It would take just a few minutes to process a gift card, he said, and beckoned her toward the nearest register.

She checked the time on her phone. A quarter past two. Not long enough to find her mother's car in the parking lot and drive to East Hanover and arrive five minutes late, certainly not if she were to first drive home and change. Of course she couldn't show up as she was, and it would be faster to pick out a new outfit here. But she declined the manager's offer. "I've got to go right now," she said and then watched as Patrick opened the plate in the floor and pulled out the mangled remains of the dress's lower half. He handed it to the manager, who handed it to Claudia. And then she was hurrying away before she thought to thank them, though hurrying to what? Back into the life she'd been living for the past decade, one distinguished by failure and compromise, given dignity only by her refusal to let it go? She tried to run in the sandals, wobbled again, and then slowed down to keep from falling. At some point, surely, she'd reach the limit, one humiliation more than she could take.

Once outside, the sun to her back and a breeze raising goose bumps on her thighs, she regretted not having taken the gift card. When would she ever be able to afford a Lord & Taylor dress again? And then she realized she'd left behind the perfume, that tiny vial so expensive it might have been full of cocaine, which she'd last tried during her month backstage for *Little Women*, bored senseless, praying for the actor playing Beth to catch the flu or sprain an ankle. She couldn't go back for it, not with her dress hacked, her ugly legs on display, the ridiculous person she'd always been revealed for everyone to see. Had she ever managed to hide it? You're good at playing yourself, a director had once told her, but this character isn't you. She crossed the sidewalk, stepped off the curb, stared into the enormous grid of cars that stretched around the mall in both directions. She had no idea which way to turn.

"Wait!"

The voice was familiar, but when she glanced behind the flare of sunlight made her squint, and she couldn't tell where it came from.

"Lady! With the dress! Your thing! Your purchase!"

Then she saw: a red-faced cowboy with unkempt hair and strong gentle hands, running to her, a little pink bag with twine handles thrust in front of him like a bouquet. She swiveled, and the sun, brighter than stage lights, struck her full in the face. She pressed the back of a hand to her forehead and, failing to swoon, tripped over the curb and sprawled face down on rough cement.

GOING TO GROUND

—<o>—

Like me, they were from suburbs of New York—Jeff from Fairfield, Rae from Massapequa Park—but I met them during the brief time we all lived in Portland. Jeff had once waited tables in a downtown seafood restaurant with my friend Mindy Weiss, when she was still married to a man whose name was either Vincent or Victor. Or maybe Rae had worked with her, and Mindy had gotten to know Jeff afterward. I can't remember. In either case, Mindy hadn't worked there long. She quit the job and the marriage soon after and started a tutoring business that was thriving by the time I landed in town. It continued to do so until the financial collapse cut her client list in half. Then she went back to school to become a therapist and tried to build a private practice that never got off the ground. The last I heard she was working for a nonprofit that had something to do with education and technology—either providing technology for schools or setting up after-school programs for kids to learn technology. We'd met for coffee, but neither of us had much time, so we didn't talk long, and I was too distracted by my own concerns—new job, baby on the way—to take in many of the details. What I did catch was that the position was only half-time and didn't come with benefits, and because she was single again and didn't need much space, she was planning to sell her house and move into a rented studio downtown. She made a crack about my worn shoes next to her recently polished boots and said to look at us you'd never know our fortunes had changed. As we said goodbye, she kissed the air next to my cheeks. That was about a year ago. We've been out of touch since.

But at the time I became acquainted with Jeff and Rae, in the late summer and fall of 1999, I spent three or four evenings a week at Mindy's house, a little bungalow she'd recently bought and begun renovating herself. I'd just turned twenty-six and knew few people in town; Mindy had hired me to tutor a pair of clients she couldn't fit into her jammed schedule, a high school junior and her freshman brother, both of whom took for granted that "tutoring" meant I'd write their essays for them. I didn't think I'd stay in Portland long. Maybe two years to save up money before heading to a bigger city, one where, though I couldn't live as cheaply, interesting opportunities might readily present themselves. This was how I believed life happened then: you put yourself somewhere you wanted to be, and avenues of possibility would open in all directions. So far, my approach had led to a handful of part-time and temporary gigs and a basement apartment with a view onto a concrete slab.

Needless to say, it was a different city then, one only just beginning to collect the kind of fashionable, sophisticated young people who'd already transformed places like San Francisco and Seattle into food and art meccas where no one could afford to live. You could still buy a condo on the edges of downtown or the Pearl District for a hundred grand, and you could pick up a dilapidated old Craftsman like the one Mindy found in North Portland, in the neighborhood between the interstate and Vancouver Avenue, for almost nothing. That neighborhood had once been known for drugs and periodic gang violence, and

Mindy's parents—who lived in the tony West Hills—thought she was crazy to buy there. But even then Mindy knew she'd made a good investment. The first couple of restaurants had opened on Mississippi Avenue, and it would be only a few years before the place was booming with boutiques and coffee shops and brewpubs, the long-time residents, most Black, pushed out by rising property taxes.

At the time, though, the neighborhood still had a threatening edge. Three times in as many months my car was broken into right beside Mindy's driveway. The first time a box of CDs went missing, the second my jack and lug wrench. The third time there was nothing left to steal, so instead the intruder gouged the armrest between the front seats—with a pocketknife, I guessed, or something larger—and yanked out a handful of foam stuffing.

But this never put me off visiting. If anything, the potential danger beyond the bungalow's sturdy walls charged the evenings I spent there with an urgency I might not have felt otherwise. At twenty-six I was still hungry for a kind of adventure I'd only tasted while traveling the year after college, and even then sporadically: on the night I'd spent in a deserted hotel in the High Tatras mountains of Slovakia; or the day I got lost in a forest on the border of Hungary and Croatia; or the time I stumbled upon a party in a five-hundred-year-old barn in the haunted valley of Glencoe, one of the few buildings left standing after the devious Campbells massacred their MacDonald hosts and burned their homes to the ground. In these moments I felt the boundaries separating me from a broader, more mysterious world partially dissolving, and even several years later I carried them around with me like tiny flakes of gold that suggested full veins yet to be discovered.

Why else would those evenings at Mindy's house have felt so important, even when, at first, little happened there? Mindy spent all her time tinkering with repairs and improvements, yanking out sketchy wiring, repainting a dented claw-foot tub, patching a hole in plaster, while I listened to music and read books. Jeff and Rae would show up an hour after they'd said they would, with dusty bottles from countries not well-known for wine production: Macedonia, Uruguay, Bali. The wine was heavy and dark purple and left a film on our teeth. Mindy hadn't unpacked her dishes yet, so we drank from plastic cups. Nor had she bought any furniture, only a dozen or so throw pillows, big square ones with velvet covers, and we lounged on these as Mindy drilled holes or spread joint compound or cut molding with her chop saw. Often, to keep from electrocuting herself, she turned off all the power at the breaker, and we'd either light candles or just watch the beam of her flashlight moving across the exposed studs of the walls she'd torn open.

And how I savored the sound of Mindy pounding in a loose floorboard, the taste of syrupy wine in the back of my throat, the sight of Jeff and Rae sprawled on pillows in candle-light—Jeff lying perpendicular to Rae, whose head rested on his belly—while the shadeless windows above us darkened. Though I knew nothing of them beyond these evenings at Mindy's house, I was drawn to them from the start. They presented themselves as serious wanderers, living exclusively for those experiences I treasured most. Before coming to Portland, they'd spent no more than six months in any one place, not since they'd met in their early twenties. Now they were thirty-three. Already they'd visited four continents and had plans to reach a fifth—Africa—within the year. They seemed not just content to drift from place to place, working service jobs just long enough to propel them to their next destination, but compelled to do so by a desire I felt I understood well, even if I couldn't have described it then. It was more than just curiosity or wanderlust, terms that suggested motivations too shallow, too passive to match their drive, which even then struck me as manic. They were addicted to wonder or terrified of boredom. Maybe a bit of both.

We quickly discovered common ground in discussing our travels, both those completed and those planned—despite struggling to pay my rent, I'd just booked a trip to western Ireland for the coming spring—and in exchanging our little nuggets of marvel and awe. Before coming to Portland, they'd spent a few months in the deserts of Utah and Arizona, culminating in an extended stay on the Hopi reservation. They'd stuck around here so long to save up for what they hoped would be a multi-year jaunt, and though they now had almost enough money to get them where they wanted to go, they were waiting for the winter solstice, when they'd attend a mass séance at the coast, on the end of a sandy spit that stretched into the Pacific. From there they'd head up to the border of British Columbia and the Yukon, to a spot where the earth's magnetic field was reported to wobble in a way that made the northern lights brighter than anywhere else.

"That is," Jeff added, "if the computer bug doesn't blow up the planet first."

His laughter was exaggerated but brief. Rae only took a sip of wine and showed me her purple teeth. "You should come with us," she said. "We'd take good care of you."

Doubting she'd meant the invitation seriously, I laughed and told her I'd have to check my busy schedule. Jeff clapped a hand on her thigh and said, "She gets sick of being with just me all the time."

The look she gave him, tender and full of patience, undermined his words, which seemed so disingenuous I found myself instantly irritated by them and quickly changed the subject, talking instead about the week I'd spent, three years earlier, hitchhiking in the Outer Hebrides.

"Oh, the Callanish Stones!" Rae exclaimed. "They're on our list." Had I stood in the middle of the circle? she asked. Had I felt the energy rising from it? She'd read stories about people hearing strange voices when the sun struck the inner ring, speaking an ancient language they almost recognized even if they'd come from the other side of the world.

I'd felt *something*, I said, though I couldn't have put my finger on exactly what. Something old and mysterious and—.

Before I could finish, Mindy called from the bathroom, where she was affixing subway tile behind the pedestal sink, "You felt your own bullshit rising out of your bowels."

—◦—

Mindy never took an interest in our stories. Most of the time, in fact, she was hostile toward them. She'd done some traveling when she was younger—France, Italy, Israel, the Bahamas—and in her early and mid-twenties she'd lived in three other cities before returning home. But now she'd just turned thirty, she'd started a business, she'd bought a house. She'd set down roots and wanted them to spread. She hadn't expected to find herself single, and she didn't plan to stay that way for long. She wanted a family. If she took a vacation, it would be to a sunny beach with water warm enough to snorkel in. But because there were no sunny beaches in Oregon, the ocean here freezing even in summer, and because she spent all the money she made fixing up her house, she hardly left the city. To her, our longing for adventure sounded like an excuse to avoid growing up.

But Jeff and Rae weren't bothered by her cynicism, or else they welcomed it as a challenge, a chance to prove to her how vital their experiences had been, how transformative. They described an encounter they'd had with an old woman on the Inca Trail, about halfway up to Machu Picchu. She was frail and bony, but she had a huge bundle on her back, what appeared to be a roll of blankets or rugs, and she was bent almost to the ground. They'd been walking for two days by then, and they were tired and hungry. To keep their own packs light, they'd taken less food than they needed, and one of the bags of dried meat they'd bought in Cuzco had gone rancid. They wouldn't have enough for the walk down, and they worried about keeping up their strength. Still, Jeff offered to carry the bundle, and the old woman thanked them repeatedly, with emphatic gestures, smiling a toothless smile.

She accompanied them the rest of the way, chattering in a language they didn't understand—Rae was fluent in Spanish—but as soon as the ruins of the Temple of the Sun came into view, along with the massive stone of the Inti Watana, she disappeared. Jeff searched for her while Rae rested, walking half a mile back down the trail, but there was no sign of her. She was just gone. They waited for her to return—half an hour, an hour, two.

"By then we knew she wasn't coming back," Rae said. "And we knew the bundle was for us."

Inside the rolled cloth they found fresh bread, purple potatoes steamed inside a thick wrapper of leaves, smoked alpaca meat. Enough food to get them all the way back down the mountain.

"Man, was it good," Jeff said. "Best meal I've ever eaten. Except maybe for the paiche and camu camu fruit when we made it to Omagua. But that gave me the squirts for the next three weeks."

From there they launched into a description of the various illnesses they'd contracted in the Amazon, and the bugs they kept finding in their shoes, with no further commentary on the old woman and the bundle she'd left them. Were we meant to take her for a benevolent spirit or deity, the ghost of an Incan princess? Who knows. This was the way they ended most of their stories, moving seamlessly from the otherworldly to the earthly, as if it were all equally compelling.

The way they took their strangest experiences for granted, as if they were only mildly unusual, was part of what made them seem eccentric to me then. It certainly wasn't their appearance, which couldn't have been called anything but ordinary, though maybe the plainness of their looks made what they said more intriguing. They weren't the type to call attention to themselves with tattoos or unexpected piercings or even flashy haircuts. Jeff's hair was closely cropped and gelled, the teeth marks of his comb visible along the part, and he wore only khaki pants, blue or black polo shirts, and stark white sneakers. The uniform of a waiter at a golf club, maybe, or a private resort. He'd once had dreadlocks and a beard, he told me, and though I didn't question him, my face must have betrayed skepticism. The next week he brought an old passport. It hadn't yet expired, but he'd replaced it anyway, he said, because immigration officers never believed it was him and constantly hassled him at border crossings. And I didn't blame those immigration officers. Imagining the figure in the photo without dreadlocks and beard, I still couldn't match it to the person in front of me. The nose was too big, the forehead too broad. And I had a hard time believing Jeff could even grow such a thick beard. Unlike mine, which sprouted a shadow five minutes after I shaved, his cheeks were clear and smooth every time I saw him, never a hint of stubble or razor burn.

If Jeff's looks were nondescript, Rae's verged on homely. She had wiry brown hair with a tendency to frizz, pushed over her ears and flyaway in back. Her face was round, just shy of chubby, with a blunt nose and big front teeth. Her body was oddly shaped, long narrow torso above flaring hips and chunky thighs, which she usually hid beneath long skirts or baggy jeans. And yet her voice, deep in pitch but silky—a singer's voice, I thought, though as far as I knew she'd never sung—along with the liveliness of her eyes whenever she spoke about traveling, made her unaccountably sensual in the flickering candlelight, stroking Jeff's hand where it rested on her shoulder.

Eventually Rae's voice would draw Mindy—sweating in tank top and shorts, bare feet stuck into unlaced work boots—away from whatever project she was working on to settle on the pillows with us. Her looks, in contrast to Rae's, were unequivocally striking: obsidian hair cut into severe bangs over carefully plucked eyebrows and heavily lidded eyes; full, downturned lips; shoulders broad from swimming; legs cut with muscle. I wouldn't have called her pretty—her features were too sharp for that word, her gaze too intense, her smile too guarded—but when she sat beside me, those strong legs stretched from her pillow toward mine, her sweat overpowering the smell of candle wax, I suddenly felt the effect of the wine, a woozy flush making me lie back, hands behind my head.

Once with us, she grilled Jeff and Rae on the details of their stories, looking for holes or discrepancies, trying to make them admit they'd invented or exaggerated. But even if they couldn't answer her questions, they only shrugged and smiled dreamy, tolerant smiles, as if Mindy were missing the point entirely.

"Who knows if anything happened the way we remember it," Rae said. "You know, the mind's a landscape all its own."

"That's why I don't need to fly to Liberia," Mindy said. "I can just close my eyes and picture all the starving kids I want, right here in the comfort of my own home." She did close her eyes then, tilting her head back and giving a dramatic sigh. "Ah, what a ride."

I suppose what bothered her most about our conversations was their effect on me. We weren't a couple, but we'd been spending more and more time together, feeling each other out, quietly inching toward intimacy, and over those months Mindy must have imagined a possible future with me as I had with her. She didn't want Jeff and Rae seducing me into fantasies of far-flung adventure, inviting me to join them on their trek to the polar vortex. When I started a story of my own, about a guest house I'd stumbled upon in the old walled city of Levoča, in eastern Slovakia, run by a family of midgets, she didn't let me get far before cutting me off. "Little people," she said. "Aren't you worldly travelers supposed to be culturally sensitive?" When I tried again, she said, "Enough with this pissing contest. I need help lifting a cabinet."

Rae gave me a knowing look, her heavy eyebrows rising as if to say, *Go on, I know what it's like to have a jealous lover.* I followed Mindy into the kitchen, more tipsy than I realized, the dark wine making my head feel loose on my neck. As we wrestled the cabinet into place, Mindy repeatedly bumped my shoulder with hers, and then she tucked herself in front of me, bracing her leg against mine while running her drill. It took all my concentration to hold up the weight while the screws went into the stud with an angry and insistent grinding. Before long Jeff and Rae peeked around the door and said goodnight. "Going already?" I asked and hoped they'd reconsider and stick around for another hour. With Mindy's hair just under my nose, her bare shoulder an inch from my chest, a triangle of sweat making the thin fabric of the tank top stick to her back, I felt my breath coming up short. I wasn't sure I wanted to be left alone with her.

Rae called out, "May your night be full of surprises." Her voice was warm and encouraging, and I told myself I should just calm down, let things follow their natural course. Wasn't this what I'd been imagining for weeks now? But instead my nervousness only intensified. I had to restrain myself from calling them back, from telling them to wait for me, that I was leaving, too.

"Lock the door behind you," Mindy said. Then, as soon as she was sure the cabinet wouldn't topple when I let go, she turned and stepped into my arms. "You're not going anywhere," she said.

◄◦►

At the time, I credited Jeff and Rae with bringing us together. Later, I blamed them for it. Without their influence, why would Mindy have considered me a prospect for long-term attachment, young as I was, underemployed, inexperienced at any romance but the fleeting sort. I was nothing like her ex-husband, slender, scruffy, and bookish where he was broad chested, clean-cut, and athletic. Everything else in her life suggested a focus on the future, on building something stable and certain. That she chose to include me in her plans I could see only as an aberration, a backsliding into living for the present. Just as Jeff and Rae's stories tempted me toward transience, they seduced her into spontaneity and abandon to the whims of heart and loins.

The night after Jeff and Rae left us alone together, or maybe on a night soon after, we lay on our backs on her bed—the one piece of furniture she had bought—staring at the gutted ceiling crisscrossed by newly strung wires, a rectangular hole where she'd soon install a heat register. Mindy whispered, "Feels like home, right?" In her raspy voice, always edged with sarcasm, I couldn't tell if she was talking about the house or our bodies pressed together, legs twined. From outside came the sound of shattered glass—maybe down the block, maybe across the street. "My car," I said, but when I tried to sit, Mindy held me down. "Just a bottle," she said. "Car windows don't pop like that." I didn't believe her and listened for more sounds of destruction. But then she rolled onto me, and I decided a broken window would be no less broken in the morning.

The truth is, being with her did feel like home, but I didn't think that was something to recommend it. I'd moved across the country to break free of the known and the comfortable, to make distance from the claustrophobic, anxiety-ridden lives of my parents and childhood friends. But I couldn't shake the feeling that Mindy and I had known each other long before I'd begun the tutoring job, that we'd spent time together as kids though we'd grown up on opposite ends of the continent. "Are you sure you never lived in New Jersey?" I'd asked more than once, and each time she responded with a squint and ruffle of her dark bangs. "What, you think I'm lying?" She'd lived in Portland until she went to college in Santa Cruz, then spent five years in San Francisco—where she'd met Vincent or Victor— before returning home. Her only extended stay on the East Coast was a summer in Manhattan with a college boyfriend, an aspiring actor—"He was good at playing a raving asshole," she said—who had an internship with a small uptown theatre company. She'd hated everything about it: the noise, the traffic, the overpowering smell of garbage, the muggy breeze off the river, the pushy people.

And yet it was so easy to imagine her fitting into the world where I'd spent my first eighteen years, as forceful and aggressive as any of those people crowding Manhattan sidewalks or driving New Jersey freeways. At our first meeting—the first, that is, about which I had no question—I was so sure I did know her I let out a laugh and gave her a hug. I couldn't have named a specific memory then but rather a range of memories that might have included her: playing in a backyard, swimming in a lake, eating a holiday meal. Had our families spent Rosh Hashanah together, or maybe the second night of Passover? She accepted the hug, but it clearly took her by surprise. We were meeting to talk about a job, after all, and this was supposed to be an interview. But the setting was informal—a bar downtown—and soon after glancing over my résumé she told me I was hired. We spent the rest of the afternoon talking about books and music and movies and food.

No, our paths had never crossed, she insisted when we parted that evening, or maybe some days later, and I asked again if she was certain. She'd never set foot in New Jersey, unless you counted a layover in Newark on the way to Jamaica, and she'd never been close to North Carolina, where I'd gone to college, or to Edinburgh, where I'd lived for most of the year after. She hadn't spent more than half a day in Corvallis, the Oregon town where I'd gone to graduate school before floating, without much purpose other than to end up somewhere new, north to Portland. "I guess you just dreamed about me," she said and let out that raspy laugh that always sounded more pained than joyful, one degree away from a sob.

Those early weeks we were getting to know each other my mind often clouded with blurry half-images that might have been Mindy or might have been any number of other small, dark-haired women or girls who'd passed in my peripheral vision, who'd been present in my dreamy childhood and adolescence without being fully concrete, who'd made no impression individually but only as a collective force of willfulness—powerful and oppressive and unexpectedly sexy, at once catching my attention and making me turn away. But then, out of this muddle, a concrete memory would emerge, as crystalline and ephemeral as a dream: a lake in Stanhope, Mindy—or someone just like her—sunbathing on a bobbing dock, a big snapping turtle surfacing just inches from my foot. Or even more vivid: my freshman dorm room in Chapel Hill, Mindy stopping to visit on her way to Atlanta or New Orleans, her dark jeans on my rumpled sheets, black hair set against off-white walls, half-veiled eyes taking in the posters and boyish mess—the mattress strewn with clothes, a crusty microwave in the corner, records jammed into the closet, books stacked on the cubby desk—her sardonic smile leaving me wondering whether she was amused or disgusted or both. Not even a decade had passed. If I remembered it so clearly, how could it not be real?

Though she firmly denied having met me before that drink in the downtown bar, for a time I remained not only skeptical but, privately, convinced that she was wrong. Whenever I talked about New Jersey as if she'd lived there, she gave me a look that wasn't just confused but downright irritated, as if I were messing with her, or else airing some facet of a twisted psychology. "Give it a rest, Oedipus," she said once. "I'm not your mother." And every time she swore we'd been strangers until late August of 1999, disappointment struck me a fresh and bewildering blow. I didn't know why I wanted her to acknowledge a connection that was elusive to me at best, but when she refused to do so, I was sure she was purposely holding out on me, denying the affirmation I not only hoped for but needed in a way I recognized as desperate, even if I didn't understand why.

One thing was certain: from the start there was a genuine familiarity between us, an uncanny sense of history that went beyond even the casual acquaintanceship I struggled to recall. Of course I knew nothing about her when we came together in that downtown bar—no details about her family or personality or interests, no idea where she'd gone to school, what she'd studied, who her friends had been. Many of those things I'd learn over the next few hours or the next few months, but even when we sat down across from each other, her long nails tapping the stem of a cocktail glass, slender fingers free of rings and always moving, I was aware of a certain ease in my manner, a confidence and comfort I felt around few other people, and I found myself quicker to laugh than usual, talking more brashly, with a touch of New Jersey accent I'd worked hard to scrub from my daily speech.

On this point, even Mindy agreed with me. From the start she did feel she understood me in some essential way that instantly disarmed her. She admitted this only later, in her bed, or on the pillows in her living room. "I knew I could trust you," she said, propping herself on an elbow and giving me that hard, scrutinizing stare. "That's unusual for me."

By then, however, I no longer wanted to consider the ease of our connection. As soon as we'd slept together, I wished I could believe she was unlike anyone I'd ever met. I tried to convince myself the feeling of familiarity had less to do with Mindy than with that particular time and place and my present state of mind. Maybe it was just a feeling tied to living on the West Coast, where I knew almost no one, to being young and freshly thrust into the world. If we'd met at any other point in my life, maybe I wouldn't have recognized her at all.

But no matter how much I tried to talk myself into thinking of Mindy as new and exotic, and as much as I enjoyed our vigorous, sweaty wrestling on her sheets or on the velvet pillows, I was left with the unsettling suspicion that I'd unwittingly—or even worse, purposely—walked straight back into the life from which I'd so staunchly run away. It didn't help that Jeff and Rae called attention to the change whenever they visited, which was less frequently now, one evening a week instead of two or three. It was late November, and they were working extra hours to boost their savings. They'd unloaded all the stuff they didn't need and traded the little hatchback they'd bought when they moved here two years ago for an Econoline van with a loft bed in back.

"I guess you won't be coming with us after all," Rae said and gave a big phony sigh. She lay with her head on Jeff's chest, and one of his fingers traced the curve of her shoulder up to her neck and back. "Too bad. I liked the idea of two men keeping me warm at night."

"More threesome fantasies," Jeff said and laughed his hearty, humorless laugh. "She's had them ever since we met this gorgeous Italian boy—"

"He was no boy," Rae said. "He was a god."

"You're just her type," Jeff said. "Small and swarthy. I don't know what she's doing with me."

"I like all types," Rae said. "If you set up a man buffet, I'd take a little taste of everything."

"Or maybe a salad bar?" Jeff said. "I guess I'd be the romaine. Good for every day. But sometimes you want to top it off with a little pepperoncini."

"Or a big one," Rae said.

"Got to keep things interesting," Jeff said. "Especially when all the computers are about to blow up the world."

"I wonder if we can convince Paolo to come with us," Rae said. And then, giving me a wink, she added, "Since our fresh pepper's taken now."

Then they launched into a story about Paolo, the Italian god whom they'd met not in Italy but on a trek in northern India, from Dharamsala into the foothills of the Himalayas. It incorporated their usual mix of outrageous occurrences and mundane details, with surprising twists involving a monk and a freezing night spent in a snow cave, but this time I struggled to listen. Instead of working in another room, Mindy was with us, lying in almost the identical position as Rae, her head on my chest, one hand balancing a cup of wine on her belly, the other resting on my thigh. During the talk of ménage à trois, the pressure of her fingers increased subtly, just enough for me to keep my mouth shut and stroke her neck in imitation of Jeff. The whole time I kept thinking how strange it was, these two couples mirrored across the room, one about to leave behind everything they'd known, the other hunkering down into comfort and security—strange mostly to find myself in this one and not the other. I wanted to jump up and start packing, except that Mindy's hand felt so warm on my thigh, so stirring, that I also wished Jeff and Rae would leave already—for the night, for good—so we could have the pillows to ourselves. Mindy had finally hung shades on the windows, and I was glad not to see what was beyond them. I'd begun parking my car in the driveway, right next to the house.

"If it weren't for Paolo, I probably would have died of hypothermia," Jeff said.

"He's the one who got to cuddle the whole night," Rae said. "All I got to do was watch."

"And she's been jealous ever since."

"Hell yes, I am. If you get to do it, why shouldn't I?"

"No one's stopping you."

"Just have to find the right pepperoncini. Or, you know, kosher pickle." She gave me another big goofy wink.

"This pickle's mine," Mindy said, and to prove it, she moved her hand up my thigh, stopping just short of my crotch. "And it's staying right here."

―◇―

The night before they were due to leave, Jeff and Rae stayed at Mindy's. They'd already given up the lease on their apartment and had moved out a week earlier. They'd been sleeping in the van, parking it on side streets in quiet Southeast neighborhoods, never the same spot two nights in a row. It was preparation, they said, to acclimate themselves to the small space after so many months enjoying the vastness of a one-room studio. "If we're going to drive each other crazy, we might as well figure it out now," Jeff said. "When there's still time to call it all off."

"Three days without a shower, and he still smells tasty to me," Rae said. "I guess that's a good sign."

But when Mindy offered to let them stay over, they agreed that one last night indoors would do them good. "It'll be the perfect way to launch us," Rae said. "A night of domestic bliss. So we'll remember what we're giving up."

I'd been sleeping at Mindy's most nights by then, but when I heard the plan, I said I might take the opportunity to head home to my apartment, stretch out in my own bed. "So you won't have such a crowd to deal with in the morning," I added. But Mindy only gave me her hard, squinting gaze and said, "They already know we're a couple. What are you afraid of?"

I didn't have any good answers, none I could speak out loud, so I only shrugged and said I didn't want to get in the way, but sure, I'd stay if she wanted me to, and I'd make breakfast for everyone in the morning. Her dubious look remained, even after I kissed her, and I had the feeling that she was reading my thoughts, at least the surface ones, which would have told her I didn't want to stay because I guessed it would mean spending the night chastely in her bed, given that Jeff and Rae would be just below, only the bare floorboards separating us, no insulation or sheetrock. Not that I was with Mindy for sex alone—my feelings for her were far more complicated than that—but without sex to distract me, I was more likely to brood on the nagging dissatisfaction I carried with me every time I arrived at her house, a sense that each day I spent with her I was closing off other possibilities that hadn't yet revealed themselves. It was an ugly feeling, one I was ashamed of, and I tried to fend it off by focusing on the firmness of Mindy's lips, on her quickening breath, on the thrust of her pelvis, on her fists pressing into the small of my back as she climaxed.

Even more important, I didn't want to see Jeff and Rae off, didn't want to experience the temptation of their invitation, however insincere, in the moment it would be lost to me for good, and then to watch their van turn a corner and disappear from sight. It would be too painful, I thought, to confront my own role in choosing a path. It was one thing to stumble from place to place as if I'd had no part in deciding where I should go and another to consciously embrace one future over another. I'm sure I didn't think about it in those terms, but some part of me believed that saying goodbye to Jeff and Rae would mean saying goodbye to an essential part of myself. It sounds melodramatic to me now, but that's how crucial it felt to me then, how momentous.

In any case, I told Mindy I'd stay, and as it turned out, I was already at her house, alone, building a fire in the new wood stove, when Jeff and Rae arrived in midafternoon. I let them in and told them Mindy would be home soon, but they treated me as if I were welcoming them into my own place, as if I were their host—thanking me for putting them up, asking if I was sure it wouldn't be any trouble. And strangely enough, I couldn't help feeling as if it *were* my place as I showed them into the guest room, where Mindy and I had blown up air mattresses so they wouldn't have to sleep on throw pillows, pointed out the towels we'd set out for them in the bathroom, offered coffee from the fresh pot I'd made. "The place is really coming along," Jeff said, and I soon found myself detailing which projects were on the docket next. Soon we'd sand and lacquer the floors upstairs, and then we'd paint the trim and picture rail before rolling out the walls. I experienced equal measures of pride in the newly finished kitchen—the cabinets all hung, granite countertops adhered in place, vintage appliances up and running—and chagrin at the stack of two-by-fours in the dining room. How impressed they'd be if they could see it in another month or two.

Jeff and Rae didn't look as if they'd been sleeping in a van for the past week. Jeff's cheeks were as smooth as usual, his hair gelled and combed, Rae as frumpy and cheerful as ever in a long layered dress that looked as if it had just been sewn together. But they both took their turns in the shower, each coming out a little more pink and wholesome, exclaiming over how good it felt to be clean again, how much they'd miss having regular access to hot water. Of course, while they were in Canada, they'd stop at a motel from time to time, not too often so as not to waste money early in their trip, but once they caught their flight from Anchorage to Beijing, who knew what to expect—and even less when they made their way north to Ulaanbaatar.

By the time Mindy came home from her last tutoring session of the day, we were deep into discussing their plans. We had maps spread out on the floor, tracing the route of the trans-Siberian railroad to Moscow, from which they'd head south to Kiev, Bucharest, Sofia, before hopping over to Cyprus, and then perhaps to Tel Aviv. "I've got a cousin in Haifa," Mindy said as she put down her bag and leaned over us, our heads so close together they probably blocked her view of the Mediterranean. "She'd probably put you up for a few days." It was a reasonable enough thing to suggest, a genuine attempt to participate, but neither Jeff nor Rae responded. I said something about the view from Mount Carmel, which I'd visited as a teenager. Mindy left us to ourselves.

Later she called me into the kitchen, where I helped with dinner, making dressing for our salad and a sauce for our pasta. Mindy and I bumped hips as we crossed the room, grabbed each other's behinds, snuck kisses. Once she whispered, "If we were alone, I'd take you right against the stove," and then bit my earlobe. While the sauce simmered, I adjusted one of the cabinet doors that hung crookedly, screwing and unscrewing until I got it straight. We ate dinner on the floor, Jeff and Rae cataloguing the meals they'd miss, the dishes they wanted to try when they finally made it south of the Sahara. "I always lose twenty pounds when we travel," Rae said. "If we stayed in one place I'd be enormous. I wouldn't be able to get up from here." She tugged the pillow under her and then lay back. "No discipline whatsoever."

After we finished and cleared our plates, Jeff said, "Second longest night of the year. Anyone want to go out in it?"

"I'm staying warm while I can," Rae said, inching closer to the wood stove. She and Mindy exchanged a curious glance, both smirking, and I knew they wanted me out of the way. "You two lovelies go ahead."

It wasn't later than eight o'clock but thickly dark, drizzling, water blocked by clogged storm drains overflowing the curb and filling half the street. I'd been coming to the neighborhood for months by then, but I'd never walked around here at night. A few streetlamps were out, a house at the end of the block was abandoned and falling into decay, a pair of hooded figures passed without speaking—but already I felt it changing from the vaguely menacing place it had been when I'd first arrived into something far more ordinary, the same as any other neighborhood in town. TVs flashed behind shaded windows, steam rose from vent pipes, dogs yipped in fenced backyards. Nothing dangerous, nothing novel.

"I always get tense before we leave a place," Jeff said after we'd crossed the interstate and made it to Overlook Park, the railyards below, the reflected lights of downtown smeared across the river pockmarked with rain. "I feel like we're forgetting everything we need, no matter how many times I check the van. But I can't say that to Rae. You know what she'll answer. What else do you need but me?"

"Don't send me any postcards," I said. "They'll just make me jealous."

"You won't even remember us in a couple weeks," Jeff said.

"I doubt that."

"Every computer in the world—"

"Right. Kaboom."

"If things don't work out with her, you can always take off," he said. "You're not signing away your life."

"You ever consider going off on your own?"

He laughed—not a false laugh this time, but one full of discomfort. "She wouldn't last five minutes without me. The second I'm gone she'll wander off a cliff or get sold into a brothel."

If only someone were to step out of the shadows and hold us up, I thought on our way back, then I might be satisfied, might let go of my doubts. But the best I got was a pair of rats crossing a power line over the street, scurrying over a roof, dipping under eaves. The house was warmer than I remembered, and Rae and Mindy sat close together beside the fire, those sly, conspiratorial smirks still playing on their lips, as if they'd decided something while we were gone. Rae struggled to stand, and Jeff helped her up.

"We should turn in," she said. "We're aiming for an early start." They'd likely be gone before we woke, so they'd better say goodbye now. I turned away to keep from choking up. She hugged me, kissed both my cheeks, and then leaned back as if to check for lipstick smudges though she wasn't wearing any. "Maybe you'll convince her," she said, tipping her chin toward Mindy, "to come meet us in Crete next spring. If all she wants is a warm beach, we might as well make it one with ancient ruins nearby. Anyway, we'll stay in touch."

◄○►

"You were right," I whispered when Mindy and I were in bed, listening to Jeff and Rae settle onto the air mattresses under us, their voices a low murmur through the slits between floorboards. "They're completely full of shit. I don't believe a word they say."

"Shut up, and give me that pickle," she said.

We made love slowly, quietly, biting each other to keep from crying out. It was the most intimate exchange we'd had, and it left us both trembling as we clung to each other, breathing each other's breath. She fell asleep that way, but I lay awake, listening to Jeff snoring below. Or maybe it was Rae snoring and Jeff silent beside her. The windows were drafty, the makeshift curtains fashioned out of bedsheets ghosting up with a breeze I couldn't feel. I knew I'd carry this moment with me the same as those I'd kept from my travels. And every other moment, I thought, each more precious the moment it was gone. The room smelled of sweat and sex and fumes from joint compound. A soft clicking sounded overhead. Probably just branches brushing the roof, though I pictured those rats crossing the wire, claws tapping over shingles.

An hour passed, two. I gave up any hope of sleeping. And then I heard another sound: the crack of glass, familiar but loud, emphatically close. This time I was out of bed before Mindy could hold me down. I yanked on a pair of boxers, bounced down the stairs, threw open the front door. No shoes, no jacket, the rain coming harder now, achingly cold on my skin, bare feet sliding on mud. My car was up in the driveway, right in front of the garage, but there was the van parked in shadow at the curb, the nearest streetlamp blocked by the thick branches of a maple hacked so it grew on either side of utility wires running through its middle. I felt the glass before I saw it, and heard it, too: a crunch underfoot, corners cutting into the soft meat between heel and arch. My cry roused whoever was inside the van. A shape appeared in the empty space where the passenger window had been, no features, just a shadow deeper than those around it. Then the door swung open and knocked me over. That shadow lingered above me a moment, and I had the same feeling as when I'd first met Mindy, that I'd seen it before, that it had been with me for as long as I could remember.

But then it was gone, and I lay on my back on the sidewalk, which was humped and cracked by the maple's roots near my head, my feet in a puddle deep enough to submerge them to the ankle. I couldn't have been there more than ten, fifteen seconds, but it was long enough for me to imagine spending the night there, waking up to the dim light of the shortest day of the year. And then someone was at my side, asking if I was okay, lifting me up by the armpits. Rae's voice, no less sultry for its urgency, so full of concern that I answered *fine, I'm fine*, though the pain pulsed through my foot all the way to my knee. Each step back to the house made me grit my teeth. After the third or fourth, I could no longer keep from groaning. Rae muttered uncertain comforting sounds, her frizzed hair even wilder from sleep than usual tickling my neck.

Only when we got to the door did Jeff come out, fully dressed. He brushed past us without a word and hurried to the van. I was shivering by the time we made it inside. Rae lowered me next to the woodstove, but only a few coals still glowed behind the glass. My wet boxers soaked the pillow under me, and blood tracked across the floor. "Good thing we didn't sand it yet," I said when Mindy came down with a blanket. She didn't answer, just wrapped me and reached under the blanket's edge to pull the boxers off. Then she went to find tweezers. I heard her scrabbling in the bathroom, cursing. "What were you thinking?" she said, coming back empty-handed. "What if he had a knife? Or a gun?" She went off again, came back, threw up her hands. Then she squatted and began pulling out bits of glass with her fingernails, scolding me as she worked, her robe falling open when she leaned forward so I could see the small firm breasts I'd kissed a couple hours earlier, the red mark on her collarbone where my teeth had clamped down. Rae stood above us, in sweatpants and an oversized T-shirt—not only plain but sexless, I thought, the last person I could imagine to inspire a threesome.

Jeff came back inside and announced that the only thing missing was the stereo. He didn't thank me, only asked Mindy where she kept her garbage bags. "Sucker used batteries wrapped in duct tape. Window's history." His usual composure was gone, his voice high and agitated as he rushed to the kitchen and back, unfolding the plastic as he went. His wet hair clumped and showed scalp underneath. "I need towels, too. Otherwise the seat. If it mildews—"

"No stereo," Rae said. "I'll have to listen to you talk the whole way?"

He was already heading to the door. Over the next hour he ran in and out, reciting his plan, trying to calm himself. They'd head to the beach, stay for the solstice, and then instead of driving straight for the border, they'd stop in Seattle to get the window fixed. If necessary, they could stay with a friend for a night while the van was in the shop. "But we can't leave it here the rest of the night. If the sucker comes back and rips off our supplies—"

"We'll just drive to the beach now," Rae said. She watched him carry towels to the door without offering to help. "It's no big deal. Just a small setback. We've had worse."

"I knew this was a mistake," Jeff said. "I wish you'd listen to me."

Mindy cleaned and bandaged my foot. I winced at the slightest pressure. I wanted to tell her definitively I was happy to let Jeff and Rae go off on their own, that I wanted no part of their desperate rambling. But I couldn't. Because I wanted no part of her house renovation, either, or the coming takeover of the neighborhood by upscale restaurants and hip boutiques. It was only moments that I craved, and now that I had some, I wanted to secret them away, guard them, keep them safe.

When Jeff finished covering the window and drying the seat, he was cheerful again, laughing the spurious laugh and brushing off the whole episode as nothing more than a nuisance. What did it matter if the kid stole everything in the van? What else did they need but each other? "Not like it's the first time we've been robbed," he said. "Did we ever tell you about the pickpockets on the Budapest subway? There were three of them, two girls and—"

"I love waking up at the beach," Rae said. "Nothing better than hearing waves before you open your eyes. This all works out just fine."

Their goodbyes were hasty, Jeff hugging Mindy and reaching down to shake my hand, Rae blowing us kisses from the door. I waved and wished them well. Séances, polar vortexes, trans-Siberian railways: all of it sounded like a joke to me now, details from a comic novel I'd read a long time ago and mostly forgotten. Mindy watched from the front porch until the van pulled away from the curb. Then she shut the door, turned to me, dropped her robe to the floor. "I know how to make you forget about your foot," she said and switched off the light.

Even beside the warm stove, the blanket tucked under my chin, I kept shivering. Gradually the outline of her naked body against the unpainted door, surrounded by exposed studs and loose wires, came into sharper focus. She was perfect that way, and I didn't need anything else but to keep looking at her. I made a silent wish for her to stay where she was. But then she stepped forward, and the moment was gone, lost among all those that followed

Acknowledgments

I am deeply grateful to Amina Gautier for choosing my manuscript for the Chandra Prize; to Ben Furnish and Cynthia Beard of BkMk Press for shepherding this book into the world; to Sheryl Johnston for getting it into the hands of reviewers; to Marjorie Sandor for a lecture on midrash that gave me the courage to mine the gaps; to Natalie Serber for help with a story that was giving me fits; to my colleagues and students at Willamette University and the Rainier Writing Workshop for years of inspiration and support; to my family for putting up with my obsessions; and to the editors of the publications where some of these stories first appeared:

DIAGRAM: "Squatter"

Chicago Quarterly Review and *Best American Short Stories 2020* (Houghton Mifflin Harcourt): "Liberté"

2 Bridges Review: "One of Us"

Alaska Quarterly Review: "Sweet Ride"

Fugue: "Caught"

Natural Bridge: "Safe and Sorry"

Chautauqua: "Perfect Together"

Grist: "Trust Me"

Ploughshares: "Butterfly at Rest"

The Main Street Rag: "The Depths"

Brief Encounters (W.W. Norton): "Parental Pride"

Pembroke Magazine: "Enzo's Last Stand"

Community College Humanities Review: "Last Bus Home"

J Journal: "The Cake"

Notre Dame Review: "Going to Ground"

Scott Nadelson grew up in northern New Jersey before escaping to Oregon, where he has lived for the past twenty-four years. He has published four collections of short stories, *The Fourth Corner of the World*, named a Jewish Fiction Prize Honor Book by the Association of Jewish Libraries; *Aftermath*; *The Cantor's Daughter*; and *Saving Stanley: The Brickman Stories*; and a memoir, *The Next Scott Nadelson: A Life in Progress*. His novel *Between You and Me* was published by Engine Books in 2015.

Winner of the Reform Judaism Fiction Prize, the Great Lakes Colleges Association New Writers Award, and an Oregon Book Award, Scott's work has appeared in a variety of magazines and literary journals, including *Ploughshares*, *The Southern Review*, *New England Review*, *Harvard Review*, *Glimmer Train*, and *Crazyhorse*, and his work has been cited as distinguished in both the *Best American Short Stories* and *Best American Essays* anthologies. He teaches at Willamette University, where he is Hallie Brown Ford Chair in Writing, and in the Rainier Writing Workshop MFA Program at Pacific Lutheran University.

BkMk Press is grateful for the support it has recently
received from the following organizations and individuals:

Miller-Mellor Foundation
Neptune Foundation
Richard J. Stern Foundation for the Arts
Stanley H. Durwood Foundation
William T. Kemper Foundation

Beverly Burch
Jaimee Wriston Colbert
Maija Rhee Devine
Whitney and Mariella Kerr
Carla Klausner
Lorraine M. López
Patricia Cleary Miller
Margot Patterson
Alan Proctor
James Hugo Rifenbark
Roderick and Wyatt Townley

CPSIA information can be obtained
at www.ICGtesting.com
Printed in the USA
BVHW070852181220
594987BV00002B/7